Chosen

(The first part of the Chosen Few trilogy)

by

David Leadbeater

Other Books by David Leadbeater:

The Matt Drake Series

A constantly evolving, action-packed romp based in the escapist action-adventure genre:

The Bones of Odin (Matt Drake #1)
The Blood King Conspiracy (Matt Drake #2)
The Gates of hell (Matt Drake 3)
The Tomb of the Gods (Matt Drake #4)
Brothers in Arms (Matt Drake #5)
The Swords of Babylon (Matt Drake #6)
Blood Vengeance (Matt Drake #7)
Last Man Standing (Matt Drake #8)
The Plagues of Pandora (Matt Drake #9)
The Lost Kingdom (Matt Drake #10)
The Ghost Ships of Arizona (Matt Drake #11)
The Last Bazaar (Matt Drake #12)
The Edge of Armageddon (Matt Drake #13)
The Treasures of Saint Germain (Matt Drake #14)
Inca Kings (Matt Drake #15)
The Four Corners of the Earth (Matt Drake #16)
The Seven Seals of Egypt (Matt Drake #17)
Weapons of the Gods (Matt Drake #18)
The Blood King Legacy (Matt Drake #19)
Devil's Island (Matt Drake #20)
The Fabergé Heist (Matt Drake #21)

The Alicia Myles Series

Aztec Gold (Alicia Myles #1)
Crusader's Gold (Alicia Myles #2)
Caribbean Gold (Alicia Myles #3)
Chasing Gold (Alecia Myles #4)

All genuine comments are very welcome at:

davidleadbeater2011@hotmail.co.uk

Twitter: @dleadbeater2011

Visit David's website for the latest news and information:
davidleadbeater.com

DEDICATION

For Erica, my amazing wife, and Keira and Megan, my beautiful daughters.

Chosen

1

NEW YORK CITY - U.S.A.

The lights went out.

Johnny Trevochet's breath froze in his throat.

A hush fell over Madison Square Garden; a hush laced with so much tension and suppressed excitement he had never experienced the like of it before. The rock group Supernatural were about to kick off a kick-ass concert, and the anticipation was palpable.

Amidst the whispers, the whistles, and the rising wave of noise he turned to smile at his wife, Natalie. This simple act was harder than he could have imagined before the accident that took away the use of his legs and destroyed his acting career. The wheelchair didn't give like normal seating. He had to turn his entire body like a damn robot.

"Hey, Johnny," she winked and leaned forward to whisper in his ear. "Remember Harvard?"

His discomfort slipped away as a rare smile came to his lips and he remembered a perfect day more than ten years ago. A day when smiles came naturally, before Fate took its greedy bite out of him. It had been one of those unforgettable Boston, Massachusetts, mid-Autumn afternoons: a bracing wind, a crisp golden light that splintered through the trees, and the promise of winter snapping at the air.

"Remember what?" he teased her and delighted in the way she threw back her head to laugh. It was his greatest pleasure, watching his wife laugh. It was the reason he hadn't taken the easy way out after a drunken attorney put an end to his acting career one snowbound New York night.

Natalie leaned in closer, her words falling like drops of honey. When her lips brushed against his ear, tingles spread from his brain to his toes, never mind the numbing paralysis. Then, Supernatural made a tumultuous appearance, and the rest of her sentence was lost in uproar.

Powerful rock music drowned out everything except the spectacle of light and dancing that erupted before them. People rushed to the front of the stage. Due to his recent disability and his luminary reputation, Johnny had been able to secure front row 'disabled-area' tickets to the gig, the hottest of the year. He'd heard that Supernatural were the new wave; an all-girl rock group who knew how to play, how to write, and sure as hell knew how to dress.

He stared for a moment, then blinked, swallowed, and pretended he hadn't been staring. "Good. . .erm. . .start," he shouted.

Natalie raised her eyebrows, still laughing, and again he was catapulted back to Boston. One evening, in the gardens of one of the quieter halls, they had enjoyed a picnic of cheese and wine whilst hiding themselves away among the shedding trees. They had taken blankets too, and had spent the night there, keeping the cold at bay with each other's bodies, toasting Chardonnay to the frosted stars, and making the conversation of two people who were destined to be with each other beyond youth and into old age. It had been the best night of their lives.

Johnny was dragged back to the present as the first song came to a rowdy end and the lead singer of

Supernatural, Emily Crowe- a dynamic girl with raven-coloured locks, shouted: "CAN YOU HEAR ME?" in a booming voice that belied her size.

The crowd responded immediately, Johnny and Natalie included, roaring their approval. Without delay, Supernatural launched into their second song; electric guitars screamed, and the drummer went into a frenzy. Johnny let the atmosphere take him. After all, he thought, if you couldn't forget your worries at a rock concert, along with twenty thousand like-minded people, you might as well be dead. You might as well have breathed your last on that snow-ridden New York street.

The crescendo of noise swelled around him. People were dancing in the aisles. He turned to Natalie.

"I wish. . .I just wish. . ." he shouted, and then a crushing sadness fell over him, causing a break in his voice.

"I wish I could take you to Central Park after this," he said. "I wish I could take you ice skating."

He saw his own hurt reflected in Natalie's eyes. And then the sudden strength. And the belief. "One day," she said, then added "Spanky."

And just like that she made him smile. 'Spanky' was her pet name for him. A few years ago, the producers of his soap-opera had green-lighted a humorous spanking scene with his pretty female co-star. He had come home sheepish; terrified his wife would be angry at him for agreeing to do it. Instead she had fallen about laughing and had never let him forget it.

Now, he leaned forward, trying to ignore the wheelchair's restrictions. "If I said you could go anywhere this summer, see anything in any part of the world, where would you choose?"

They were silent for a moment as the music rolled and swelled around them. Supernatural's lead singer strutted back and forth not ten feet away, chomping so hard at her microphone Johnny wondered if it was made of cookie dough.

"You'd think I might say Boston," Natalie said at last when the music stilled. "But I'm thinking something different. England, I think. And not London. There are supposed to be castle walls in York you can walk along around the city."

At that moment, Johnny experienced a peculiar sensation. He had the nauseating sense that everything around him receded and then returned instantly, like some special-effects trick. Time seemed to shift, as if one moment hadn't quite melded with the next. His head span. It happened so fast he couldn't be sure anything *had* happened, but then the sick expression on Natalie's face and the confused commotion around him confirmed it.

What the-?

The music faded. A guitar barked discordantly. On stage, Emily Crowe and her leather-clad lead guitarist stared at each other and then into the crowd.

"Johnny. . ." Natalie sounded puzzled.

"Shhh. . ." Johnny held up a hand as a new sound arose. A terrible knowledge hit him. He struggled to turn around in his chair.

"Oh my God!"

Behind them, twenty thousand people were stampeding.

This can't be happening. My God, not now.
Johnny Trevochet turned back to his wife.
Natalie sat frozen, her face white with fear.

4

A terrible undulating wave of noise swept through the Garden. Johnny knew that sound. It was the primordial sound of terror. The sound of a speeding car breaking your legs.

He snapped his head to the left when the swell of people smashed some unfortunates against the stage. Screaming and the sound of crushing bodies rent the air. Up on stage, the members of Supernatural watched in horror. Johnny saw bodyguards rush on and try to drag them away. The lead guitarist ran back to her microphone, shouting something that was lost in the mad cacophony of human terror that rose like a killer wave.

"The stage!" he screamed at Natalie. She didn't respond, so he got right up in her face. *"The stage! Get us up on the fucking stage!"*

Natalie snapped out of it and began to drag him forward. Around them other people were clambering and struggling in the same direction. The stage was eerily deserted now, lit by a single spotlight, strewn with wires and instruments. Johnny shook his head in disgust. If the members of Supernatural or their bodyguards had elected to stay, they could have saved dozens of lives.

Something dark was rising, he could sense it. It filled his lungs like a malignant cancer. It filled the Garden up to its rafters with malice, curdling the very air they breathed. A high-pitched wail sliced through everything. Not human, Johnny thought before his wheelchair toppled over and he landed face first on the sticky floor, amidst a plastic carnage of broken chairs, paper cups and bottles.

It was a desperate moment. He thought: *this is it; this is where I get trampled to death,* then Natalie was down on her knees beside him.

"Come on, Johnny," she breathed. She hauled him up.

He blinked in disbelief at the chaos that filled the Garden. To his right, uniformed guards tried to stem the stampede. Johnny saw one of them swept away in a panicked rush; he saw another elbowed in the face and trampled underfoot. He saw blood spraying from the crowd in errant patterns as if a coked-up painter had decided to decorate the Garden in crimson.

This couldn't be happening. Denial still dulled Johnny's wits even as a man fell snarling at his feet. Johnny reached for him, but the man kicked out, at the seats, at anything that might lever him back to his feet. Johnny stared, unable to help the man even if he'd wanted to. He sat with his back to the stage and faced the surging tide of humanity.

It was Natalie and him against them all. Natalie crouched beside him, looking him dead in the eyes.

"Be safe." She said.

She moved back, then ran and jumped, catching the edge of the stage. In a few seconds she had hauled herself up, then rolled on to her front and wriggled to the edge of the stage to reach back down.

"Come on, Johnny!"

She caught his hands and heaved, struggling with his dead weight. Shame and humiliation rushed through him as he tried to shuffle the top part of his body over the edge of the stage. His dead legs dangled uselessly, giving him no leverage. Other people were clambering up now, some reaching back to help loved ones, some reaching back to help just anyone. Others stumbled straight for the stage exit without even a backwards glance.

Natalie hooked her hands under his arms, positioned herself so they were face to face, and then heaved. Johnny could feel the strength dwindling out of her. He sensed more than felt his heavy bulk slide up onto the stage. Natalie collapsed and Johnny shuffled his head back around.

"Holy shit!" he muttered, biting his lip in fear, in shock, in confusion.

He stared out over the battling sea of humanity in sheer horror. The panicked screams of thousands smashed and reverberated off the walls, swelling towards the ceiling where they were swallowed by the eager darkness.

"What the hell is causing this?" he said aloud, to no one in particular.

The man called Loki stared out the window of his hotel room on West 34th Street, the hard approximation of a smile curling his lips as he watched the panic take hold fifteen floors below. He laughed as pathetic streams of the damned tripped and fell from the blood-soaked exits of Madison Square Garden. Their screams were muted by the triple-glazing. *Shame,* he thought. He itched to be among them, to feel their distress, their suffering. He laughed again, a sound lacking any trace of humour. He shook his head as the cops arrived- the so-called forces of good- red lights flashing, as if that was going to help. They had *no idea* what was happening. They were no match for what was coming.

"Hey, George," a feminine voice floated from the room behind him. "Would'ya look at this," he heard the sound of the TV as she turned up the volume. "Something's happened at the Garden. They say it's the worst thing since 9/11."

Pathetic moron, he thought. Typical home-grown bitch. The vice he never should have allowed himself but indulged to help make the waiting that much sweeter. He felt nothing but contempt for her. Here he watched real life and death unfold, whilst in her room she lay sprawled on the four-poster bed, clad in lace, sipping wine and watching television. It was the same the world over, he knew. Untold human hordes sat around their squawking boxes, insulated from reality, happy in their sublime ignorance, ingesting the fast food that was killing them. But then, why did they need real life experience when they had Hollywood blockbusters, Sony PlayStations and the World Wide Web?

He padded back to her, a force of nature, his every movement seemingly effortless. He sneered at the half empty bottle of California red before turning cold eyes on the girl.

He reveled in her expression of fear. His nostrils flared. This was it. This prime piece of American sweetmeat had a body like a Victoria's Secret model: tanned skin, a flawless face, eyes that drew you in like warm, liquid gold; narrow hips, and an ass so soft and smooth it was like resting your balls on a Versace cushion.

"George," she swallowed nervously and waved towards the TV. "Have you seen this? I really need to go," her eyes were wide. "My brother was at this concert. He's *in there.*"

"You have been fully compensated for the whole night," he told her, lips stretched with cold mirth. "After all, what do you Americans say? A deal's a deal?"

"But...my brother-"

"Take off your robe," he told her. "And put your head against the window. That way you needn't miss a thing."

He laughed as she complied. He could tell she was already exhausted from the evening's previous efforts. He didn't care. She meant nothing to him. She was soft candy, bought and paid for. A sack of sugar with no name. He would use her tonight, then throw her away as he continued to prepare for the coming battles that would bring Hell itself to this aimless world. "For *Gorgoth!*" he whispered into her ear as she watched distressing scenes below. She would bear witness to that what those on the ground could not- the twisting malevolent vapours that teased and trickled their way up through the Garden's roof, drifting higher and higher into the ever-darkening New York night.

2

YORK, ENGLAND

My mobile vibrated. I fished it out of my pocket and checked the screen.

Number unlisted.

A bolt of fear shot through me. For the last twenty-three months I had sprinted for the ringing phone or the chiming doorbell, always hoping it would be Raychel, my wife, getting back in touch.

I was still waiting.

"Hello?"

"Is that Mr. Dean Logan?"

The voice held that formal quality that could freeze the breath in your throat.

"Yes, it is."

"I'm ringing about your daughter, Mr. Logan. I'm ringing about Lucy."

Lucy?

"There has been an incident, sir." The voice was steel, intended for the delivery of bad news. "Lucy is okay, but she cut herself tonight. I can't go into details over the phone, but could you come to York District Hospital? You may want to pick up some of her things from home first."

I closed my eyes tight. *Oh, Lucy. You're all I have left. What have you done now?*

As I wrenched open the door to my house, I saw my own shattered face reflected in the broken mirror that dominated the hallway. Blood smeared the glass.

My daughter's blood.

Oh, God. First, I'd failed my wife, now I'd failed my daughter. I wanted to scream, to put my fist through the door. Instead I glanced at my best friend, Holly.

"Wait here."

The TV was blaring away to itself. I heard something about a disaster at Madison Square Garden. A high-class hooker thrown off the top floor of a twenty-storey hotel room opposite.

Holly reached out to wipe away the tears that ran down my cheeks. I blinked, unaware I'd been crying.

"Not a chance, Dean. I'm coming with you."

I headed straight for the stairs, then stopped at the bottom and just stared. "I...I don't know what to do."

Lucy. My daughter had faced up to her mother's mystifying disappearance the way a coward takes on a prize-fighter- by hitting the canvas and covering her eyes. I wished she would share. I would gladly take her pain with my own. I blamed myself when she cut herself the first time. But now? Had I neglected my own daughter yet again?

Would they take her away from me?

"Dean," Holly had been around me long enough to gauge where my thoughts were heading. "Just go upstairs and pack her an overnighter. Now."

I started up, feeling numb. I entered Lucy's bedroom. A typical teenager's domain, complete with the mess of books, magazines, school clothes, sports equipment, bobbles, conditioner, *pre*-conditioner and CDs filed everywhere except in the CD rack – a room filled with my daughter's fast-moving life, but not with her.

Holly stood before me, deliberately filling my vision. "*Listen to me, Dean.* This is not your fault. It's not Lucy's fault. It's *hers.*"

Holly pointed towards one of only two framed pictures of Raychel that remained in the house.

"Raychel left you," Holly said. "Without a word. She didn't care about her husband or her daughter, or how her leaving would affect you both."

I was still struggling to cope with Raychel's disappearance, whilst Lucy lived life with a slab of guilt fixed around her shoulders. Guilt that was unfounded, yet undiminished with the passage of time.

I found one of Lucy's sports bags and filled it. Ten minutes to the hospital.

My wife, Raychel, had left us one cold, winter's day in 2005. In the morning she was there, in the evening she was gone. We'd heard nothing from her in twenty-three months. Not even a false alarm. At first, the police had been suspicious, but no longer, which in some ways was even worse.

All that remained was a shattered husband and a seriously fucked-up kid called Lucy- once a ray of shiny happiness- who now believed she had caused her mother to abandon the family home.

I had turned to the bottle. Lucy had turned to self-abuse. It had taken a life-altering moment- me stumbling into the bathroom, whisky bottle held upright like a guiding light, to see my daughter sobbing in the bathtub, hair and clothes and face covered in sweat and puke and tears, her blood sprayed across the white shower curtain, to shatter my depression and recognize hers. That and the loving help of Holly, who had always been around.

Now, I teetered above a black abyss of guilt, unresolved loss and deepening money troubles. One day, I feared, I would embrace the abyss. But I would never let it happen whilst Lucy needed me.

We entered the hospital. I walked the stark corridors. My throat was dry. I recognized the craving for a spirit that I thought I had exorcised over a year ago.

I finally found Ward G3 and turned to Holly before going in.

"I'll be right here." She found a plastic seat.

I took a deep breath and walked into Lucy's hospital room. Pain and weariness enveloped me as I saw Lucy lying on the hospital bed like the palest flower against the whitest sheet. In sharp contrast, her locks of wavy brown hair were spread out all over the pillow.

She blinked at me. "Hey, old man."

It broke my heart. For six years she had made fun of my age, and in return I made fun of her youth, calling her youngling, or munchkin, or worse, but not tonight.

Tonight, I just couldn't get past the heart-rending sight of her.

"How are you feeling, Luce?"

"Okay, I think. I should be okay for squash next week."

Lucy was a great player. National standard. Lately I'd begun to think it was a way for her to channel aggression. "We'll do our best."

"They made me turn my mobile off."

I glanced towards the muted TV. Saw the same coverage of the Madison Square Garden tragedy I'd overheard back at our house. I turned away, got a look at Lucy's bandages. One was wrapped around her upper right arm, and two smaller ones covered her wrists. I felt my control slip. "I thought we'd gotten past the worst, Luce."

Her eyes flashed.

"Your mother *left us*," I tried again. "All I'm trying to do is keep our lives together."

"By ignoring it?" Lucy hissed. "By pretending it's all alright and nothing changed when she left?"

"We don't even know where she went. We're left behind without a single clue."

Tears sprang from Lucy's eyes. "It was because of *me*," she sobbed. "I drove her away. We had...we had an argument."

"No," I said gently. "Your mother loved you. *Loves* you. Christ..."

"Did you make her go? What did *you* do?"

"Nothing!" My denial was loud, as much with the shock of the question as its abruptness. "One day everything was fine, the next..." I spread my arms. On the TV I noticed they were interviewing Johnny Trevochet, a survivor of the Madison Square Garden tragedy, a one-time American soap opera star. A strange tingle travelled the length of my spine when I saw him, though at the time I had no idea why.

Then I said: "*She* was a fine actor. I'll give her that."

Lucy looked at me through her tears and sniffed. "What do you mean?"

"If something *was* wrong. If *I* did something wrong. I never knew."

She turned away.

"When your mother left, I wanted to give in. Remember? I couldn't think straight. But do you know what you're doing now?" I put my hand lightly over one of the bandages.

Lucy said nothing.

"Not winning," I said. "The only thing you *are* doing is pushing away the only parent you have left. The one who cares."

I let that sink in for a moment, then said: "They could take you away from me, Luce."

Raychel, I hate you for this.

A bewildered expression fell over Lucy's face as if a thousand conflicting thoughts hit her all at once. It must have caused a considerable amount of pain, but she leaned over and held her arms out to me.

"Dad, I'm sorry. Please don't leave me."

I took her into my arms. "I'm not going to leave you. I want you to trust me, Luce."

I hugged my daughter as tightly as I dared, and my eyes happened on the muted TV where a breaking news channel was flashing up new stories about more tragedies around the world. I closed my eyes against the horror, vowing to give Lucy all the time she needed.

I wasn't going anywhere.

3

MIAMI, U.S.A.

Marian Cleaver bobbed and weaved around the heavy leather bag, then came up and punched with a powerful left, rocking it to the right. It felt good tonight. The rhythm, the rock and the roll, the shuffle and the jab. Even the smells were right – stinging antiseptic mixed with fresh sweat, old sweat, and blood. It was all here tonight. Fear, determination, hope. And the old men sat around watching, their rheumy eyes bright with memories of younger days. Cleaver loved it. These nights came around once, maybe twice a year.

It was after midnight. Earlier, he'd watched the tragedy unfolding at Madison Square Garden. Then he'd started wondering if it was the start of something more, something related to him, and his duty.

He'd felt the need to hit the leather. Hannigan, the old pro who ran this place, usually locked the door around eleven but let his guys train until they were spent. Cleaver dropped a shoulder and pummeled the bag once more, grinning as the thought struck him that only those who led seriously fucked-up lives would ever train and sweat at this time and place.

Marian Cleaver was a member of the celebrated HC Detective Agency. HC stood for Hector Clancy, the ex-marine who owned it. Imaginative. But, in addition, Cleaver was also one of the most capable field-operatives of a covert Global organization called Aegis.

His beeper went off. He threw some easy punches to

cool down. He stopped and stared at the bag, breathing heavily, a tall solidly built man with day-old growth springing from his chiseled features. He had a face that both men and women found dependable, and a twinkle that could attract females like waffles attract maple syrup. Out on the street he was an enigma, a mix of reliability and violence.

In South Miami he was a legend.

Once an upcoming boxer, all controlled fire and natural skill, he had gone from ruling the ring to occupying his own prison cell in two easy hours. Young, fearless, and impetuous he had stolen a car. And, wanting to impress some friend who had faded away faster than his career, he had driven it fast.

He had collided with a boy named Josh Walker.

Cleaver killed that same boy every night in his dreams. When it got too bad, he came back here, to Hannnigan's. To take it out on the leather.

Through the years he tried to make amends. He worked for the detective agency, helping where he could. And he worked for Aegis, an organization that remained anonymous whilst helping to save the world. If he could do more, he would.

He walked over to the peeling window-sill where he'd left his belongings. On the way, one of the old men caught his gaze. The man's unforgiving glare seemed to say *'you lost it, kid. You had it all and you lost it all. Look at me- I never had nothing, but you could'a walked outta this place wearing gloves of gold...* Cleaver imagined the old man was thinking nothing of the sort, but gnawing guilt told him otherwise.

With a fumble he picked up his beeper. Its message, from HC, glowed electric green.

911. They never used 911. *Fuck!*

No time for a shower or even a change of clothes. He headed for the exit and rolled his eyes at Hannigan, a battered old black guy, and one of the few men Cleaver trusted.

"The agency. I'm heading out."

"Worked that bag pretty good," Hannigan's voice was a heavy whisper. "You come back any time you need it, Marian. Any time."

Cleaver smiled. Hannigan was also the only person in the world Cleaver knew would never twist his first name into a form of mockery. Once outside he flipped open his phone, hit speed dial, and tucked it under his ear.

An agent answered. "Elliott."

"Clancy paged me."

The big boss was scornfully nicknamed Clanger outside the range of listening equipment by those who knew about several big balls he'd dropped.

There was a short silence, a whir of machinery, and then Clanger's voice. He sounded excited. "Cleaver? Great. Get out to South Beach. You know Liberty Avenue near the convention centre?"

"It's after midnight, sir, and technically my day off."

"Who cares? Just go. Now."

"After I shower and change-"

"No," Cleaver rarely heard Clanger stressed. "You've always been chasing the *big one*, Cleaver. Well, our cases don't come much bigger than this."

Cleaver's curiosity piqued. "Please explain."

"No time. Just get going. Gomez, Moore and Day have already left. You'll be late but I want you on point. You're my number one, Cleave; did I ever tell you that?"

"Constantly," Cleaver said, thinking *but only when you*

want the envelope of risk pushed that little bit further.

Clancy was still droning on. "Don't waste time setting up an OC. Just call me back when you're close. And listen, don't get emotional on this one, just do it by the book."

"I know my job, sir," Cleaver wondered what the hell *that* was supposed to mean. *Don't get emotional?* He cleared his throat. "Who's the client?"

"Tell you later. Oh, and Cleaver?"

"Sir?"

"This one's definitely got your name on it."

Cleaver scratched his chin as the old tingle passed through him. A long time ago, back when he was setting up his very own security firm, a client had set him up. Some Latino scum-suckers had wanted to take out the man who'd flat-lined their dope operation- *him*. So, they'd hired Cleaver anonymously. Everything checked out, even when Cleaver met them. But he'd been warned by that special tingle, that sixth sense. Fuck, call it Spidey sense, he had it in abundance. Something he put down to his years of surviving in the boxing ring. Suffice to say that the above-mentioned scum-suckers died screaming.

He felt that tingle now as he closed the cellphone. To his knowledge HC had never sent more than one employee to any client.

The Liberty Avenue job warranted four.

As he neared ground zero Cleaver put his game face on. His cell rang. It was Clancy, speaking like Schumacher used to drive his Ferrari.

"Cleaver? You there yet?"

"Almost."

"Listen up. You've got a houseful of hostages. Kids, ranging from ages eighteen to twenty. Sossamon's made a few enquiries and says there was a frat party going on. Probably a damn orgy. You with me so far?"

"All the way," but Cleaver thought: *kids?*

"Right," Clanger rushed on. "Best case scenario is *thirty kids.* But here's the kicker. Miami PD says there's only a single hostage-taker. Heat sig' and a couple of sightings seem to confirm what they're saying."

"I don't get this. Who's our client?"

"The kids have all been forced to huddle up against a wall, and our bad guy, who is actually a bad *woman,* is sat in a Lazee-Boy, feet up, watching them."

Cleaver was silent for a moment, thinking: *you didn't answer my question. Again.*

Something was warped out of shape here.

Eye on the bag, Hannigan used to say. *And always on the sweet spot. Never lose your focus on that damned sweet spot.*

He focused now.

"Do MDPD have shooters on her?"

"Sure. But they can't tell what she's hiding, if anything."

Cleaver frowned as he swung the car around a sharp left. Clanger was right. The woman could have a major weapon up there. Even a bomb.

"Could there be more hostage-takers mixed up with the kids?"

"Don't rule it out."

"I'm guessing there's been no negotiations, no contact." He used his ID to weave through stalled traffic and pull into a mini-mall parking lot. He sniffed at his armpits, got a whiff of stale sweat, shrugged and exited the car. He breathed in the warm night air and started to make his way towards the scene, cell tucked under his chin.

"What?" Clanger's voice faded in and out.

Half a dozen radio units were strewn haphazardly in front of a length of crime-scene tape, their bubbles painting the surrounding buildings in lurid red flashes. Cleaver raised his voice. "I asked if there'd been any contact."

"Well, yeah, just once," Clanger hesitated. "And this is where it gets weird. And I mean 'off the chart' weird. Hold on, I'm gonna quote you the exact words."

Cleaver stopped with the cell tucked between shoulder and chin, casting his eyes over the staging area. He wondered what could possibly make this scenario any weirder. The building in question rose ahead, stone clad, three storey's high and half a block wide.

"Okay," the Clang-man was back on the line, shuffling papers. "You still there?"

"Right here and waiting."

"Then let the weirdness begin. To quote this woman: 'My name is Mena Gaines. At this time I mean you no harm, but I will do what I must to complete my part successfully. I will sit at the head table of...ummm...*Gorgoth*, beside Loki. I will let your children live a little longer when you send me the man who represents Aegis. You know him by the name: Marian Cleaver," Clanger paused. "I guess that's you."

Cleaver's legs buckled with shock. *This was about Aegis! And Gorgoth!* Clanger was firing out questions, but Cleaver didn't hear them above the thunder that filled his ears. This was end of the world stuff.

It's all about Aegis. My God, it's beginning already. For a moment dark spots danced before his eyes.

This woman is our client.

He knew the name Mena Gaines. She was one of the six evil Destroyers who would engineer the doom of the world, who would be arrayed against the world's eight Chosen in the final battle. Marian Cleaver, naturally, had volunteered to help protect the Chosen.

Mena Gaines might well be his nemesis.

4

YORK, ENGLAND

If I knew Lucy, she would show happy-face on the outside and save the real hurt for when she was alone.

I looked away from a TV full of doom and gloom towards what we called our Victory Wall. My part of the Wall consisted of photographic prints I'd sold over ten years. If it didn't sell, it didn't get framed. The other, larger, part of the wall was full of Lucy's squash trophies and photos of her receiving awards. Lucy's part was now encroaching on my part. The daughter starting to outdo the father. The wall boosted her confidence. Almost every day I saw her admiring a photo or a sparkling trophy.

But tonight, I don't think the wall was giving either of us much inspiration. Major events were shaking the world. The stampede at Madison Square Garden, something about a roller coaster collapse at Sea World, a devastating earth tremor in Costa Rica.

In my house, in my chair, in this city hundreds of miles away from any scenes of destruction, I began to feel unsettled.

I'd never seen so many people so scared, so many witnesses showing outright fear. And now there was something going on in Miami; something about a bunch of college kids being held hostage by a mad-woman. And someone said a bomb was involved. A wave of terror was sweeping the world.

"What's going on, Dad?" Lucy asked, her first words in twenty minutes. "Are we safe?"

I frowned, wondering if the more insignificant occurrences were being lost beneath the information deluge that accompanied the devastating events? For a moment I felt relieved that my business partner, Tom Acker, was looking after our new enterprise whilst I spent time with Lucy.

I nodded. I flicked off the TV before it sent us both reeling towards deeper depths of despair. "Take away?"

"Cool."

"Preference?"

"Mmm, maybe Italian. Mauricio's?"

"Maybe not," I shuddered, having heard bad reports. "I thought Oscars was your favorite?" And I knew they had a two-for-one deal on deliveries before seven.

She leapt for the phone. "Quick, before he changes his mind!" Lucy's presence filled the house, and it felt good. I shook my head. Yesterday she lay in a hospital bed; today the event was history.

"Bring it on," I said to the guy who answered the phone. "Everything we can have on that two-for-one deal. Garlic bread, beer-"

"Wine?" Lucy interrupted. "Let's not forget who's sixteen in a few days."

I coughed. "Not in this decade."

Lucy gave me a narrow-eyed look.

"*Diet Pepsi*," I said. "For the tweenie. No ice."

"Loser," Lucy grumbled, but it sounded good to my ears.

The meal arrived, steaming hot. She grabbed my beer and downed a mouthful before I could get a hand on it. I gave her a pretend glare, but couldn't keep the twinkle from my eyes, and it was like we were a normal father and daughter for about three minutes, which was when a knock at the door made us both sit up. Outside were two serious-looking guys in suits.

"Mr. Logan?" The taller one spoke.

My instant thought was of Raychel, and a rush of fear swept through me. Then I thought they might be here because of Lucy's recent hospital visit. Either way, my heckles rose.

"Mr. Logan?"

"Yes."

"My name is Ryan. My colleague here is Geoffrey Giles. May we have a moment of your time, sir?"

I frowned. They seemed an odd pairing. Ryan was tall and all business. Giles, on the other hand, looked uncomfortable, apologetic even, which was alright by me, and gave me pause. Giles rooted a finger around his collar as if unused to the fit of a shirt and tie.

"I am with my daughter," I said, stating the obvious.

"If we could have a moment to explain," Ryan's tone softened.

"One minute."

I noticed them flick their eyes at Lucy, hopping silently behind me. "Umm, it would be better if we could talk alone," Giles said uneasily.

Lucy rolled her eyes." Christ, what are you guys? The Fucking Bureau of Investigation?"

I felt my good feelings beginning to evaporate.

"You can talk in front of her." I said. "Or leave us to our meal."

I heard Lucy's sharp intake of breath at that moment of unconditional trust. Good. We all trooped into the living room.

The tall guy, Ryan, gave a tight smile that turned his lips bloodless and said: "Quick version. The world's going to shit. Have you seen the news?"

I glared, saying nothing.

"The disasters you've heard about so far?" his voice was

pitched deliberately low. "They're nothing compared to what's coming. May I?" he gestured at my forgotten slice of garlic bread.

I blinked, thrown by his cheek. He took my silence as agreement and bit off a large piece. "Right," he mumbled. "Where was I?" .

"World's going to hell, gonna get much worse, yada yada yada, ooh I'm so hungry," Lucy summed up.

Ryan narrowed his eyes. "Thanks. Which brings me to you, Mr. Logan?"

I wondered if Holly had hired these two clowns as a joke.

"Look-" I said. "The circus left town a while back, and-"

"Dean Logan," Ryan said quickly. "Owner of a new business venture called Logan's Tours. Your best friend is Holly Green. Wife, Raychel, disappeared without trace back in '05. Daughter here is called Lucy. School, City, and County squash champion."

Giles said. "We represent an organization called *Aegis*. Please give us the chance to explain things to you. A lot has happened in the last few days, Logan, and our people are still playing catch up."

"So, *what* has happened?" Lucy asked. "Don't tell me Britney's pregnant again."

"Madison Square Garden," Ryan almost hissed in his frustration. "The woman thrown out of the hotel window opposite. The roller-coaster collapse at Sea World-"

"I watch the news," I said shortly. "Christ, even Lucy watches the news."

"Thanks, Dad."

Now Giles stepped forward, all but shouldering his partner aside. "The incidents are all linked. I will explain, but you *must* believe me when I say that Aegis have identified you as one of the eight living people who can save our planet."

With that, both men stopped to gauge my reaction. I stared back in disbelief, then rolled my eyes at Lucy and watched her face go through a dozen comical changes, from amazed, to scared, to downright curious.

I threw up my hands in despair. "Alright! That's it! Who hired you two fucking clowns?"

Lucy's eyes were dinner plates. I paused, taking a deep breath to stay calm. "Look," I spread my hands. "Joke failed. It backfired. Never mind, at least you tried. Now run along."

And yet why would a practical joker mention Raychel in front of Lucy?

Ryan stepped forward and bent down until his lips were level with my ear. "You've felt the darkness, haven't you?" he whispered. "By watching TV. You've seen just a few of *thousands* of fragile areas around the world where evil is leaking through," his voice lowered still further. "this evil is rising, Logan, in response to an approaching cataclysmic event."

I flashed back to witnesses speaking and crying with an intense, unfathomable fear in their voices.

Ryan continued. "Something is forcing its way up from below, Mr. Logan. It is evil rising to meet its maker. We need only an hour of your time to prove all this."

My heart was beating fast. Those words: '*Something is forcing its way up from below* struck an ominous chord. I suddenly had no doubt that, however mad they were, these men believed their words. I recalled Lucy's scared question earlier tonight: *Dad, are we safe?*

I spoke succinctly, each word a sentence. "What. Do. You. Want?"

"One hour," Ryan said, straightening up. "We'll tell you everything."

I handed them my take-away bill.

"You're paying," I said to Giles, ever money-conscious.

We followed Ryan and Giles patiently down Parliament Street. The May weather was balmy, attracting both tourists and locals into town. The pavement cafés were full.

At length we entered an upscale area where each home was large and close enough to the city centre to be worth upwards of a million pounds apiece. Our two guides stopped by a discreet doorway marked only by an unassuming brass plate that read: *AEGIS*. Giles punched a code into a keypad and opened the door. A dark exterior passage widened out into a pleasant inner garden paved with random Indian stone. Lucy shuffled next to me. I laid a protective arm around her shoulders, which she promptly shrugged off.

"Through there," Ryan gestured towards an archway ahead.

What was I getting us into?

5

MAUI, HAWAII, U.S.A.

The man named Loki, leader of Gorgoth's armies, exited a taxi in a busy part of Lahaina, Maui's most popular tourist town. He paused to get his bearings, shading his storm-cloud eyes.

The Hawaiian heat tempered by a cool sea breeze hit him immediately. He set off down the high street, past busy shops, blending with and laughing at the oh-so-happy tourists who wandered around like lost sheep awaiting the slaughter. They had no inkling that the whirlwind already moved among them.

He laughed aloud when he spotted a small church and noticed a couple of locals walking in. What the hell was the Big Kahuna going to do for them? Their God was a lazy God, a fat walrus grown complacent whilst feeding off the uncontested worship of two thousand years.

Things are gonna change. Believe me...

Loki walked into a coffee shop opposite the art gallery where his target worked and ordered a cappuccino. And a muffin. If there was one thing this world did right, it was these skinny orange and lemon muffins. The downside was that they were fast becoming Vice Number Two. His lip curled. He'd only been in America for two weeks and already the vices were starting to mount. He looked around. Maybe they'd let Starbucks stay open when this world went to hell.

Seated by the window he turned his attention to an art gallery across the busy road. Devon Summers worked there, a local woman ignorant of her potential. She was one of the Chosen – a group of eight humans who possessed enough untapped ability to rip Gorgoth's plan apart. But they could only do that if those abilities were nurtured by the Aegis organization in the appropriate manner. Loki's job was to see that never happened.

Two minutes later his quarry exited the art gallery and headed home. Loki rammed down his muffin- temporarily assuaging Vice Number Two- and started after her. He knew her address already, but kept following for this woman was the epitome of Vice Number One – his insatiable lust for beautiful women.

He shadowed her until she vanished into her house. He waited three minutes and then pounded on the door.

Flustered, she answered immediately, as he'd gambled she would. "Yes?"

Tall, athletic, stunning, purring with a dormant ability that she would never fulfill, Devon Summers was a sight to behold. Red hair flowed in waves over her shoulders to the middle of her back. Striking green eyes, bright with intelligence, studied him with an unsettling innocence and curiosity.

"Are you Devon Summers?" Loki settled into a strike position.

Look at her, he thought. She senses nothing. Suspects nothing.

And she is one of the chosen eight?

The people of this world would succumb like fields of grass mown down by a master's blood-coated scythe.

"Yes, who-?"

Eight seconds. A lot can happen in eight seconds. You would never imagine that a man at your door could force his way inside and kick and punch you in vital areas, rendering you helpless and all but dead on the hallway floor, your body a world of hurt and your limbs unresponsive, in just eight seconds.

But it can. And when Loki paused one second after that to close the door behind him he was pleased to see the only response Devon Summers could manage was to roll her terrified, gloriously green eyes.

"You don't know me," he said with a snarl as his self-control began to slip. "So I have you at a great disadvantage, Devon Summers of 311 Lahaina Garden Court, Maui, Hawaii. Devon has a hidden ability that could save the planet. She likes to dine out regularly around the eastern shore where it's less touristy. She likes to surf at the weekend. Oh, and she likes to leave work early," he sneered. "And as for dislikes? Well, let's see, shall we?"

6

YORK, ENGLAND

We entered a spacious room dominated by an oak table. Around the table were at least thirty people. The noise and aggression levels were tremendous. I winced in shock, unprepared for this.

I tried to take it all in. Demanding the most attention was a slim woman dressed in a crisp business suit. She was on her feet, gesturing angrily. When Giles cleared his throat, she looked straight at me.

Giles said, "Ah. Myleene, excuse me. This is Dean Logan. And his daughter, Lucy."

There was a sudden silence that gave both Lucy and I a moment to adjust. I put a hand on Lucy's shoulder. An impression of intelligent exasperation dominated the room.

Surreal? I could have had a field day photographing all the contrasting expressions.

"Mr. Logan," Myleene said. "Welcome to Aegis."

"Cheers," I said dryly.

Shaking my head, I noticed a dozen seats to our right arrayed in cinema-like rows. I counted ten more people, including an oriental guy and a striking blonde in leather trousers. She caught my eye and held it. Her gaze seemed sharper than the rest, glinting with secret appraisal. Eyes like that would look stunning in portrait. They might even make the front cover of Photographer's Monthly. Or Vogue. I glanced away, but her face stayed in my mind's eye like a lingering flash image.

I couldn't help myself. I looked back again. Now her

expression was slightly mischievous. She wore a t-shirt emblazoned with the legend: *I'll be nicer if you give me chocolate.* The sheer force of her gaze made me want to offer her a Kit Kat Chunky or something.

Myleene offered a strained smile. "Try to keep up, Logan. You know, you shouldn't have brought your daughter into this."

I put a protective arm firmly around Lucy's shoulders. "She stays with me."

Myleene nodded as if to say *your funeral*, and then looked to my left. "You may be our fucking leader, Giles, but-" Myleene brought her fist down on the table hard enough to rattle the ice in the water pitchers. "All this bloody bickering won't help! It's all we ever do. It's why we sectored the organization around the world in the first bloody place. Just remember this-" Myleene took a deep breath. "while we fight, our enemies grow stronger. They pick off our hopes one by one."

Squeezing Lucy's shoulder for moral support I said, "Will someone just tell us what the hell's going on here so we can get back to our rudely interrupted father-daughter evening?"

Blank looks greeted my request. I was about three seconds from walking out.

Then an American-accented voice said, "You guys are unbelievable."

I turned as the blonde girl strode to the centre of the room. My interest was piqued. She stood five-six and tanned, with eyes like blue lasers and a poise that came over as both elegant and lethal. Her muscles were clearly defined but not bulging. Straight blonde hair framed her face and brushed over her shoulders. She stood out as the most positive and capable person in the room.

"These guys have no manners," she said. "They forget

themselves in their anxiety. Hi, I'm Belinda." she held a hand out.

I shook it, feeling her smooth, warm skin. "Dean Logan. My daughter, Lucy."

"Cool," she held my gaze and said, "So what do you know about Vampires?"

My eyes narrowed. "Bill Compton from True Blood's good," I started, but the intensity of her stare turned saliva to ashes in my mouth.

"Let me guess," I said. "They're all real?"

"All as real as I am," she put her hands on her hips.

I said, "Ummm-" Classic male recovery.

Beside me, Lucy coughed and giggled at the same time.

Shit.

"Fine," I said, reddening. "I believe you. Can we go now?"

Belinda relented. "We'll tell you everything you need to see, Logan. And what you *don't believe,* I'll prove to you later," she gave me a slow wink.

I knew this act. She projected a playful exterior, designed to shield the person within. She was a mini dynamo, brimming with boundless energy, sexually charged and exuding a sparkle and confidence that perked up the entire room. For that, at least, she deserved my respect.

I said, "You've got five minutes."

"Cool," she winked. "Aegis has discovered there are eight people capable of saving the world, and that six so-called 'Destroyers' will be sent against them. You, Logan, are one of the Eight, one of the Chosen."

I stared at her, struggling to believe. I took a deep breath. "And you can prove that to me? How"

Belinda shook her blonde hair in a spray of pale gold and grinned. "Tonight, I'll take you to meet some of them."

7

YORK, ENGLAND

One minute I was this cash-strapped guy trying to kick off a brand-new tourist business, striving to make greater efforts with his heartbroken fifteen year old daughter and to ignore the aching absence of her mother, the next I'm listening to Myleene haranguing Giles. "Let's agree on this then. We call a one-time crisis meeting. Everyone involved. We give them the make-or-break scenario. Let them decide, what do you say?"

"*Everyone* involved? Don't be stupid, Myleene." Giles said. "Ubers as well? At this stage?"

"They have to be involved. Vampires practically *rule* this world. And as for the easily pleased Lycans and the few Elves that are left. . .well, it's their world too."

Giles was again tugging at his collar. I found myself wishing he'd just take the bloody tie off. "We don't *know* anything yet. About our enemy, I mean."

Myleene kept her cool. "I know that, but the text will convince them."

At this, all conversation died. I took the opportunity to raise my hand. Well, I raised Lucy's hand since she was the youngest.

"What text?" I asked.

Lucy made a face beside me. "And what's an *Uber?*"

Belinda shifted in her chair, leather pants creaking. "Uber is short for Uberhuman. It's what we collectively call the 'alternate' species'."

I got it. "And the text?"

Myleene said, "The text. Well, the text is what started-"

"The latest crisis?" Belinda finished for her.

"Latest," Giles sighed. "And most bloody awful."

I scratched my nose. "I guess someone found out something they weren't supposed to?"

Myleene nodded. "Isn't that always the way? You've heard of the Library of Alexandria?"

"Yes," I said. "Old place, destroyed ages ago."

"A place where all the wisdom of the world was once collected. Well, at the time of Alexandria, *our* library- the Library of Aegis- rivaled if not *exceeded* that one. Only a handful of people around the world know it exists, and even less its location. Now if you imagine how much was lost at Alexandria- add another seven hundred years of learning to that, and *then* add the countless volumes added by our Uberhuman friends, you might guess at what we have."

I was genuinely shocked. "Sounds...cool."

Belinda laughed. "That's what *I* said."

"It is the seat of learning and knowledge and absolute power. It is the very axis of the world."

I took the rebuke with a humble nod. "Go on."

"So, we knew our enemy was planning a raid on the library," Giles prompted.

"Right," Myleene nodded. "First, our enemy should not know the Library's location. Second, why a small *raid*?" Myleene said around a sip of water. "Why not an all-out assault? Why now? And more importantly- *what were they bloody-well after?*"

Eyes twinkling, Belinda said, "In a nutshell. I watched the Library. I followed the raiders. I caught them red-handed. I slapped their arses."

I grinned.

Myleene gave a short laugh. "Yes, well, luckily our enemy miscalculated and sent humans to carry out the raid. Belinda directed the *questioning* of the thieves and we learned they'd come to find and *destroy* a certain document. The Text of Arcadia."

An air of silence and wonder had fallen over the room that set my heart racing. Lucy, I noticed, was enthralled, not even rubbing the bandages that covered her wounds.

"The Text of Arcadia," Myleene continued. "Has been translated and reviewed by some of the most learned people on the planet."

"What does it say?" Lucy asked.

Myleene took a breath.

"And such a time shall come to pass when dark shadows drive through the very crust of the Earth where it has grown weak," Myleene spoke in a voice force without inflection or emotion and purely from memory. *"Earth and Air, Fire and Water- it will all warp. Disaster shall be visited upon the innocents, and they shall no longer remain innocent. Gorgoth will send Trickster, Spirit, Malevolence, Eradicator, Warrior, Conjuror and Sorcerer, the six Destroyers- precursors to the coming of his armies- and these six Lieutenants shall wreak havoc upon the world as they seek out and destroy the eight chosen souls. The Eight are powerful alone, but forged together and standing side-by-side at the site of the Last Battle their powers will save the world. Protect the Eight, for if they do not stand together against the coming of Gorgoth at the end, at New Babylon, our fair earth will be lost."*

8

MAUI, HAWAII, U.S.A.

About three minutes before Devon Summers died the man called Loki stopped hurting her and stepped back to admire his handiwork. For two hours his pleasure and her hell had mounted in unison. Now it was all about to come to a frenzied end.

Devon stared up at her murderer through the pain. Her body felt like it had been run over by a steam roller from the neck down. How had things come to this senseless end?

Who was he? This killer? A jilted lover? An unhappy customer? An irate pedestrian? It didn't take much these days to commit an act of violence. The killer stood over her, eyes locked with hers, reveling in her final moments.

"It was good to kill you, Devon Summers," she heard him whisper. "You are the first to die. Your power will never be realized, not by Aegis and not by you," his hateful eyes travelled the length of her body. "You could have saved the world."

He turned away and passed beyond her sight. After a minute she heard the door click softly. Her killer was gone. *At least he left me to die in peace,* she thought.

Later, midnight chimed out on the mantelpiece clock. She could not move. His blows had long since broken all her major bones. To blink and roll her eyes and use her brain was the sum total of her collapsing world. It was ironic in a way, for she had never spent a single day in hospital. Never suffered a single bout of flu. Germs couldn't touch her, but stark, shitty life could. It could take away everything she had ever experienced.

Devon forced her eyes open, not wanting to slip away. She had wonderful memories. She had dreams and aspirations.

All about to be scattered like autumn leaves in a winter storm.

Oh, God!

Devon ached to live. Tears slid from the corners of her eyes, running down her face to pool on the carpet. She willed herself not to die, willed it with every fiber of her being.

And then she sensed something inside, something rising. Like a wave it flowed from her very core, gathering momentum, rushing from her toes to her scalp. Her eyes flashed bright green, the glow discernible even to her. She groaned. Heat blossomed within her.

She curled her fingers into fists. She moved her right leg.

She gasped, and then held herself immobile. Something was happening. Something miraculous. The parts of her body she could see were no longer broken, just bruised. *And were the bruises paling away even as she watched?*

Then the front door clicked open again and she stifled a shriek of fear. The killer was back to finish the job. Her panic hit a pinnacle when she saw a stranger walking towards her.

But the concern she saw in his face made her want to weep with joy.

"Devon Summers?" the man was so upset she could see tears glistening in his eyes. "Oh no. Are you Devon Summers?"

She managed a nod, dumbfounded she could even manage that.

"We're too late," the man collapsed to his knees, shoulders shaking in misery. "Oh, God, we're too late." The man reached for his cell phone.

Then he noticed her rapidly vanishing bruises and the protruding bones that were painlessly knitting themselves back together. He noticed her amazing emerald eyes ablaze with power.

"You are the *healer,*" he whispered in awe. "They thought they'd killed you, and left you for dead, not realizing *you are the healer!*"

Devon reveled in the newly awakened power within her.

The man jabbed at his cell phone. After a few seconds he said, "This is Michael. Devon Summers is alive, by a miracle. Get a team here. We have to get her to safety *now.*"

9

YORK, ENGLAND

I didn't understand the Text of Arcadia yet but leapt upon one point. "And you guys think *I* am one of these...these eight Chosen?"

Myleene shook her head. "Logan, we *know* you are."

Others nodded. Even Belinda gave me an encouraging smile.

"But *how?*"

"The planet's most powerful coven of witches used the Arcadia text as a focal point to concoct a location spell. A few days ago, the spell located the Eight, scattered around the world. Aegis has dispatched people to bring them in safely. But-"

I swallowed. "But?"

"The Six Destroyers, though stretched, are already out there, Logan. The spell sought them also, and they are very, very close. We even have their real names. Of course, the Destroyers know more about this crisis than we do. We don't even know how many of the Eight remain alive."

"Wait," Lucy spoke in a tiny voice. "It's...it's just you keep saying *six* Destroyers, yet you spoke *seven* names."

"Nice," Belinda grinned in appreciation.

"Yes, you are right. Well done." Myleene nodded in respect. "*Trickster*- the seventh Destroyer is a shape-changer, always concealed, almost impossible to find. We think it's the Text's way of pointing that out to us."

"Listen," I pinched the bridge of my nose and breathed slowly. "It's all very well rabbiting on about unknown powers and apocalypse, but in *my* reality I need to concentrate on stopping my house from being repossessed. Do you think my power might achieve that?"

Giles gave me a tight-lipped smile. "Who knows? We believe everyone's power is unique. Individually it will be fantastic, possibly devastating. But first, it needs coaxing out."

"Through hard *training*," Belinda added with a smile.

"Have you found *any* of the Eight?" Lucy asked. "Apart from dad?"

Myleene nodded towards the oriental guy who sat with his legs dangling over a chair arm. "Say hello to Kisami. Belinda flew him in from Hong Kong yesterday. He was the first we found."

Kisami said, "I speak small English. No?"

I widened my eyes.

"Look, I think we're done here," Giles said. "Go to your contacts. Get this meeting organized for tomorrow night. There has never been a more important meeting in our two thousand year history. We're at kill or be killed." With this last word he finally unknotted his tie and threw it on the table.

I sat there, scared. "Does this mean..." I swallowed. "Does this mean my daughter and I are in immediate danger?"

Belinda slid out of her chair and came over to me. "I'm with you now, Logan. You'll be safe," she winked. "And warm."

I heard Lucy choke back a laugh. I thought about my house, my business, and my friends.

"But seriously," Myleene drew my attention. "We do know that one of the Six is here, in York."

"In *York?*"

"Uh huh. A woman by the name of Ashka."

Fear twisted my gut. Nice bombshell.

I indicated Lucy. "My daughter needs to be safe. Plus, she needs to be back in school in a few days," I knew school weren't expecting her for a while following the hospitalization. "And I have a business, and bills."

"We'll work it out, Logan. Your daughter is safer with Belinda than with anyone else in the world right now. And you are safer in York, under our protection, than in any other city. Take some solace in that."

"So," Belinda held out a hand. "You gonna sit there all night, Logan? Or do ya wanna meet Bill Compton?"

10

MIAMI, U.S.A.

Pure adrenalin surged through Marian Cleaver as he approached the building where a crazy woman was holding thirty kids' hostage.

A stocky guy with a buzz cut was talking into his radio-mike behind a mini-van. Cleaver approached him

The stocky guy held out a hand. "Whoa there, partner. Been jogging?"

Cleaver winced, remembering the state of his sweats. "Just left your wife, bud. What's the activity here?"

"No one's gone in or out since we got here. And by the way, do I know you, *bud?*"

"What's the layout?" Cleaver ran a hand through his sweat-drenched hair, trying to look jaded, set for the long haul. None of these guys knew he was the man Gaines had named.

"Thirty to thirty-five hostages, ages eighteen to twenty three. Mixed race. No obvious motives," buzz-cut pointed to a room. Second floor. Left hand corner. "All in there."

"And the perp?"

"Sat watching them."

Cleaver frowned. "So not a single hostage has made a move? Not one? What the hell has this woman done to them?"

"We're just kicking it here, waiting for the brass. I'm really going to need to see some ID now."

Cleaver mulled it over. Gaines had to be holding something horrible over those kids. Out of all the dross his mind picked up on one thing.

"I wonder why they've been herded together."

"Who cares," buzz cut winked. "They're only college kids, right?"

Cleaver fought hard to restrain his natural tendencies. "Get a team together," he snarled. "Get a negotiator over here. And move the fucking press back," he pointed to a circling helicopter. "I don't want this playing out over national TV."

The Miami PD guy looked impressed, and then rushed off without questioning Cleaver's ID again. Cleaver took a moment to check his weapons, donned his trusty brown duster and made sure its heavy bulk was hiding both shotguns and all three automatics. And an array of knives. And a highly illegal cattle prod. A weapon for every occasion.

He slunk among the shadows, hugging the garden wall all the way to the house. A rattle of the front door found it locked. He pulled out a set of custom-made picks and finessed the lock. Seconds later he was inside.

A dark corridor ran to the far side of the house. Cleaver started down it, pausing frequently to listen. What the hell was he doing? Risking his career? And all for an ancient, secretive organization that denied its very existence. He muted his cell phone and sent a text message to England. His life wasn't as important as other things going on in the world right now. People needed help, whether they knew it or not. He wouldn't fail them.

Cleaver found a staircase. To his left, dirty windows overlooked a neglected garden and beyond that a Shell station that had been evacuated. Vivid lights bathed the scene in stark relief. He saw a bunch of kids one block over sitting on a wall, sucking down 20oz Dews and shoveling in fast food as if they had front row seats at the local Cineplex.

No sound came from the floor above. *Thirty-five kids? No sound?*

His cell phone lit up. An incoming text message from Aegis. He owed them. They had saved him, honed his boxing skills into fighting expertise, turned him around and given him a purpose- to watch over events here in Miami and report as they unfolded.

And Miami was about to become the most important place on the planet.

He read the message. *Do not confront Gaines. Eight still not found. Stand down.*

Cleaver bowed his head and leaned against the wall. *Stand down? Bullshit.* It wasn't that simple. Ever since Josh Walker died all those years ago, Cleaver had never left an innocent in trouble. He couldn't start now, Aegis directive or not.

He took out his gun and proceeded up the stairs. Staying low, he reached the second floor and located the room that held the hostages. Without a sound he crept towards the door, put his head to the wood, and listened.

Suddenly the door opened. A young girl stood there. She had shoulder-length jet black hair and a tanned face that would have been attractive if not for her red-rimmed eyes and trembling lower jaw. Her face paled at the sight of the gun.

"You have to come inside," the girl whispered. "She will kill one of us if you don't."

Cleaver was at a loss. He motioned with the gun. "Stand aside."

The girl moved. Through the gap Cleaver saw the hostages in various states of dress, huddled in a far corner of the room. They looked lost and helpless, and terrified.

Maybe Clanger had been right for once. Maybe this had been some kind of sex party.

Cleaver stepped through the door, ignoring the voice in his head that demanded he let Miami PD handle this by the book. As he entered the room his senses were assaulted by the cloying smell of mixed fear and tension, a smell he knew intimately. It was the smell of the ring. Some fighters came crawling through the ropes, their terror-stink so thick it used to fill Cleaver's nostrils like thousand dollar cologne. Some fighters masked it well behind a bullish exterior; others basked and wallowed in it like a hippo in his favorite mud bath. But there was no mistaking it.

Cleaver's nostrils flared.

In contrast, Mena Gaines, lounged in her Lazee-Boy, one white leg dangling over the padded arm. Cleaver locked eyes with her.

"So you are Marian Cleaver," Gaines rose with languid ease. "And we meet here, at New Babylon, for the first time."

"New Babylon?"

"The site of the apocalypse. Don't you know? This is where Gorgoth will be born. Do you have any idea who I am?"

Cleaver said nothing, but let his mind drink it all in. Gaines was tall, over six feet, and athletic beyond the point you might call obsession. Catwalk models had more fat. She wore an ankle-length black skirt with waist-high slits on both sides and a loose-fitting white sweater. Her black hair was straight and framed a once-pretty face that now looked haunted in the pale light. Cleaver likened her to a chandelier stripped of its glitter, still imposing and bright but missing that quality that made it really *live*.

He levelled the gun at her.

Gaines flicked a tongue across her lips. "I am Eradicator."

47

"Cool name. Put it on a T-shirt. Let the kids go."

"They are sitting on a cleverly-contrived pressure plate. If their combined weight shifts even a few ounces either way, it will trigger an explosion that will destroy this entire building."

Fuck and damn. "Including you."

Gaines shrugged.

"I thought you were a fighter."

Gaines looked delighted. "Well, I have many talents, Marian," she smiled lasciviously.

"You're not even *human*," Cleaver spat the words at her in disgust.

"Of course I am. I am imbued with the power my Master saw fit to give me, but I am as human as you, Marian."

"Stop calling me that!"

"Then don't say I'm not human," Gaines took a step forward. Her feet were bare and white against the oak floor.

"We are the second of our respective powers to meet. It is a shame you are not one of the Chosen, one of the Eight. Maybe Loki has murdered them all by now, eh? But we can still fight," her eyes flicked towards the sobbing huddle of kids. "Winner takes all."

Cleaver saw terrified faces staring back at him. "How do I release them?"

"The disarm button," Gaines motioned towards the arm of the Lazee-Boy. Cleaver saw a rectangular plastic object like a remote control.

"What guarantee do I have that it won't just set the bomb off?"

"Ummm," Gaines put a finger to her lips. "You got me there."

Cleaver wondered if he should risk just shooting the bitch. But the mocking expression on Gaines' face stopped him.

At that moment a voice blared out, amplified through a bullhorn. "Mena Gaines! This is the police! Is there a way we could talk to you?"

A splash of light, most likely from a helicopter, swept the windows.

Gaines danced forward, moving easily in her slit skirt. She flexed her shoulders and settled into a fighter's stance before the main window.

"Winner takes all," she said again. "In New Babylon. Here and now. Just think, Marian, you're not only trying to save the kids, you're trying to save the world too. And you get to do it on prime-time television. Isn't America cool?"

Cleaver stalled for a few more seconds, hoping a sniper might take a pot shot. To take out one of the Six so soon and so easily would give Aegis and the Chosen a massive boost.

Gaines indicated the remote. "Or I could put everyone out of their misery right now."

Cleaver dropped the gun and leapt at her.

11

SAN FRANCISCO, U.S.A.

The Porsche twitched and the engine screamed as Ken Hamilton slammed his foot down on the accelerator.

"What the fuck's going on, man?" he shouted. "Who the hell are you and who's that crazy bitch back there?"

The man in the passenger seat, a short, balding individual who spoke in a clipped British accent said, "I do have a vague idea who that is, Ken. Though I'm not about to make any assumptions. Especially at this speed."

"Do I look like I enjoy being attacked by a mad woman?" Ken shouted angrily. "Huh? And especially one with a fucking *sword?*"

"Well, in truth, Ken, you strike me as a young, rather roguish surfer dude who hates authority and makes snap decisions, making him very unpredictable."

Ken shrugged. "Well-"

"Eyes on the road please," the man grimaced as the Porsche veered towards oncoming traffic.

Ken twisted the wheel in a violent motion. Bright headlights zoomed closer in the rear view.

"Damn. We lost three seconds there."

Ken breathed out slowly, forcing himself to relax. He sent up a hand to smooth out his wild, blonde hair.

"Please listen to what I am saying," the Englishman enunciated clearly. "We have little time, and I certainly do not fancy coming between you and that bloody sword *again*. Do I have your attention?"

"Yes," Ken sulked. He hated being told what to do.

"Well, thank the Lord. We have a major problem, my man. First let me assure you the random atrocities you have seen on Fox and CNN recently are not random at all. The odd shadow phenomenon you have heard dismissed by reporters and news anchors is not an anomaly, rather it is a *cause*. And you, Ken Hamilton, though somewhat insubordinate and far too good looking, are rather more than you seem."

Ken kept his eyes on the road. "Stop the bullshit *Jeeves*. And stop saying *Ken this* and *Ken that*. It's annoying."

"Vampires," 'the man said. "werewolves and other species do not solely belong to the fictional realm, *Ken*. I ask only your indulgence, and an hour of your time, to prove it."

Ken tousled his hair in frustration, and then straightened it out again almost without realizing. It was a bad habit, and drew the wrong kind of attention. Girls thought he was vain, guys thought he was a dork. He didn't really love himself. Not too much anyway.

"And the sword-bitch?" he pressed, jerking his head towards the car close to their rear.

"A rogue element. A secret weapon of our enemies, I fear, sent to kill you. She is not one of the Six Destroyers. I fear she is something else."

"Like what? A *vampire?* Are you saying Kate was right?"

"Kate?"

"*Beckinsale*. You know, the Underworld babe? Mentioned some bullshit about a war going on for centuries, between vamps and werewolves."

"Well, as much as I respect Ms Beckinsale's work, our story is a little different."

Ken swung around a slower car. "Sure it is, man. So where do I fit in?"

"You have a latent ability, Ken. A *power*, if you will. You are one of eight people who might be able to save the world."

Ken grimaced. Listening to this crap was starting to freak him out. There was a reefer stashed away in the glove box, and Ken's fingers were itching to make a grab for it. He gritted his teeth, trying to focus. It'd be a mistake to zone out at this speed, not with that bitch hot on his well-tanned ass. He risked a quick glance at the Englishman. The only reason he hadn't broken the dude's bald head was that he'd beaten off 'sword-bitch' back there, saving Ken's life.

Ken shook his head mockingly.

"Dude, after a few smokes and a crate of Bud I might buy that," he made a quick, thoughtless decision and decided to end this. He slammed on the brakes. Cars all around him swerved and honked and flashed their lights. Oncoming traffic slewed left and right.

The Englishman's nose ended up an inch from the glove box. "Whilst I encourage unpredictability in a student," he said softly. "I must say that if you don't get this vehicle moving right now and get some distance between us and that mad woman, I'll break your fucking arm."

Ken goggled at the small man. Whoa, the dude was serious. And not just about his threat, but about everything else too. Ken could see it in his face. For the first time since they met forty minutes ago Ken felt an icy finger of fear slide down his spine. What if all his fancy words were true?

He gunned the engine. The Porsche took off like a missile, tyres squealing. The bitch came alongside them for a moment. Ken got a brief look at her, and what he saw made his fear turn into undiluted horror. The woman looked insane. Her eyes were inhumanly wide. Waves of dirty white hair framed her snarling face. She had more teeth than a Ferrari gearbox and a mouth so crooked it could probably bite off her own left ear. She gestured threateningly at him with a well-muscled arm. Rings of bone were set at every knuckle. Necklaces of small skulls jiggled around her throat.

"Man," Ken breathed. "She sure looks crazy."

He swerved as she tried to ram their car, narrowly missing the guard rail. He juiced the accelerator and the Porsche leapt forward. Before them a great sense of space suddenly opened up.

"Oh, man, it's the Golden Gate," Ken blinked rapidly, tensing with stress. "What are we gonna do?"

"Keep going. Watch the road," the Englishman barked. "What's the problem?"

"It's the fucking *Golden Gate*, you English fruitcake," Ken loved insulting people who thought they were in charge. "The bridge will be snarled. Do you wanna end up fighting her on the Golden Gate?"

The Englishman narrowed his eyes and turned to Ken with a wry smile. It was the first time Ken had seen the guy lighten up.

"Swords clashing on the Golden Gate Bridge?" He said dreamily. "Now there's a vision"

"How do you *know* me, man?"

"Stop when you get near the bridge. I will distract her. You must drive through San Francisco to the *old* Hard Rock Café, the new House of Aegis. They will explain everything," the Englishman smiled sadly. "I wish I could have trained with you. I wanted to see your power revealed."

53

Ken's mouth tasted like sand and blood. "What the crap do you mean? Spill, man. Who's the bitch?"

"Dementia," the answer held a tone of deep terror, as if they were talking about the Angel of Death. "She is not one of the Six Destroyers. She is a legendary demon of Satan's top Hierarchy, someone we believed to be a kind of 'bogeyman' figure, dreamt up to scare vampires and lycans. My, God, why the hell would she ally herself with this World-Ender? This Gorgoth. It makes no sense at all."

"Fuck me! You're telling me that this Dementia is a *demon* dreamt up to *scare vampires?*"

"Maybe a secret weapon of the enemy, and perhaps their most powerful, as Belinda is to us," the Englishman set his jaw. "I will hold her back as long as I am able."

"*What?*" Ken didn't like the way this was going. "What are you saying? That you're going to *sacrifice* yourself for me?"

"You must live, Ken. The fate of millions could depend on it."

Ken made his decision in a millisecond. "Fuck that."

He swung the wheel hard and wrenched at the handbrake, grimacing as the Porsche executed a squealing one hundred and eighty degree turn.

In a split second they were now facing their enemy's onrushing car.

"The Porsche Turbo," Ken breathed. "Off the mark, it's still one of the fastest cars in the world." His hands gripped the steering wheel until the knuckles turned white.

Ken trod heavily on the accelerator. The Porsche fired itself forward as if it had been shot out of a gun.

Headlights rushed at them. Blinding them. Dementia showed no signs of slowing down.

"It's also the most maneuverable," Ken threw the vehicle into a sideways spin at seventy miles an hour. Asphalt screeched and bits of rock and debris shot from beneath the wheels like bullets. The car slid in a graceful arc across the blacktop. Dementia's vehicle twitched towards them. Ken wrenched the wheel quickly in the opposite direction, executing another perfect arc.

The Porsche glided gracefully around Dementia's car, the two deadly masses of metal and glass clearing each other by a matter of inches. Ken, holding on for dear life, got a full-face glare from the legendary mad-dog killer, and then the cars were skidding apart.

Dementia's car hit the guard rail, then shot across to the other side of the road where it struck the other guard rail, bounced back, and rolled onto its roof. Tyres spun ineffectually at the air. Nothing moved in the wreckage.

Ken finessed the drift expertly until they were facing back towards the Golden Gate. "Wow!" he said. "I know I'm cool. And, God knows, I'm pretty. But man, can I fucking *drive!*"

"She won't be dead," the Englishman looked suitably green. "But we can't spare the time to finish her off. The police will be here soon. Ken, thank you. Now, will you please drive to the city? Let me take you to the safe house. Give me an hour to prove what I have told you."

"Now *that's* more like it," Ken gave him the full beam smile. "You say *please,* you get my attention!

12

MIAMI, U.S.A.

Cleaver leapt forward. Mena Gaines danced away, leaving him flailing awkwardly. He was not a graceful fighter. He was brutal power with minimum finesse.

Gaines had retreated towards the remote. Cleaver had been hoping she would move away from it. She smiled at him, as if reading his mind.

Harsh light washed through the windows. Vaguely, he heard someone shouting his name through a bullhorn. With an effort he pushed it aside, narrowing his focus until everything except Gaines faded to background noise.

This was the zone. The way of combat. Let the rest of the world die away to static.

What remained was the spring in the floorboards, the random obstacles he might use to his advantage, the way Gaines hopped from foot to foot not favouring left or right, the location of the remote, his many weapons.

Gaines came at him. Cleaver half-turned to one side, left a stiff arm for her to run into, but she slipped under it. Cleaver double-stepped instantly, delivering a hook to the small of Gaines' back. Amazingly, it hit, sending Gaines sprawling. Cleaver watched her fall, knowing he had a millisecond to decide.

Grab the remote. Or press forward, maybe kill Gaines.

Save thirty frightened kids or risk the lives of millions.

Cleaver went for the remote as Gaines scrambled to her feet. Cleaver gritted his teeth, offered up a silent prayer, and pressed the disarm button. There was a faint click, and then nothing.

But the grin on Gaines' face was truly evil.

Cleaver stared at her. *What now?*

"Oh, Marian, you've been found wanting," she spat at him. "You had the chance to take me out. *You!* But you chose to save thirty not-so-innocents, and you've gambled the world. This test has shown that Aegis is weak. My master will be pleased."

"Test?" Cleaver said. "All this is just a *test?*" The pride he felt in beating Gaines, the brief flicker of hope that he might have made some small atonement for his past mistake withered and died like love betrayed.

Gaines laughed. Spittle flew from her lips. "You didn't *beat* me. I *analysed* you! And now you will reap the whirlwind! Miami is the New Babylon and soon it will start to explode with rage and passion and death." Gaines spread her arms wide. "You will soon wish you *had* all been blown to bits!"

Gaines ran. Cleaver thumbed his cell phone. Bewildered, angered, and aware that he might have made the wrong choice, he phoned in the all clear.

13

YORK, ENGLAND

My first concern after my daughter was for my best friend. As Belinda drove us out of York in her white Nissan I reached for my mobile.

"Who you calling, honeycakes?" Belinda glanced at me briefly, pulling up at a red light.

"I'm calling Holly. Making sure she's alright." *What the hell had she called me?*

Belinda blinked at me. "Who's Holly? Your girlfriend? Your dog?"

I ignored the snort of laughter from the back seat. Patience before pride.

I nodded at the traffic lights that had turned green. "My best friend," I told her. "She's helped us out...a lot. I can't *not* warn her about this."

And I'd seen movies. The bad guys *always* came after your friends first.

Belinda snorted as she started moving again. "You've watched too many movies, sugarcakes. But, go ahead, ring her. Christ, maybe we can make a night of it- drop by for pizza, go shopping, meet the vampire. You know, normal stuff."

I pressed speed dial 2, trying to tune her energized chatter out for a few seconds. She was still babbling on about *slay a demon, catch an old Five-O episode, crack open a crate of Bud*...when Holly answered.

"Dean? Are you okay?"

The digital readout on the dash glowed *11.21* and I

heard the concern in her voice. "Hey, Hol, I'm fine. Listen, are you alone?" In truth I didn't feel okay at all, my chest was aching, and my head was pounding with a combination of stress and shock.

"Very funny, Dean. Har har."

"Holly," Lucy said from the back seat. "You really need to listen."

I paused in surprise. Hearing Lucy speak that way was music to my ears.

I turned to grin at my daughter and saw a light in her eyes that I'd doubted would ever be rekindled.

Holly's voice held a note of surprise. "Lucy? Is that you?"

"Yeah, Hol."

I spoke quickly. "Listen, Hol, there's something important that I have to do," I paused. "That *we both* have to do. Lucy and me. It may take a few days. I want you to stay safe, Hol. Be safe. Okay?"

"What? Has...oh, God. Has *she-*"

"No," I rushed in immediately, realising that Holly meant Raychel. "Nothing like that."

"But what about the business? What about school?"

Belinda turned into a dark, tree-lined driveway and slowed down.

"I have to go, Hol. I'll call you tomorrow."

I snapped the phone shut, forestalling any protest. After a second, I muted it as well.

Belinda smirked. "Sounded more like your mother to me, muffin."

"She cares, that's all."

"Well, you sure handled it well. I guess we can rule out your special power as being the art of persuasion."

"Shut up, smart arse," I said. "And what's with all the bloody *cake* references?"

Belinda affected a dumb blonde expression as she exited the still-ticking car. "Don't know what you're talking about."

I cracked open my own door. My rebuke had washed over her like warm summer rain. "C'mon, Luce," I said. "The girl's nutty."

Belinda stood near the front of the car.

"This is *his* house," Belinda said. "Don't expect too much. It's not a castle. He's not Dracula. In fact, he's just a tall white guy with cool eyes and pointy fangs. Apart from that he's pretty normal. Gets his stakes from Asda-" she smiled at her own little joke. "Oh, and believe me, he's *definitely* straight."

I frowned, then thought: *don't even ask.*

"What's his name?" Lucy asked as we crunched over gravel towards an impressive looking portico.

"I am Ceriden," a voice said in silky tones and both Lucy and I jumped as a dark presence materialized next to us.

"He's a vampire," Belinda shrugged. "You have to let him do that."

Ceriden approached us so fast I barely saw him move. I took a step back, making sure I was beside my daughter.

"I am *so* pleased to meet you," Ceriden stuck out a pasty hand. The fingers were adorned with jewelry, mostly gold rings, and the wrist hung limply.

I stared, transfixed, at my first vampire. My stomach churned with an acidic mix of stress, fright and nausea. I didn't like how my beliefs had changed in the last few hours, and how readily I had come to accept it.

Ceriden's gaze fell on Lucy. "Oh, what-a-*darling,*" he gushed, taking me completely by surprise. He bent towards her. "Oh, dear," his eyes found her shoes.

"Fashion victim. *So* rip-off, my dear. And *so* not the way to go."

Ceriden squinted sideways at me. "Do you make her wear these *outside?* In the *open?* Bad man!"

I gulped, bewildered, unable to form words. Belinda, judging by her ear to ear grin, was enjoying herself immensely.

"And those jeans," Ceriden tutted. "What *are they?*"

"Top Man," I blurted, feeling shame.

"*Oh my God!*" Ceriden turned to Belinda in absolute horror.

I just stared. Of all ways I could have pigeonholed a vampire, this was not one of them.

Now Ceriden sniffed haughtily. "A little birdie tells me you are seeking proof that certain, ah, *supernatural* races exist. Am I right?"

I believed already, but I managed a nod. The vampire moved closer until he towered over me. The only flesh on view was bone white, making me think he'd lived his entire life in shadow. His eyes were deep, something almost hypnotic sparkled in their depths. I saw his nostrils flare, and wondered if my fear had a scent.

"Like an old Gautier cologne," Ceriden murmured, barely moving his lips.

Had he just read my mind?

Ceriden rolled up the sleeves of his expensive sweater. "Throw me your knife, Belinda darling."

"No," I blurted out, getting a lurid image of Lucy's self-inflicted wounds in my head. "No knives."

"Very well," Ceriden huffed. "Mr. *Top Man.*" His gaze conveyed power, wealth, and absolute confidence. "Come, Belinda, dear, I don't have all night. Important people are awaiting my return. Important *wealthy* people," he made eyes at me. "I know *all* the most powerful people, you know. Including Posh and David," to my horror he giggled.

Again, I stayed quiet.

The vampire sent a frown towards Belinda. "Your crucifix, Bee."

She hesitated. I saw it in her face. A half second of doubt, and then it was gone. She stepped forward and dropped a little crucifix into Ceriden's outstretched hands.

A hissing sound and a cloying, burning stench filled the air. I watched in rising horror as a thin curl of smoke spiraled up from the vampire's hands. Ceriden bore it for a few seconds then tossed the crucifix away. Belinda made no effort to retrieve it.

"Only blessed religious items affect me," Ceriden said. His palms were raw, the wound edged with a black crust. Lucy's hand slipped nervously into my own and I squeezed it. Ceriden took out a black velvet handkerchief embossed with the gold Versace symbol and dabbed at the burned flesh.

He went on. "Holy water. Sunlight. A well-placed wooden stake. But we are a cautious race. Most of us take no blood that is not freely given." Ceriden showed me his fangs. "For three hundred years I have followed this tradition."

Three hundred...

Ceriden's gaze lingered on the handkerchief. "I knew Gianni, you know. And later, Donatella- but that girl was so wild. No time for me."

Lucy goggled at our new friend. "Do you know Burberry?"

Ceriden laughed and ruffled her hair so fast I didn't see him move. "Puh*lease!* Stick with the eternal Italians, my dear. Gianni, Georgio, and Guccio. And maybe Enzo. How old are you?"

"Fifteen," I said.

"Nearly sixteen," she shrilled in my ear, and added, "Soon."

"We need to get you an *outfit*," Ceriden eyed me. "Assuming the Grumpmeister here will let you have one."

"Look," I said. "I don't mean to be rude, and especially not to a vampire, but –"

At a sudden loss for words, I gestured at Belinda.

Help? Please get me out of here.

She grinned. "Background info- Vampires, the good ones like Ceriden here- take what they call 'shades.' Willing men and women who stay with the vampire for life, almost like a soul-mate, if you like, allowing their master to feed off them and slake his blood lust. If he is careful a vampire like Ceriden may need only a dozen shades in his entire life, never feeding off an innocent."

"I thought vampires lived forever?" Lucy asked, recovering her voice before I did.

"No, dear, Hollywood overestimated us there I'm afraid. Vampires are not immortal," Ceriden flashed his fangs at her like a benevolent blood-sucking grandfather. "We reach our peak around three-to-four hundred before beginning the dreadful slide into obscurity and senility," he glanced pointedly at me. "Death occurs after roughly five hundred years. A vampire that old literally falls apart."

"Gross," Lucy said.

I wondered at her mounting confidence. Was it because she had been given new purpose? Or was it because her old dad was floundering?

"These human shades," I picked up on one of the many things bothering me. "Are they your slaves?"

"Not at all," Ceriden flapped a wrist. "A shade may walk away at any time. After a few years they will recover and be able to lead a full life. No after effects. But the *rewards* of being a vampire's shade far outweigh the downsides."

"Why?" Lucy was quick to ask.

"Too many to count, little one," he said. "And not for the ears of one so young. Maybe another time."

I gripped Lucy's hand, thinking *don't count on it, fang-face.*

Belinda gave Ceriden a big hug. "You know about the big pow-wow tomorrow night. All the little chiefs should be there. Fate of the world and all that."

The vampire nodded. "Fear not. My well-tailored buttocks will be seated beside your own sweet cheeks, my dear. And I will pass the word."

"That's it then," Belinda waved her hand to and fro in front of my face. "Still wavering, Logan, or did the fence just collapse beneath you?"

What could I say? I thought of our Victory Wall back home, of all those professional photographs taken by yours truly. If it didn't sell, it didn't get framed. Maybe I could make one exception.

"So tell me," I said to Ceriden. "Do you photograph well?"

By the time we arrived back at Aegis' safe house I was feeling beyond bone weary. It was well after midnight. Lucy had been quiet the whole way back and didn't protest when I agreed with Belinda's suggestion that we stay the night. At the time I put it down to her exhaustion. How naïve of me.

Lucy's room was spacious, dominated by a large double bed. I tapped on her PDA for a minute, leaving a note reminding her to change her bandages in the morning. I kissed her on the forehead, and then left the room.

My daughter. It would be a mistake to believe she wasn't really dying inside, still blaming herself for her mother's absence. The dark watches of the night bring into sharper focus those things that torment us the most.

I headed into the kitchen and threw a weary glance at Belinda. She returned my look with eyes that held too much wisdom for someone her age. I wondered what she'd gone through in her short life.

"Quick drink?" She asked.

"Oh, yeah," I said. "A chamomile tea if you've got any. I don't know what's harder- meeting a vampire or trying to talk to my daughter."

"Sure you don't want anything stronger? We could share *vodka*." She spoke the last word in a terrible Russian accent.

"No alcohol."

She fixed the tea, explaining that Aegis had bought up this entire six-house row, and then knocked each house through until it became an extensive warren of plush carpeted corridors and high vaulted ceilings. I couldn't imagine how many rooms there were in the whole three-storey high building, or how much the place was worth.

As Belinda delved into the floor standing freezer and came out with a half-empty bottle of Grey Goose, I plonked my weary frame down at the kitchen table and thought seriously about Raychel for the first time in weeks. Mostly now my absent wife was a fleeting distraction. I had dwelled on her far too much during that first year. But Holly had taken every foul word and petty incident I had thrown at her with almost inhuman patience and forgiveness. I owed her more than I could ever repay.

I had learned to compartmentalize. My method was in

keeping busy. By design, there was rarely a moment these days when I got chance to sit down and dwell.

My story is simple. One day my wife disappeared, taking nothing with her but a platinum ring inscribed with the legend: 'To Dean, all my love forever, Raychel'. At first I was a suspect in that disappearance, but now everyone believed my wife had just run away. Happened all the time, apparently. I'd spent a year clicking away on the internet, searching for sightings, for missing persons. There are websites for that, you know. I guess you need to be in my unique and desperate position to find out about them.

And sometimes I still clicked away after Lucy had gone to bed when she wouldn't hear me. I entered Raychel's name in all its guises, her old mobile number, her old addresses. I checked Google and more recently Facebook and Twitter.

Imagine my torture when the phone rang. Or there was a knock at the door.

Back then, I'd hit the bottle hard. I'd ceased to care about my life and the lives of those closest to me. I blamed myself for Raychel's vanishing act. I had failed her. I had failed Lucy and thrown away my career. Why the Hell would anyone make me one of the Chosen?

I swallowed a lump of pure guilt as Belinda finally came over, a glass half full of clear liquid in her left hand, my cup of chamomile tea in her right.

"Shall we toast?" she said.

I stared questioningly at her.

"To doing the right thing," she gave an easy smile.

"You always drink that much?"

Belinda grinned in that carefree way of hers. "It's a 'Belinda-shot', sugarcake. Just enough to take you *there*."

I stared into her eyes, shining with health and wit and wisdom. It was a wisdom she concealed well, and purposely, behind a light exterior.

I briefly wondered why.

Then I raised my cup. "To friends," I said simply, knowing she would understand. "Both old and new."

14

YORK, ENGLAND

I slept poorly for a few hours, my dreams haunted by a beast I could neither name nor remember. I climbed out of bed, then pulled on yesterday's clothes and headed down to the kitchen, following the smell of freshly-brewed coffee

Belinda was already seated at the table, a steaming cup in front of her. She looked the opposite of me, fresh, bright-eyed and perky. Today's t-shirt read: *'Innocent'*. I almost smiled.

"Just brewed," she said, indicating the expensive-looking coffee machine. "It's Komodo Dragon blend. Myleene brought it back from the States a few weeks ago."

I poured a cup, then nearly dropped it when I noticed a short girl with masses of bouncy hair and a wide, wicked smile stood behind the door.

"Meet Felicia," Belinda waved at her. "This here is Dean Logan. One of the Eight. Go easy, poodle, you're his first Lycan."

I stared, feeling rude but unable to stop. Felicia looked soft and sweet and all things cute. A silver ring sparkled at her navel and two more at her earlobes.

Felicia gave a pretend growl, showing sharp canines. "Don't worry," she said. "I've already eaten."

I closed my mouth with a clack of teeth and turned my attention back to my coffee. I wasn't about to poke fun at a werewolf no matter how light-hearted she seemed.

The coffee was dark and smooth, with a hint of liquorice. Belinda said, "Like it? I'm a coffee connoisseur. Don't laugh."

"She's a geek," Felicia breezed past, heading for the coffee maker.

I said nothing, feeling intimidated. Ceriden breezed in a few moments later and walked across to the fridge. It soon became obvious the kitchen was a kind of sounding stage where views were aired, and reactions evaluated. More decisions were ground out here, I wagered, than in any official meeting room.

Felicia seated herself beside me. I noticed her send a wicked grin in response to Belinda's warning look. "We Lycans are a loose affiliation, Mr. Logan. We like our freedom, so tend not to linger in once place for long. We move in groups of three or four, but rarely more. I am the only Lycan within a hundred miles of here," she winked. "At least, the only one worth knowing."

Felicia was about to continue when someone else entered the kitchen. I recognized Myleene, dressed in a black, well-cut business suit.

"Now there-" Ceriden said approvingly. "Is a woman who knows how to dress." he turned to me. "What does her look say to you, Logan? Power? Dominance? Some Vivienne Westwood mixed with a little S and M?"

Felicia giggled.

"The meeting," Myleene cut across us. "Is about to start. Everyone must assemble in the meeting room within five minutes."

I heard the tension in her voice. It reminded me that these discussions would affect the future of our planet. I glanced at the apprehensive faces of all the fantastical beings arrayed around me in the kitchen. It was their expressions that, above all else, drove home the indisputable fact that we were facing the severest crisis in our history.

***

The meeting room was full to bursting. I sat with a bedraggled looking Lucy as unobtrusively as possible. A tall row of windows marched away to my left, looking out onto an ordinary York street. People walked there- mothers pushed prams, little girls held their fathers' hands, a postman delivered letters- completely unaware that on the other side of those opaque windows the fate of the world was being decided. I recognized few people by now, Myleene, Belinda, Felicia the lovely Lycan, Ceriden the vampire and the oriental guy, Kisami, sitting a few rows in front.

And now how I wished for my trusty old Nikon. The camera is the physical extension of the mind, and my mind captured grainy studies in tension, fear and anticipation.

Myleene brought the meeting to order by indicating the quad bank of video screens mounted on the wall, facing us. "Soon we will see Tristran, Master of Vampires. Cheyne- the Witch Queen. And Eldritch- King of the Elves. Their representatives in the room are Ceriden, whom you all know, and-" Myleene paused as if in awe.

"Eleanor, the wife of Eldritch. Queen of the Elves."

My jaw dropped. I knew enough to be stunned by the presence of a being even vampires said were rare and reverential.

Elves? I thought. *Am I dreaming?*

I saw a diminutive figure give a slight nod from the front row. I craned my neck to get a better view, then noticed Lucy doing a complicated neck-wrenching manoeuvre beside me. I patted her knee. "We'll catch her later," I winked.

Myleene had recovered her poise. She flicked a switch

and the screens flickered to life allowing the momentous meeting of the true leaders of the world to begin.

Giles, the world leader of Aegis, said nothing. Myleene stayed on her feet, taking the spotlight. I thought they'd probably worked out a routine where she took the limelight and he kept to the background, taking time to think. The idea was sound.

Myleene spoke up. "First the good news. Devon Summers, of Maui, has been successfully extracted. Our enemy got to her first but made a mistake," she smiled. "Devon is our healer."

There were a few positive expletives around the room.

"Devon is on her way to York. And Ken Hamilton, another of the Eight, has been found, though he is proving a tough nut to convince."

"Just put me in line for a crack at that," Belinda said.

Ceriden cooed. "*Belinda!*"

I guessed they knew something about Ken Hamilton that I didn't.

"*All* eight Chosen have been located," Myleene said with obvious pride. "And *all* are alive. We'll do our best to keep them that way. But we haven't yet contacted the majority of them."

"How long do you anticipate?" Eldritch asked.

"Twenty four hours," Myleene said. "That's all we need."

"Make it quicker, please," Eldritch said, somehow making his order sound like a reasonable request. "The Eight are all that stand between us and oblivion."

Tristran spoke up next. For a master vampire he didn't sound good. His voice shook as he spoke. "Any luck with triggering their latent. . . powers. . . yet?" Tristran's words ended in a series of wracking coughs.

"We haven't started yet, Tristran."

"Then what happened with Devon Summers?"

"We believe her powers surfaced in response to a near-death situation," Myleene sighed. "Let's hope it's not the only way to do it."

"We can at least start their training," Eldritch said "Perhaps Eleanor could help? None are better at training humans than the elves. If anyone can coax their powers out it is Eleanor, our finest."

A voice answered from the front row. "I am grateful for the opportunity, husband."

I noticed Myleene relax. I realized there was more diplomacy going on here than it appeared.

"I'm sure there is more to learn from this text," Cheyne said. "This text of Arcadia. I don't need to mention that no one has located the *seventh* Destroyer yet, Trickster. I would like to continue spelling the text here in the library."

Cheyne was a true beauty, with the bearing and appearance of a model, but nothing could take my attention away from her nose. More like a beak, it was practically double-jointed and crooked. It was as if God had said *okay, I'll give you all this power, I'll make you a true witch, but you'll live with* this *in return.* And *bam!* She'd gained a conk only a shade shorter and slightly less crooked than the Grand Canyon.

I heard Lucy stifle a giggle-cough beside me.

"Don't say a word," I leaned towards her. "I don't want my daughter turned into Shrek."

Cheyne went on, folding her tanned legs beneath her and sipping from a crystal wine glass at her side. "I want more specifics about this last battle. And I'd bet my ribbed broomstick that there's more to discover about Gorgoth.

He's the coming world-ender, of whom we know nothing."

That made me frown. We knew *nothing?* Myleene and the gang had kept that fact quiet.

"What of the threat to the library?" Myleene said.

Felicia then found her voice. "I offer the services of Hugo's pack. They hunt not an hour's run from the Library of Aegis."

"And I offer Eliza's help, and that of her shades," Tristran said around a choking cough. "Eliza...is our best... by far."

I heard Ceriden whisper, "*Do you think I should offer the services of David Beckham?*" and blessed him for lightening the moment. The guy was an odd card, sure, but was he a Joker or an Ace?

Belinda said, "I wouldn't mind being offered the services of that ribbed broomstick," under her breath.

"Good enough," Myleene said, taking Giles' silence as affirmation. "Now, I know this will cause contention," she paused. "But. . .Marian Cleaver?"

Felicia surged to her feet. The small Lycan looked out of place, but her words carried true conviction. "He should *never* have been left in Miami to face this alone. *Never.* "

Giles replied immediately, holding his hands up as if in surrender. "Fine. I was wrong, you were right. I made a mistake leaving Cleaver vulnerable. I wanted to...give him a righteous goal, if you like. But it was a decision we all took, and something he *wanted*. Needed even," Giles said carefully. "And I will not take all the hits for it."

The Aegis leader loosened his tie.

"A mistake that can be rectified," Ceriden put in. "Now."

Felicia nodded so hard I thought her masses of blonde curls might fall off.

"I hear you," Giles pulled on his shirt collar for ventilation. "Eldritch will meet up with him soon."

"And since we now know Gorgoth will first appear in Miami," Ceriden said. "Perhaps we should start to gather more teams there," his bony hands were steepled together on the table.

"Later," Giles told him. "I want to know more about Gorgoth and his Destroyers before we take any major action. Also, it might draw attention to *you*," he flapped a hand generally. "To Ubers, I mean."

"Agreed," Tristran overruled Ceriden. "Unfortunately, the only clear facts are that we must protect the Eight and learn more about this Gorgoth."

"And what of this brand new threat?" Cheyne asked between sips of wine. "What of the Hierarchy of Demons?"

Myleene looked confused. "New threat?"

"Dementia has surfaced in San Francisco, and she is a *demon*," Cheyne spoke with care. "Not a Destroyer. Something is not right there. . ." she trailed off.

There was a long silence. Cheyne, it seemed, had raised a point no one else had considered.

"That is new." Myleene allowed.

Cheyne was scratching at her chicane-like nose. "Summoning Dementia is an act without reason. Demons are demons, loyal only to Lucifer- the Devil Himself. I'll be burned at the stake if I can't figure out why they would ally themselves with this Gorgoth, this world-ender." Cheyne ran a hand through her dark, curly tresses. "And more pressing needs mean we have to focus on Gorgoth and worry about the Hierarchy later."

A lull followed. If only someone had continued *that* line of conversation.

Tristran coughed. "It seems that we Ubers are taking on

the role of protectors and seekers of knowledge," he said, his voice wet. "What will be the role of Aegis, I wonder?"

Giles stood immediately. "To find the Eight," he said. "To unite them on the training ground. To overlook *all aspects* of every operation. In short, we will police this whole undertaking."

I saw Felicia shift uncomfortably. Ceriden sniffed. I could tell Giles' words didn't sit well with them. As I thought, diplomacy wasn't his strongest suit.

Myleene sensed the sudden tension. "We all have a part to play," she said. "And we have to rely on each other. If we lose this one, we don't get to try again next year. We lose our world. "

"Learn what you can from the text," she inclined her head at Cheyne. "Tap all resources for information on Gorgoth. Someone out there knows something. They *have* to."

"And use any means," Tristran added.

"Yes," Giles made a fist around his tie. "We're already playing towards the endgame here and we know *nothing*."

Belinda rose to her feet. "There are no trophies," she said. "No rewards. We fight for the right to exist, and for the good and innocent people out there who make the fight worthwhile."

My mouth was dry. I squeezed Lucy's hand in reassurance, as much for me as her.

We'd been shown the full weight of the task being laid upon us. I prayed I had the strength to bear my part of it.

15

MIAMI, U.S.A.

Marian Cleaver climbed the flight of stairs that led to his door, then stood and leaned his head against the cool glass. Taking on Mena Gaines had challenged everything he stood for.

You have been found wanting.

But she was a snake, at best. A lying, conniving piece of evil that slithered and crawled its way along whichever filthy gutter her master commanded.

Aegis was sending help. Was that a good thing? Miami was the staging area for an end of the world event. But at least the kids were safe; he'd saved the day. And yet judging by the type of questions fired at him earlier by the goddamn feds you wouldn't fucking think it.

He entered the house, lost the duster, and cracked open the fridge. A single lonely slice of congealed pizza stared back at him.

Mmmm...tempting.

He threw his weapons on the kitchen table and checked the cattle prod. The sound of his cell phone ringing shattered the predawn quiet. Cleaver closed his eyes and wished for a moment's peace.

"Cleaver here."

"Clancy. Where are you now?"

"At home, Hector. I told you I was going home, so where else would I be?"

"Well, Sir Cleaver, I'm sorry to have to do this to you," Clanger didn't sound sorry at all. "But you're needed downtown. Now."

As he listened to his boss Cleaver heard distant sirens. Lots of them.

He bit his lip. "What's happened?"

Clanger was silent for a moment, then launched into nervous mode, his words falling faster than water in a rainstorm. "Don't know with any certainty, but a large group of people have attacked the Coconut Grove shopping mall. You know, the open air one? A part of it is on fire. And people...people have been seen leaping into the flames. And your Gaines woman is involved in this one too."

Cleaver breathed out slowly. Mena Gaines' words resounded in his head: *Miami is the New Babylon and soon it will start to explode with rage and passion and death!*

"I'm on my way, Hector," Cleaver said slowly. "I'm on my way."

16

YORK, ENGLAND

By the time I'd returned to the kitchen it had occurred to me that the world hadn't yet stopped turning. I had a business to run, bills to pay, and a daughter to care for. How the hell was I going to trade that off against this latest crap?

Whilst I waited for the coffee to brew, I called my office manager, Tom. By the time it arrived, made by Belinda, I was dwelling between contented and concerned. Our new venture had generated several enquiries, but one thing was missing. *Me!*

"Zambia Terranova Estate," Belinda broke into my thoughts and placed a mug before me. "It's a Black Apron coffee. The best."

I nodded, shaking my head at that *Innocent* t-shirt. Lucy filed in. She stared at me. "You know it's a school day?"

"I thought of that, Luce. Then I remembered...they're not expecting you," I looked briefly at her bandaged arm, now covered by a sweater.

"I didn't mean for *schoolwork,*" Lucy made a face as if she was talking to the dumbest person in the world. "I meant to see my friends."

I rolled my eyes. "*Fifteen* year olds."

"Almost *sixteen.*"

I sipped the delicious coffee, trying to ignore both Lucy's birthday reminder and the unfathomable looks being directed at me by a particularly playful lycan. My mobile vibrated in my pocket, making me jump. I hadn't turned it off silent mode. When I managed to fish it out, I saw that I had a voicemail from Holly.

Recorded three minutes ago.

It went: "Dean, I know I sound stupid, but I keep remembering what you said about staying safe. Well, there's a woman outside and I'm *sure* she's watching the house. I don't like it, Dean. I'm going out to talk to her."

Holly! My face went ashen. I turned to Belinda.

"You mentioned that one of the Six was already in York. I can't remember- was it a woman?"

"Yes." Belinda frowned at the stress choking my voice. "Ashka."

"Would she target my friends?"

Lucy shifted in her seat. "Dad? What is it?"

"Yes, for several reasons. To distract you, to draw you out, or to cause you distress. Why, Logan?"

I pressed speed dial two, holding the phone tight to my ear and praying my best friend would answer.

Please, Hol, please be there.

Belinda walked over to me. Felicia leapt off the worktop. Ceriden pushed his seat back.

Holly answered, "Dean?"

"Holly, thank God! Are you okay? What's happening over there?"

"Just- oh, hang on, there's someone at the door. Probably that bloody woman."

"Wait!"

I think we all held our breath, except Ceriden, who didn't breathe.

"What is it, Dean?" Holly sounded scared now.

"Just wait," I said.

Belinda pulled her car keys off a hook by the door.

"Hold on!" I shouted down the phone. "Hide. Keep your mobile with you. And *please*, Hol, don't talk to that woman!"

Belinda ran for the kitchen door, Felicia close behind. I stared after them. "I'm coming," I said. "She's my best friend."

"Dean, what the hell is-" Holly sounded half scared, half-amused.

"We're coming to get you," I hissed. "We're ten minutes away. *Do not* go near that woman."

I ran after Felicia, glancing back at Lucy as I exited the kitchen. She was staring after me with huge, anxious eyes. Guilt shredded my will. Maybe I shouldn't leave her like this. A depressed child would fear the worst- that her father might die. I could almost see our new, fragile bond tear at the seams.

"I'm coming back," I told her. "Don't worry."

Ceriden made his way around the table. "Since it is daylight and I can't accompany you," he patted my daughter's shoulder. "I will look after your Lucy."

I hesitated. It felt wrong. It cut deep when I noticed Lucy's eyes brighten. But by then I was out the door.

I was committed.

Ten minutes. Did you ever wonder how many thoughts-happy and sad, positive and terrifying- can race through your mind in just ten minutes?

By the time we pulled up outside Holly's house I was wound as tight as a chartered accountant paying for his daughters' wedding. Sunlight blasted us as we jumped out of Belinda's Audi. Felicia was fast beyond belief, leaping sure-footedly between the bushes and hitting Holly's garden at a dead run. Belinda was right on her heels. I flailed about behind them. In truth I am no slouch. I am fit and capable, but man, I'm only human.

Felicia slowed. I came up beside Belinda who was bouncing on the balls of her feet.

Standing in Holly's doorway was a tall woman with eastern-European features.

"Hi," Belinda said warily. "And you would be?"

The woman gave us a sly smile. "I would be Ashka. One of the six Destroyers of the world."

Felicia padded to her left, Belinda fanned right. I remained where I was, merely a distraction. A heavy tension fell over us and I felt an utterly surreal moment. Here we stood in a sunlit garden in the heart of York, surrounded by the steady hum of traffic and the constant din of the everyday world, yet we might as well have been in a different dimension. A death scent of savage intentions infused the air, giving me a rush of adrenalin and a feeling of self-preservation stronger than anything I had ever known.

I didn't take my eyes off Ashka but remained aware of every movement Belinda and Felicia made through my peripheral vision. I stopped breathing when the killer's eyes fixed on me. They were dark. Even in the daylight I could see they were flecked with red. Bright with evil desire. I suddenly felt vulnerable and foolish. What the hell had I been thinking?

Holly. My friend.

Belinda said, "You made a fatal mistake coming here, you big-boned demon-slut bitch."

I grimaced. There was nothing like Belinda's attitude to ease the tension. She was the best at what she did, and I admit that I was perversely fascinated to see her unleashed.

81

Ashka took a step forward, setting her balance. Confidence shone like a challenge from her hellish eyes.

She pulled out two short knives from the waistband of her jeans.

Belinda tried to taunt her again. "Only three inches, darling?"

She was playing for time. Myleene had dispatched a second car to help us. The Elf, Eleanor, was three minutes away. It spoke volumes for Ashka that someone like Belinda, with Felicia backing her up, was stalling until help arrived.

The smile that darkened Ashka's face could have eclipsed the sun. "You will feel every inch, girl, believe me."

The door behind Ashka opened and Holly stood there. "Dean? Dean, what's-"

Too close. *No!*

Everything went crazy. Ashka spun at Holly, slashing, and I saw blood spatter the white door, but then Ashka spun right back as she realized that both Belinda and Felicia had struck. I gaped in disbelief, hardly able to comprehend how fast they moved. Belinda leapt at Ashka with a flying kick, falling purposely short, then landing and spinning in one fluid movement, her trailing leg stuck out to trip her adversary. This was all designed so Felicia, coming in low, could rip at Ashka with sharp fingernails, aiming for a tendon or a vein.

Ashka backed away. She evaded Belinda's sweep, then somersaulted over Felicia, landing poised and un-flustered.

Her movements brought her to within eight feet of me. I could count the blood-red whorls in her eyes. Then Belinda was there, assailing Ashka with a series of elbow, knee and palm strikes, each one aimed to kill. Through all her defence, Ashka found a millisecond to flick a knife towards Holly which Felicia incredibly intercepted. Holly was down on one knee. I could see blood on her hands. In that instant I accepted that none of this was a 'capture' scenario. This, and everything that was happening all over the world, was a fight to the death.

In that instant, I accepted it all.

Something inside me began to swell. I staggered, feeling nauseous.

Belinda maintained the attack, not only to keep Ashka away from me but also to buy time. The second car couldn't be far away now.

I took deep breaths, trying to keep my breakfast down. A flare of embarrassment lit my face. God, Belinda shouldn't see me like this. What the hell-?

Then a pleasant sensation began to pool in the pit of my stomach. I lifted my face. Energy flowed through my limbs. I felt rejuvenated, energized, as if I'd been given fresh batteries.

Six feet away Belinda and Felicia struck viciously at Ashka, but I could sense that the Destroyers attention was fixed on me. She was using their own efforts against them, purposely being driven in my direction.

She had used Holly to draw me out.

Suddenly Ashka threw her head back and screamed. Raw energy lit her face as if a floodlight had been turned on inside, sending her skin almost translucent. Power shot from her in a twisting bolt of black that made her hair stand on end.

"I am Malevolence!" she screamed. *"All who oppose me will shudder and die!"*

The wonderful sensation trickling through me suddenly

stopped. Ashka flung her hands in the air and suddenly her body was wreathed in black flame. I felt something strike my mind, a dark comet of terrifying images. From nowhere came a vision of Lucy, a sickening vision of my daughter lying helpless, alone, her veins opened up, and her body dried out, a grimace of terror stretched across her white face. Her lips moved in a final breath, and I had to strain to make out that last word: *dad...*

I staggered, landed on my hip. A jolt of pain shot through me. I held my head in my hands as it threatened to explode.

Lucy! No!

A headache threatened to split my head open.

"It's her power!" I heard Belinda's tortured voice cry. "She...she's Malevolence. She shows you your worst fear!"

I put my hands on the ground, feeling the soft, real earth. Already the Lucy-vision was fading. A pair of feet landed softly in front of me. I lifted my head.

Ashka was right there. She said, "So you are Logan. I have come around the world to take your pathetic body apart, sliver by rotting sliver."

I knelt before her, rooted to the spot. Where was my power? Where was my *fucking* power when I needed it? The Lucy-vision had struck hard and Ashka gave me no time to recover.

Hands wreathed in black fire reached for me. I stared into her face, into her glistening, sinful eyes, and I couldn't look away.

Death laughed at me.

I heard: *"No!"* and Belinda landed a kick on Ashka's spine, sending her staggering past me. I saw Felicia raising herself from the ground, a haunted look on her face. Then she too launched herself at Ashka.

"Keep her off balance," one of them said. "She can't cast if she's too busy to think."

And then Eleanor arrived. My God, if I'd thought the others were fast then the elf was a rapid freak of nature. Dealing out two blows for every one of Belinda's she forced the evil Destroyer back across the garden towards the tree line.

I watched, awestruck. Eleanor led the attack, complimented by Belinda to her right and Felicia to the left. Working together as a unit they ensured Ashka was simply too preoccupied with self-preservation to be able to fling any more incapacitating visions our way.

A moment later Ashka took hefty blows from three sides, which gave her that precious second needed to summon her fire. She fell heavily, but then black flame exploded all around her and I cringed as a devastating bombardment of mental assaults floored us all.

But this time it was different. This time I saw Belinda. *Why?* I almost wept as I saw the dynamic blonde crawling through a heap of severed limbs and plague-riddled corpses, a chain looped around her neck, and a fiery demon holding the handle of her leash, standing behind her with a wicked sword held high.

A demon? A terrible thought swept through me as the vision fell away. *What if this is a premonition?*

In another second, I raised my head to see the others gaining their feet. But Ashka was gone. She had used the vision-attack as a diversion.

She had chosen to fight another day.

I took a breath. Around me the simple hum of city traffic and normal life continued, but how different it was in here, in our deadly circle of the world.

Belinda regarded me with haunted eyes. What had *she*

seen? Felicia and Eleanor stared at each other in horror. And I could hear Holly crying.

Please don't let them be premonitions.

17

YORK, ENGLAND

We wasted no time bundling Holly into Belinda's Audi, then heading back to Aegis. I asked Holly to wait for explanations. After what she'd just witnessed, she was in no state to argue. Ashka's knife had ripped her forearm open.

I sat in silence the whole way back, wondering if my latent ability had surfaced briefly. If so, it had failed.

"Those damn visions nearly killed me;" Belinda's eyes met mine in the rear view. The false vision of Lucy's last breath threatened to overwhelm me.

"And Ashka's only one of six Destroyers against us." Felicia shivered as if trying to shake the memory.

And beyond the Destroyers was their *God. Gorgoth.* The world was falling apart as we talked and planned and hoped our powers would surface.

I couldn't handle any of it right now. I sat and chewed my nails to the quick, compelling it all to go away.

Once back at the house I found and hugged Lucy like I hadn't seen her in months and then, ignoring everyone else, I took her and a freshly bandaged Holly up to my room. We sat on the bed and stared at each other in silence.

"Nice place," Holly said, meaning the house itself. "One of York's darker secrets?"

I tried a smile, but it didn't quite touch my face. Holly looked even more scared. Holly was short, with flame red hair and a vivacious smile. Her spirit was strong, a glowing flame that usually roared, sometimes wavered, but never died. I walked over to the window and spent a moment looking down at the sprawling gardens. I hesitated, then looked over my shoulder at Lucy.

"Give her the low-down, Luce." I said. To explain any of it would make it starkly real.

And if some of it was real, then *all* of it was real, and some world-saving power existed inside me. A power that would fail. And it meant that Ashka's visions could also be real.

I let it wash over me, listening distractedly as Lucy enlightened my best friend. The excitement in her voice passed me by, as did Holly's amazement, her disbelief, her slow acceptance. I didn't even look around when a new vampire was brought into the room as final, irrefutable proof. I heard the newcomer's name- Mai, but barely noticed the odd tone in my daughter's voice that said this new vampire wasn't a total stranger to her.

I made a call. Checked in with Tom. The business was scraping by.

At that moment the door opened and Belinda sauntered in. She had changed back into her leather pants and a new t-shirt. This one read: *everyone loves a woody!* I tried not to laugh, but stared, whilst trying not to.

I cleared my throat. How was I supposed to hide in my room when Belinda could just waltz in without knocking? "Did you want something?"

"Thought I'd let you know, honey muffin. Another one of the Eight just joined the party. Devon Summers, from Maui."

"She's Hawaiian?" Lucy asked with sudden interest. It was the only place she'd ever wanted to visit. Something to do with palm trees and open-air malls, Waikiki Beach,

Jack from Lost, Sawyer from Lost...you get the picture.

"The healer?" A foreboding suddenly crept through me. Devon Summers had embraced her power. Mine had deserted me.

"Yes," Belinda said to me. "And yes," she gave Lucy a wink. "She doesn't know Jack or Sawyer though. I already asked."

I snorted. "Women."

18

MONACO, EUROPE

Stars shone in the night sky and the air was alive with easy chatter. Lysette Cohen swung her long, bare legs out of a rented limo. It had been a short drive from her apartment in the principality's centre to Monaco's least famous casino. If all went well tonight, she'd be leaving with another year's rent.

She preferred to enter through an inconspicuous side door rather than follow the obvious route taken by security guards, celebrities, and tourists. After all, she thought, in her calf length, sheer, split-to-the-groin Donna Karan dress; she was noticeable enough as it was.

She'd styled her black hair upwards in a complicated do. Diamonds twinkled at her ears and iced her neck, none of them as striking as her blue-eyed gaze. She looked a million dollars- the look that blended in and said, conversely, that here in Monaco she wouldn't be remembered past tonight.

"Thank you," she mouthed to the doorman who ushered her into the casino's inner sanctum. Once inside she was surrounded by an unmatched elegance and a sense of barely-contained excitement. The ultra-wealthy played it to the bone here and the air was ripe with sophistication. Lysette threaded her way through roulette tables and Black Jack stations, heading towards the back of the casino, where the real game was played.

Poker.

A game she'd played twice in her life. She'd learned the

basic rules off the internet. But her winnings to date were over two million Euros.

"New player?" The question was asked as she sashayed past an assured looking young man dealing Black Jack. Her slightly mocking expression told him she knew *his* game. Half the men working here had learned their craft in order to bed gorgeous, wealthy women. It helped their cause that half the women who came in here had married for money.

Lysette ignored the man as she laid eyes on a playable table. Two spaces were available. She sidled into one.

"Bhouka," she said, affecting an accent which she'd perfected listening to CD's.

Whilst Lysette waited for the dealer to get on with it she studied the players. Time to get serious. Gucci Tie was to her left, a vacant Playboy bunny stood behind him, dangling a heavy wrist of Bvlgari swag over his steroid-enhanced shoulders. Gay Blonde was to her right, nicely-ripped boyfriend standing to his left. Stud Muffin was dead ahead, a playful smile lighting his eyes. The only other player was Old Hag, a conventional wealthy crone in her late sixties, wearing too much make-up, too much hair coloring, and much too little clothing.

Lysette watched the dealer- Secret Transvestite- toss down the cards. Her method of keeping track of everyone she met was to give them nicknames. It also afforded her a bit of private fun.

Her drink was placed before her along with two cards. Her hole cards. She checked her luck, a pair of threes, and flicked them back down, turning her attention to the other players. In truth she hadn't a clue about body language, she hadn't a clue how to look for 'tells', she just had a...gift.

A gift that had taken her out of Hell and saved her life.

Lysette kept her eyes low, staying inconspicuous. Even so she knew Gucci Tie wasn't happy with his cards, Gay Blonde was neutral, and Stud Muffin was trying to hide a smile.

Old Hag pulled out. Everyone else stayed in.

Lysette smiled sweetly. She didn't dislike these people. She just wondered at their indifference. Two years ago, she'd had been trapped in a living nightmare – penniless, adrift, and trying to endure the nightly ordeal of watching her husband, Richard, drink away their joint wage and punish her for his troubles with ready fists.

Now she sipped her drink. Strong liquid burned the dry ash of memory from her head. The dealer flipped over four cards. No one looked too impressed. But then they wouldn't, would they.

Lysette started to *push*.

Her life had changed one snowy January night. Richard had come home after a particularly bad day, banging through the door with a fresh pizza and a dangerous attitude. Ten minutes later he was on straight whisky. Without knowing what she was doing Lysette had pushed. At least, that's what she called it later.

Pushing.

When she *pushed* she read a person's mind. And at that exact moment she'd read her husbands'.

That night, he would either break her for good, or kill her.

Lysette was running within the hour, running for her life and her freedom. To all intents and purposes she disappeared, flying to Paris and then taking trains and taxis, contacting no one. She carried no baggage- nothing that would tie her to her past. She would never allow anyone into her heart again.

And so, she'd ended up at this poker table, a stranger among strangers. This was her life, this loneliness. Endured, respected, required.

Her power was both savior, and curse. How could she ever love again when she could read everyone's thoughts?

Lysette pushed.

Gucci Tie had nothing; he was bluffing his way to an early exit. Gay Blonde was running for a flush but doubted he was going to get it. Lysette guessed that a round of extravagant betting would soon send his well-shaved arse into his boyfriend's willing lap. Stud Muffin was the real danger here, in more ways than one.

Lysette wanted them all to stay at the table for a few more rounds to raise the stakes. She shuffled her chips and clipped off a small stack.

"Four thousand." Her voice was even.

There were a few smiles, a smirk from Old Hag. Good. They thought she was a pretty girl with a sugar daddy out to donate a few Euros. Predictably, they all stepped up to the cause.

It wasn't pretty. She fleeced them. She read them, *pushed* them, played on their fears, and their desires. By the time she finished most of them were drunk, and Stud Muffin was as edgy as a pig who'd won a Busman's Holiday in a bacon factory. When she'd finished ,she moved her chair back and took her sweet time about dropping the dealer a hundred. She left the table, feeling Stud Muffin's eyes on her clear across the floor.

At the gate, she cashed out. Took a banker's cheque and slipped it between the soft velvet folds of her designer purse.

Outside, the limo was waiting. She stopped for a moment to take in the crisp night air. The smell of success and filthy money greeted her, but best of all was the sweet scent of freedom. She unfastened her hair, letting loose a black cascade around her shoulders and down to the middle of her back.

Alone was good. To be able to *push* was good. It ensured she would never be ensnared again.

The man who approached from the tree-line looked uncomfortably hot and grossly out of place. Lysette eyed him as he walked towards her. She told herself all was well. A casino guard stood six feet to her left.

"Lysette Cohen?" the man huffed as he reached her. "Christ knows why I had to wear this bloody tie to speak to you *outside* the bloody casino."

"Who are you?" Fear slid uncomfortably down her spine like a caress of skeletal fingers.

"I'm so sorry, Ms. Cohen," the man's voice was unmistakably English. An ex private school boy for sure. "My name is Geoffrey Giles. I represent a company called Aegis." He yanked off his tie and blinked at her.

"I really need to talk to you, Ms Cohen."

"You don't need to," Lysette stopped pushing, suddenly feeling light-headed. "I just read everything in your mind. And saw the truth of it. The first pure truth I've seen in three years." She smiled at the man's priceless confusion. "I don't mind going to York with you, Mr. Giles, but you'll have to put a different name on my passport to get me there."

19

MIAMI, U.S.A.

Marian Cleaver crossed into the wealthy Coconut Grove area of Miami, arriving at the shopping mall a few minutes later. The scene could be described in two-no-*three* words. Utter fucking chaos. Cleaver flashed his I.D. to get inside the perimeter. Police cruisers were strewn everywhere. Unmarked vans took up several spaces in the parking lot. Police and plain-clothes agents made up the bulk of manpower, but there were others scattered around he didn't recognize, most likely agents from anonymous agencies.

Beyond the staging area he saw palm trees on fire, their splayed branches crackling and spilling blazing globules onto the sidewalk. Beyond them flames licked through the mall's shattered windows. Cleaver could see inside the main entrance to the food court. Tables and chairs and fake palm trees and benches and other debris had been piled high and was the source of inferno. Vague shapes danced and flitted around the bonfire. Occasionally a shot rang out.

Cleaver unclipped his cell phone.

Thankfully his contact at Aegis answered quickly. "Yes?"

"I'm at the mall, Myleene. No sign of Gaines."

"Is anyone with you?"

"Not from Aegis. Not yet. I don't have much time. What's your input here?"

"Eldritch is coming to you. We just aren't ready to commit everything yet."

Cleaver watched a tower of smoke plume into the sky. He jammed a finger in his right ear as Miami PD ran by, shouting into their radios. "Best be ready sooner than later, Myleene," he said. "This place is going to hell."

"Any sign of the shadow phenomenon?"

"Some of the smoke is moving against the wind."

"Those people in there," Myleene hesitated. "They...well...we know evil is rising through the cracks in the world, the weak spots. It no doubt attracted them. If they weren't openly criminal-minded before, they will be now. It will have consumed their minds."

"Meaning?"

"Bleeding hell, Cleaver. Use your brain. Ever see Dawn of the Dead? Resident Evil? Gaines might be planning to send them into Miami. Don't forget, you are at the epicenter. Miami is New Babylon – the focal point of everything evil that's rising. Stay safe, Cleaver. And *don't* rush into this one."

"They're just people in there," Cleaver wondered if Gaines might be testing him again. "They didn't harm anyone before today."

"Remember this – evil attracts evil. There's a reason those people answered a calling to visit the mall tonight, and I'm guessing it's not for Popeye's chicken and biscuits. You might have every child molester and serial killer in the southern States running amok in there."

"Radio says people have been seen leaping into the flames."

"I understand." Myleene's voice was a disturbed whisper. "But-"

"Understand this-" Cleaver snapped his cell shut mid-sentence.

If you're gonna save the world, you gotta pick a time

to start, Cleaver thought as he pulled one side of his duster apart.

His shotgun, concealed by a shoulder holster, swung into sight. He began to thread his way through the haphazard lines of police cruisers. Miami PD began to move. Cleaver's thoughts were all about the innocents who might be trapped in the mall – the women with young kids and babies in strollers. The schoolchildren out for a Coke and a smile. The families, the geeks, the students. All the potential Josh Walker's. If he could help them, he would.

The noise level grew as he approached the front line. At that moment there was a commotion ahead. Shots rang out. Everyone ducked for cover. Cleaver bobbed down behind a civilian Chrysler, suddenly finding his view blocked by a large guy with the SWAT legend across his back.

Cleaver raised his head cautiously. He saw a policeman caught half way between here and the mall entrance, frozen in fear like a deer trapped in a searchlight. And people were rushing from the mall, chasing him down.

People covered in blood, with open wounds, wielding makeshift weapons.

"Shit!" Cleaver was up in an instant, sweeping his duster aside like a cape and freeing his shotgun. Officers around him read the situation and began to shout at their colleague to get the hell out of there.

Taken by surprise, almost everyone stood and watched. Or shouted. Or scratched their heads.

Cleaver was already two thirds of the way to the stranded cop. The officer caught sight of him. Cleaver saw his eyes go wide with fear. The cop didn't know if Cleaver was one of the good guys.

More gunfire rang out. Cleaver watched in horror as the

cop spun in place, spraying blood. Cleaver reached him a second later, catching him with one hand and firing his shotgun with the other. Reloading one-handed Cleaver scooped the cop up and backed away. Officers behind him laid down covering fire.

There was a hiss like gallons of water boiling and then a white streak shot from one of the mall's windows. A SWAT truck exploded in a roiling mass of metal and flame.

"*Fuck!*" Someone cried. "They just fired a fucking *missile!*"

A second streak shot from a different window. Screams of warning filled the air. Cleaver automatically ducked as the missile flew over his head and struck something big behind him. He heard the whoosh of a huge explosion and then a blast of heated air drove him to his knees. Cleaver used the distraction to drag the wounded cop the last few yards over the police line. Other cops rushed to help, eyeing Cleaver with quiet respect. A medic rushed towards them.

The blood-soaked people were returning to the mall.

Cleaver took a deep breath and then turned around to a scene of bedlam. At least four cruisers had been destroyed by the second missile. Nothing but twisted metal and flames remained. Cleaver saw three cops lying nearby, unmoving, broken as if they'd been thrown from the uncaring hands of a passing giant.

Uniforms ran in and out of the turmoil. Someone shouted on a bullhorn to pull back the perimeter. Cleaver turned once more to the burning shopping mall.

Was this 'all Hell' starting to break loose?

20

YORK, ENGLAND

I woke in the dead of night. The rain beat against the window and a wind blasted around the eaves. I climbed out of bed and padded to the window. The garden below was under assault from the elements. Security night-lights flicked themselves on and off as trees and shrubbery waved. I stared harder, wondering if there were any vamps or lycans down there.

If I woke at this time normally, it would be because of an old, unresolved guilt called Raychel. Mentally, I shook my head. Memories of Raychel inevitably led to raw reflection on Lucy. The thought of an early coffee in the warm security of the kitchen beckoned me, along with the chance that I might bump into Belinda.

The kitchen was occupied, but only by Felicia. I hesitated.

"Come on in, Logan," she said with a smile. "I won't eat you."

I sniffed the air. "Coffee?"

"Belinda's finest," Felicia smirked. "we all drink it when she's asleep."

I took a seat, smiling when the small lycan placed a hot mug before me. I watched as she took the seat opposite. She was perfectly formed, this *Uberhuman,* and she looked like a bundle of fun. The sparkling ring at her navel drew my attention again.

"It's not silver, it's steel," she followed my eyes.

"Is it. . . symbolic?"

"It's an Uber thing." She shrugged, then gave me a sly smile. "I have them. . .in other places too."

I did my best to ignore that one and leaned back in my chair, sipping coffee. The wind howled outside, and rain rattled against the windows.

I said, "I know nothing about Ubers. I never knew you existed before..." I paused. What day was it anyway?

"Lycans are the *best* Ubers," she grinned. "We turn when the mood takes us. We change back at will. We live among humans easily, so long as we stay clear of silver. We are completely free."

She unwrapped a chunk of expensive chocolate marked with the Ghirardelli seal.

"And vamps?"

"Chained forever by their reliance on blood. By their duty to their Shades. By their aversion to sunlight. And by their incessant need for material gain." She bit off a chunk of chocolate and pulled an ecstatic face.

"Vamps like power?" I guessed. "And all its trappings?"

"Ceriden owns two Maserati's and uses a Bentley for the grocery run. His home is worth millions. Tristran, his direct superior, lives in Las Vegas, in a new apartment built on the Strip. The complex has its own beach. The saying among Ubers goes: *behind every great man, there's a great fang.* They're everywhere."

I tried to keep the shock off my face as my view of the world shifted. "Wow."

"Vamps bask in power."

"But lycans are free? Why do you say that?"

Felicia smiled, masses of blonde hair framing her perfect face. "Okay, Logan, I'll try to explain." She didn't sound condescending, just earnest. "It's the freedom of being here in this house today but knowing I could be just as happy in the depths of a forest or on the wild moors tomorrow. It's the freedom of being able to mingle with anyone, anytime. We don't need anything material to be happy. We just need the Run, passion, sex, excitement. All the best things that makes your blood hot. Could *you* say that? Could any other species?"

Felicia took a breath and fixed me with her deep saucer-like eyes. "But, most of all, it's the wild, uninhibited sense of the Run. When we change, we are raw nature, untamed and unbound, beyond regulation and rule. The Run is true freedom, Logan, the passing of tree and root, the caress of the harsh sun or the silvery moon upon your flawless body. When you're given that kind of release, well, that's when you howl."

I didn't know what to say. She made it sound so good.

"Don't believe a word," a new voice boomed from behind me. I started, almost spilling my coffee as I whipped around.

Ceriden said, "Sorry, Logan, dearest. Us 'material-beings' tend to move without making much sound."

I lifted my mug. "Grab a coffee."

"Is it double blended?" Ceriden asked. "With blood and a pinch of Bram?"

I certainly hoped not, but before I could speak Ceriden went on, "Felicia, I simply *love* the way your belly-button ring sparkles when you twist it, but *please* give it a break." He made a nauseous sound.

Felicia screwed her face up. "*This,* coming from a *vampire?*"

Ceriden waggled his long fingers at her. "Felicia misrepresents us, I feel. Have you been on the 'Shrooms again, poodle?"

"'Shrooms?" I questioned, as Felicia giggled.

"Magic mushrooms," Ceriden smiled. "Are a lycan delicacy. They have the same effect on lycans as cannabis does on humans. Or Bram does on vampires. They make her *frisky*."

I stared at the blonde wolf in human form. "You mean she's high?"

"Most of the time." Ceriden reached into the freezer, levered out a carton of blood and placed it in the microwave. "Emergency ration," he said to my appalled look.

"Well, Mr. 'fashion-victim', I hear your powers might have started to surface?"

"Not really."

"What did you feel?"

"Sick. I almost threw up."

"Almost? Well, try studying your dress sense. That should help you finish. Anyway, avoiding the situation will not change it."

"It's not *your* situation. Maybe I'm the wrong man. And what the hell is Bram exactly?"

"You don't want to believe it." Ceriden ignored my question and slid with perturbing speed and grace over to the table. He picked up a copy of Cosmo and started leafing through it. "That's fine. But you *did* feel something. Sweet-cheeks told me, and it was a response to the danger your friend was in. Devon Summers had a similar response to the danger *she* was in. Devon, however, had no choice but to embrace her powers."

I met the vampire's gaze. "It saved her life, didn't it?"

"Yes. And you must face the fact that soon your life will be in danger. And the lives of your friends, and your daughter. What will you do then?"

"You can't put this on me," I turned away, not liking the way my playful conversation with Felicia had turned. "I didn't ask for it. My life sucks. I have a disturbed daughter, a wife I haven't seen in two years, a huge debt, and a business to run. Do you think I need to bear your burdens too?"

"Your daughter will be fine," the vampire said a little too quickly.

"I don't want you anywhere near my daughter."

Lucy was vulnerable, impressionable, and fifteen.

"I understand," Ceriden inclined his head, diffusing the situation in a second. I wasn't sure what else to say so I turned to Felicia. "Have you guys turned anything up on this ultimate evil that's supposed to rise in Miami? Whatever's behind all this?"

"Gorgoth," Ceriden said.

"Our resources go back thousands of years," she said. "No text mentions him. No volume references him. The library is so vast. It's like looking for your favourite tree in the forest," she tried a grin. "Practically impossible."

I smiled at her little joke at her own expense. "Too many books, too little time," I said. "Maybe you're looking in the wrong place."

"Meaning?" I sensed Ceriden's sudden interest.

"I don't *know*," I said in frustration. "But it makes sense. If all your scholars can't turn up *one single thing in all of history*, then change your strategy. Look elsewhere."

Ceriden gulped down whatever the hell he was drinking, then threw the carton in the rubbish and headed for the door with his copy of Cosmo tucked under his arm. "Tristran has a hundred thousand volumes to go through. We are all doing the best we can," he said. "I think you should do the same, Mr. Logan."

Ceriden flounced out of the room, choosing the dramatic exit.

I stared after him, turning my mug in my hands and

biting my lip to stifle any pointless retort. When I turned back to Felicia, she was staring at me with a mix of sympathy and interest.

"Don't mind him," she said. "He thinks he's second in command of the master race and, who knows, he could be right." Felicia rose to her feet, and once again I was left staring at her belly-button ring.

"It's an Uber thing," she said again, then deliberately looked down and twisted it through the hole it made in her flesh.

"I hear Belinda's got one too," she said, her words making doubly sure I stared as she walked out the door. Alone in the kitchen and surrounded by the comforting smell of fresh coffee and the fury of the storm outside, I tried again to absorb everything that had been said and done in the last few days.

In turmoil, I turned to the coffee pot.

21

LAS VEGAS, U.S.A.

The man called Loki flew into McCarran airport and quickly located the nearest Starbucks. The fulfillment of Vice Number Two was paramount. After that he flagged down a cab and asked to be taken to the Bellagio hotel on Las Vegas Boulevard. He scanned the dusk-filled roads as they drove whilst punching out a number on his cell phone.

A woman's voice answered immediately. "Crowe here."

"You know who this is?"

"Yes Sir, I do."

"Good," his lips, like pale rat's tails, curled in a grimace of satisfaction. "I am His Commander. You will do as I say."

"Yes."

"I have the address. The target is there now. The Vampire race will never recover."

"We will be successful."

"We have to be. The Destroyers are busy elsewhere. Trickster is in deep cover. Sorcerer is in Barbados, and shortly Hawaii. Malevolence is in northern England. Spirit will soon be in London."

"And Eradicator is already in place in New Babylon," Crowe finished. "I watch CNN, too."

"Ah yes. I enjoyed your concert coverage hugely the other night, by the way. And one thing," Loki watched the bright procession of hotels pass the cab window as they turned on to the Strip. "This must end by midnight. We have just located another of the Eight Chosen in L.A., and I must be there by morning."

22

YORK, ENGLAND

It felt like my head had just hit the pillow when Lucy came bursting into my room, shouting: "Get up! Wake up! Something's happened! Dad!"

I tried to wedge my eyes open. "Lubbghh?"

"It's Ceriden! Something's happened to Ceriden! Mai and Vipas won't let us see him!"

I sat up slowly. "Slow down, Luce. What's happened?" And who the hell were Mai and Vipas?

"I don't know," Lucy was hopping about, beside herself. "They won't tell me."

It didn't sound good. "Ten minutes," I said. "Meet me in the kitchen. Ask Belinda to put some of that Zambian blend on." Good quality coffee was fast becoming my new addiction.

"Can't. She left earlier to collect Giles and a woman called Lysette Cohen from Manchester airport."

"Okaaaay." My daughter was quicker than Sky News. I waved at her to close the door. Five minutes later I was pouring my own coffee. I checked my watch. It was barely past seven. I turned away and headed for the patio doors, which were thrown open to allow access to the garden where several people I didn't know were gathered. I spotted Holly immediately.

"Hol," I nodded and sipped my coffee.

"James keeps on ringing," Holly said in a flat voice.

"James?"

"My tentative boyfriend. 'He who is younger than me and the source of humour to you.'"

"Maybe he can't find his school bag?"

"Bite me."

"Oh, that's topical," I cast around, pursing my lips. "have you seen Lucy?"

"Not so far," Holly nodded towards the garden. "Big morning, it seems. What's going on?"

"Don't know. Where did all these people come from?"

"They've been arriving since six," an American drawl from behind made us turn around.

I caught my breath. I had no doubt this was Devon Summers, the Hawaiian girl who had recently come into her power. Red, wavy hair fell to the middle of her back, piercing green eyes pinned us. An aura of contentment seemed to surround her.

"Hi, I'm Devon," she laughed. "You're the first of the Eight I've met."

We shook hands. Her touch was light and luxurious, like silk. "This is Holly, my friend," I said.

After our introductions some chitchat followed. I suddenly felt that I wanted my best friend to leave. I wanted to quiz this red-headed woman, Devon, who had embraced her power. I wanted to talk to her privately and admit that I didn't believe in my own ability. I wanted to see her reaction. In truth I wanted to get the hell out of there and run back to my old life like there was no tomorrow.

The garden buzzed with conversation. It was quite pleasant out here, among so many people at seven o clock in the morning. I sipped my coffee, feeling the cool breeze float over me. The finely cut grass was still damp from last night's rain.

A commotion at the door caught my attention. Belinda strode out, fixed her eyes on me, and headed over. She looked fit and fresh, not like someone who'd already driven to Manchester airport and back this morning. Today's t-shirt read: *juicy*. Behind her I saw a self-assured, dark-haired woman stepping carefully across the grass in what looked like a very expensive pair of designer shoes. Her bearing and mode of dress shouted wealth at me louder than any black AmEx card.

Belinda stopped next to me and nodded. "Logan. This is Lysette Cohen. She is one of the Eight, and recently flew in from Monaco." Belinda struck a pose in her tight leather trousers, looked me in the eyes, and then grinned.

"Careful, tiger," she said. "This girl can read your mind."

Soon after we were summoned through to the kitchen. I quelled a panic attack. Things were starting to move faster. More of the Eight were arriving every day. Could I *really* be one of them? As far as I knew only Kisami and I had yet to prove ourselves. And Kisami couldn't even speak English.

Myleene spoke up as we all crowded into the kitchen. "First the good news," she said. "Aegis' plan is working. Today, Lysette Cohen has arrived to join Devon, Kisami, and Logan."

Lysette smiled, but the expression didn't touch her eyes. Her rigid body language spoke of nerves; maybe she was a loner and the group dynamic unsettled her.

"What news of Cleaver?" Felicia asked.

"Safe in Miami. Soon we will have a hundred clans in that area. Containment is our only option until we learn more of Gorgoth and his Destroyers. Matt Black, another of the Eight, has been located in L.A. and is currently being sought by Eldritch. Hopefully, Ken Hamilton should arrive in York tomorrow."

I heard Belinda utter a low *grrr* and tried to ignore her.

"The remaining two," Myleene flicked at a wrinkle in her business suit. "Have not yet been identified."

Myleene went on in sombre tones, "It is getting worse out there. Avalanche in Colorado. Minor quake in San Francisco. Blackout last night in Vegas," I saw her eyes narrow with worry. "A fire in the Louvre where an uncatalogued item was stolen. Our contacts in law enforcement say the big dogs are starting to *twitch*."

I hardly heard her. I was wondering if Ken *'grrr'* Hamilton had also freed his hidden power. There had been no sign of any training yet. Kisami stood next to me, nodding along to Myleene's words as if he understood what she was saying. Only problem was, he smiled in the wrong places.

At that moment I saw movement behind Myleene. Ashes coated my mouth as Ceriden entered. His expression was grave, and he moved as if the weight of the world had been placed on his shoulders. The change in him was stunning. There was an instant silence as all eyes fell on him.

The master Vampire cleared his voice. "I found out, only an hour ago, that...that-" Ceriden seemed to stagger. I saw Myleene reach forward to help, but Mai was already there, clutching his elbow. She'd moved so fast I hadn't even noticed a blur.

Ceriden shook her off. He raised stricken eyes to all of us. He said, "Tristran is dead."

Ceriden's voice grated through the room like a chime of doom, like the final thud of a guillotine, like falling buildings.

"Tristran has been murdered."

23

LOS ANGELES, U.S.A.

The man called Loki motored through the balmy Californian night on the back of a big, silver Harley. This late, the roads of L.A. were relatively people-free, save for the few streets which catered for *en-vogue* clubs, the kind that swallowed and regurgitated A-list celebrities and loser wannabes at an alarming rate.

Beyond Hollywood Boulevard, and then Sunset Boulevard, he began to climb into the Hollywood hills. The Harley's heavy roar echoed back off the canyons, a sound of thunder and madness that soothed him.

He arrived at Matt Black's house and climbed off the Harley. The big bike ticked in the darkness, a beast worthy of its rider. Almost on sight it had become Vice Number Three. Loki knew he was changing. America offered vice and virtue in abundance, and sometimes one disguised itself as the other. But he had the experience and intelligence to realise that change, for good or bad, was inevitable. And necessary.

Turning his attention to the house Loki wondered if he was too late. Lights blazed from every window. Maybe the Aegis people had gotten here first.

His expression turned hard. This one mattered. With Tristran dead the vampires were in chaos. If he, Loki, Commander of Gorgoth's armies, could strike a telling blow against the humans too, the glory heaped upon him would be limitless.

His recalled Tristran's death with twisted satisfaction.

How he and the whore, Emily Crowe, had fought and murdered all who opposed them with skill and glee and unfettered bloodlust. How they had come upon Tristran and then watched the ages-old, almost-dead Vampire King try to relive his glory days. To be honest the old, dead bastard had done okay, felling Crowe and even catching Loki with a surprising burst of speed, but then Loki had switched into top gear and Crowe had conjured an image of the sun. Tristran, confused, weak and outclassed, had collapsed screaming upon his expensive, Italian-marble floor. Loki now grinned in the dark as he remembered Crowe taking out a syringe and injecting the vampire with a drug called Bram, the vampire race's own carefully-concocted drug of choice. A mix of caffeine, adrenalin, a herb called Crowsbane, and Absinthe, it was designed for mixing with blood. When ingested at the same time as blood it induced a heady stupor. Crowe had filled Tristran with the stuff and they had watched him start to float. Then Loki and Crowe had fallen on top of him, writhing, twisting, and quickly becoming naked in a lustful mix of ecstasy and violence. A short time later Tristran was dead and Loki was indulging himself in Vice Number One with Crowe beside the vampire's broken body. Ah, the perks of leadership.

Now Loki stayed in the shadows as the automatic gate that fronted Matt Black's mansion began to open. At the same time the garage doors started to rise. Loki slipped deeper into shadow as a black Hummer shot down the driveway and out through the gates.

In another second Loki was back on the Harley, twisting the throttle in pursuit, pleased with the bikes instant turn of speed. The Hummer flew ahead, its own engine roaring as its driver spotted the tail.

The roar of the two powerful beasts, like dinosaurs battling through ancient, benighted canyons, shattered the vast silence that normally settled here after midnight. Loki spotted a coyote running scared by the side of the road. Its eyes gleamed, connected with his, and then immediately disappeared. With a turn of speed, he came alongside the Hummer, cocked his Glock, and shot out the passenger side tyres.

The Hummer swerved wildly, turning back on itself in a slew of spitting gravel, coming to a shocking sudden stop. Instantly, three doors opened. Loki leapt off the still moving Harley, rolled, and came up with his Glock pointing forward.

He recognized his quarry, Matt Black, one of the Eight, instantly. A black-suited guy with a machine pistol was covering him. Probably a guy from Aegis. Then, surprisingly, a third person emerged from the other side of the Hummer. Loki couldn't get a good view of him but – the height. . .the bearing?

Loki had never experienced shock before. Thus, the adrenalin that surged through him right then turned his blood to fire. From the age of six he had known nothing but violence and combat. As a child he had been indoctrinated in battle, in bloodshed, in the hell of warfare – a modern Spartan warrior. Now, as he recognized the elven king, Eldritch, he saw one of the only beings alive who might be his equal in hand-to-hand combat. He didn't want to kill Eldritch like this though. Not with a gun. The Aegis guy was clever, enlisting the help of the elf king.

Loki said, "I will let you go if Eldritch stands against me now. In combat."

"Not happening, freak," the Aegis guy squandered his one chance to live and squeezed off a couple of shots that

kicked up gravel an inch from Loki's right arm. Loki fired
the Glock with a sneer of disdain, laughing when he saw
the bullet smash a hole through the Aegis guy's forehead,
snapping him back against the Hummer in a spray of bone
and blood.

Aegis employed so many amateurs.

Matt Black was standing alone, terrified, fully aware he
was the focus of Loki's steady sights. In all probability he
didn't understand what was happening. Loki wondered
what Black's powers would have amounted to. The man
looked like a lawyer.

He hesitated. His intelligence people had told him they
had a mole inside Aegis. Maybe Matt Black was the one.
But no, that was stupid. The traitor was deeply embedded
– he'd given them Blacks location, and Tristran's, and the
site of the fabled Aegis library, in addition to the ultimate
snippet of information – the location of the house in
England. Those issues would be acted upon shortly, but
for now Loki enjoyed Matt Black's terror for one more
second.

Then he squeezed the trigger.

Eldritch, moving faster than thought, almost took the
bullet in the chest, but the long-haired elf was half a
second too slow. The bullet ripped through his jacket,
leaving a smoking hole, then crashed into Matt Black's
chest and destroyed his heart. Black was dead before his
body hit the ground.

Eldritch stopped, staring aghast at the dead body, then
turned to face Loki.

The Destroyer made a quick decision. His goal was
accomplished. Glory was assured. Vices one, two and three
would be heaped upon him in abundance.

He might as well enjoy them for a while.

"Until next time," he said to Eldritch, then swung a leg over the Harley, tweaked the throttle and roared away, leaving the elf and the human world to their new and desperate misery.

24

YORK, ENGLAND

We'd finally begun our training.

Eleanor appraised us, appearing shy and reclusive but with a look of resolve on her angular features. It was only seven hours ago that we had learned one of the great Elven secrets.

Their species could communicate through telepathy.

Thus, Eleanor had passed on the terrible news that filled us with dread.

Matt Black, from L.A., one of the Eight, had been murdered by Loki. Before any of us could dwell on what this meant, Myleene had asked Eleanor to begin our training in the garden. We were all that remained, she said. The world would crumble or stand through our competence.

I had tried to hide a flinch that betrayed my uncertainty.

Now I paused as Eleanor held up a hand. "Relax." her face was expressionless. "Meditate."

I stood with my arms by my sides. Something prodded at my mind, invading my thoughts. Eleanor was trying to coax something inside me to reveal itself, gently probing and searching.

"Lose yourself," she said to us all. "Think of something you cherish or a place you love."

On my wall back home, the one opposite our Victory Wall, I had hung a four-thousand dollar painting by the marine artist, Christian Reese Lassen. Called *Escape* it depicted a scene in paradise, with the vibrant skies, the perfect surf and the cliff-hugging waterfalls that signified the artist's trademark work. I thought of that painting now, trying to put myself in the shack that nestled at the foot of one of the cliff faces, staring out the window at the perfect sea and the pounding waves.

Again, Eleanor's invasive prod jolted my mind. A voice whispered *don't fight it, try to accept it*. I closed my eyes, wondering how Lysette was handling someone reading *her* mind. Lysette had already promised never to try and read anyone inside the sanctuary of the house.

My thoughts were scanned and then cast aside as if someone was searching for a particular tome in a library. Images struck me briefly as Eleanor as sifted through them. The cherished memory of my wife. The life-altering anguish that marked her disappearance. The ulcer-inducing stress I'd endured every night as I trawled through the Internet looking at pictures of missing persons. Looking for something I knew I'd never find.

One day I would know the truth.

I found Felicia in my deeper thoughts, the feelings clouded and unsure. Deeper still I found Belinda and suddenly my eyes flew open.

Was this my terror? That I might find someone new only to lose them again, whether by force or by choice?

It was the same vision Ashka had hurled at me. Of Belinda captured by Demons, the last hope of mankind crawling through human debris whilst being taunted by a being of utter evil. Tears sprang from my eyes. Eleanor locked her gaze with mine, flinging the vision aside and crushing it as I watched, trying to imbue me with her own determination.

"Enough," Eleanor's voice filled my mind, spoken both

within and without. The bond between us snapped, and I felt the power slip away with a gulp of regret.

"It must develop slowly," Eleanor said to us all. "For you Devon, and Lysette, we are seeking to expand what you are already capable of. Don't fight it. Don't think you're even close to your limits."

Drained, I listened as the elf gave advice. Then, not really believing I was capable of achieving any real power I tuned her out and watched as the wind started to ripple through the trees.

A few minutes later we filed through the patio door and into the kitchen. Lucy was already there with Ceriden, Belinda and Myleene. My heart lifted to see Lucy smiling and chatting with confidence.

"Hey Luce," I said. "How long now 'til you're sixteen?"

I was rewarded with a hand-wave that declared me insignificant. I noticed that the telltale bandage bulge beneath her long-sleeved sweatshirt was gone. Draining a glass of water I wiped sweat off my brow just as the kitchen door opened and a well-built man with wild blonde hair and a big smile walked in. Being the sudden centre of attention didn't faze him at all; in fact, his smile grew wider.

"Hey, dudes and dudettes," he said loudly. "I'm Ken Hamilton. Can someone direct me to the beer?"

I pretended not to be fazed when Belinda, Devon, Lysette and Felicia – who all appeared from nowhere – descended on Ken. I made my exit and trotted upstairs for a shower. On my way out I also noticed Giles look up from his laptop long enough to frown at the new boy, and then at Lysette. I saw Lysette glance over her shoulder at Giles and then smile even wider at Ken. Grinning, I climbed the stairs, hoping those two could forge something good. Lysette seemed okay, if a little distant, and Giles was a good guy.

As for Ken Hamilton, let them have him. At least the guy who'd brought him here, Ryan – an Oxford graduate if ever I saw one – had taken the thunder out of Ken's appearance by confirming the previously-unknown existence of Dementia, some crazy demon-woman from Hell. Well, I thought, she's sure come at the right time.

After a ten minute shower and a change of clothes I was heading back down to the big conference room in response to Myleene's message that another video-call had been scheduled. Myleene wanted everyone present.

I entered the big, airy room to find everyone seated. I ignored Belinda's questioning look and seated myself between the vampire, Mai, on one side and Lucy on the other.

"Daughter," I said by way of greeting.

"Father," she said in the same deep tone. "Ceriden has been made king vamp," she whispered. "They're gonna announce it soon."

My instant thought was to ask her how she knew. But then I remembered Mai was seated to my right. Lucy seemed to be getting awful close to Ceriden and the fang-gang these days.

"Lucy, I've been meaning to ask you-"

"My arms are fine."

"No. I didn't mean that."

"What then?"

I flicked at the chair arm. "Don't get too close to Ceriden, darling. He may be a laugh, but he's still a vampire."

"How observant of you."

"Don't get mad, Luce," I dared not look at her because I thought she might see it as a challenge.

"Please, Luce. Be careful."

"I *am!* He's okay. We just talk. They're all okay. They know really cool stuff."

"I just want you to remember who you are. And what they are. And that one day this will be over, and we'll go back to things like school, and work."

Lucy fixed her gaze ahead, locking onto the video screens and refusing to look at me.

I put my hand over her arm. "You've been through enough. It's time for something normal."

In classic contradiction Myleene then got to her feet. She flicked a remote at the video screens and we were once again looking at Cheyne the Witch Queen, and Eldritch, king of the elves.

Giles rose from a chair in front of me, dressed down in jeans and a t-shirt. "First of all," he said, without preamble. "I know I speak for us all when I express my sympathies to the vampire race. Tristran was both a friend and a fine strategist. His expertise will be sorely missed," Giles paused for a second before continuing. "I am sure everyone wishes Ceriden the best as he takes Tristran's place, as King."

Ceriden nodded but didn't rise.

The vampire beside me, the girl Mai, seemed so tense and sat so straight it seemed to me that she was almost bursting with excitement. Without seeing her move I suddenly noticed that her arm was resting atop my own.

"A position he has long deserved," Mai whispered.

I gave her a tight-lipped smile.

Giles was saying, "Unfortunately Tristran's death illustrates the probability of a high-level traitor among us."

Now Giles paused a while longer, I'm guessing to let his candid statement sink in.

And judging by the absolute silence that filled the room it certainly did.

"Find this person," Giles said, staring at me, at everyone in the room, at the monitors. "Before they betray our most valuable secrets."

I found myself re-evaluating everyone. The traitor could be any one of us, or someone at the Library.

Cheyne now said, "I'm afraid that I too have bad news. We are struggling here. All the Library's resources haven't turned up a *single clue* as to Gorgoth's origins."

"It's the most terrible evil the world has even known," I said. "And no-one's ever even heard of it?"

Cheyne looked humiliated. "What can I say? If we don't come up with something soon, I fear even my familiar will disown me."

Lysette, seated two rows in front, said, "How can we destroy something if we don't know anything about it?"

Cheyne shook her head. "We can't."

"We're asking all of you," Giles filled the silence with a barrage of words. "For help. Try anything. Think outside the box, use any contact, ask your Great Grandma, whatever. We have nothing here."

I wondered what Jack Bauer would do. "You should try capturing one of them," I spoke with a nervous catch in my voice. "One of the Destroyers, I mean. Then torture him, or something."

"The Destroyers are practically *ghosts*," Myleene answered from her position at the round table. "They pop up, they commit carnage, and disappear. Only Mena Gaines in Miami and Ashka here in York can even be identified."

"But if the chance presents itself..." Ceriden's face was hard with anger. "The idea is sound."

"Any news of the seventh Destroyer?" Lucy asked. "The Trickster?"

"Help us," Cheyne said, speaking as if she hadn't heard Lucy at all. "Time is running out. We need information. If we don't stop Gorgoth, he will take our world."

The queen of the witches seemed at the end of her tether. After a few more minutes the meeting ended. I waited as Lucy scooted off without a word. I ignored Belinda. I had been expecting my daughter to flounce off and it suited my plans.

I laid a hand on the pale, thin arm of the woman next to me.

Mai, the vampire.

I said, "Tell me all about Shades."

Later, I stood staring out my bedroom window into the night-filled garden and across the windswept grounds. I was alone with my thoughts. A gust of wind rattled the window and I focused on the one thing that had tiptoed past me over the last few days.

The change in my daughter.

It put my head in a crazy place. It was impossible. Mai, in her respectful way, had explained more than I needed to know. A vampire's shade, she told me, was a willing life-partner. A partner prepared to accept that the blood they shared with the vampire was more than an impulse, or fun, or experiment, or for ecstasy. It was the exchange of pure life itself. A *shared* life. A vampire created a blood-bond with his shade and would be loyal to that bond through the shade's entire life. A shade would always be aware that they would never become a vampire, but the union they shared with their life-partner was as deep as anything you could imagine. Pure love. Pure dependence. Pure existence.

And Lucy was fascinated by this? It seemed so.

I gritted my teeth in frustration. After a second, I exited my room and walked a few steps down the hushed corridor. I knocked quietly on Lucy's door.

A muffled voice said, "Go away."

"Lucy," I said, trying to keep emotion from my voice. "I need to see you."

The door opened. Lucy stood there, eyes red, looking more vulnerable than I'd seen her since that night in the hospital bed.

I didn't know where to start, or what to say. It was one of those moments when you needed the perfect words, but I couldn't find any.

"I love you, Lucy," I said, and my heart rate tripled.

"Don't leave me," she said. "Just please don't ever leave me."

I fixed her with a stare and a promise. "I am not your *mother*, Lucy. I will never leave you, kid."

"I'm not a kid," she snuffled, and I knew I'd broken through to her.

"I know," I said. "I know. When's your birthday again? I forget."

Amidst the banter, and the next hour of father-daughter fun I managed to put aside the intensifying demands on both our lives and our relationship.

It almost felt like we were a family again.

25

YORK, ENGLAND

Our training intensified to an exhausting level. Even Ken Hamilton stopped the wisecracks. When we broke for lunch I chose to eat in the garden, sitting on one of the wooden benches with my new friend, Eleanor

"What do you make of it?" I said, around a mouthful of sandwich.

She had noticed a change in me.

"I believe you are blessed with a *linked* power. In other words, there is another you can *link to,* and the bond created will hold colossal power. Apart, you will be strong; together you would complement each other and create. . . *catastrophic magic.* The *linked* ones have enormous potential power like the Old Ones once had. The magic to work wonders, to create *and* destroy. You two- will be our vanguard."

Catastrophic magic? Jesus.

I almost asked *with whom?* But the awe in Eleanor's eyes stopped me. Clearly it was one of the Eight still out there. I hoped and prayed it hadn't been Matt Black.

It also struck deep when I realized I would be letting everyone down badly. I turned away, embarrassed, and noticed Lysette seated on a bench across the garden. Unsurprisingly, Giles was by her side. They seemed deep in conversation and were almost, *almost,* touching.

Eleanor said a little more. "I think that with this other's arrival your complementary powers will be unleashed." she smiled. "It is a *very* interesting time."

I shook my head. I looked around the garden, at Ken using his surfer-dude dialogue to impress Belinda, at Kisami standing alone in the midst of a group, unable to communicate, and I thought *if we don't all join together, we will all die apart.* And I meant everyone, not only the Chosen. Everyone.

26

YORK, ENGLAND

And still more training and scouring of my inhibitions. By the time we finished for the day the sky was turning from russet gold to patchy black, and the limited power inside me was almost available on tap.

Almost.

But it didn't change anything, I thought. It's like the rookie cop who emulates every precinct record on the practice range. You put that rookie face to face with a desperate criminal on a stormy night in a filthy alley, alone and tired. Then talk to me about your *records*.

So far, I couldn't conjure anything by will alone. It had to be forced out of me by making me upset, or angry. Eleanor pointed out it might take a true life-or-death situation to ignite the fire within me.

Lucy had joined the training session when it became more physical, much to my surprise and grudging approval. Eleanor had insisted that we should be able to handle ourselves in physical combat. It made sense. Lucy enjoyed herself and grinned at me whilst she trained. I had so far refused to take her to a boxing gym. Revenge, I thought, made her smile that much sweeter.

Now, as the sun went down and the day died, Lucy, Belinda, Felicia, and Holly sat around the table as I struggled to make enough peach and pear smoothie to serve us all. Then Myleene walked into the kitchen. Her crisp business suit looked uncharacteristically rumpled and her hair was all over the place. We all smiled at each other, but I don't think our sharply dressed leader even noticed.

"Conference room in ten minutes," she said. "Belinda. Felicia. And you Logan. No one else."

Myleene backed out, leaving us blinking and staring after her in confusion.

Ten minutes later I was sat on the back row, facing the video screens. We were like a bunch of people gathered to watch a movie. All we needed was a heap of butter popcorn and a large diet coke. A few others joined us, including Ceriden, Lysette, Devon Summers and Geoffrey Giles.

I wondered at the choice of people.

I didn't have to wonder for long. Myleene swept in, flicked a speck of imaginary dust off her finely tailored shoulder, and came over to us. Eleanor was with her, a glint of concern in her dark eyes.

"Because we cannot trust everyone," Myleene said in a regretful voice. "We have to choose the most trustworthy amongst us. What we have to say goes no further than this room. Anyone who doesn't agree can leave now."

She paused. No one moved. I felt my heart beat faster as I realized I was considered a member of the inner circle. Did I really want this?

Myleene said, "First, we have no idea as to our traitor's identity. If nothing turns up soon, I will ask Lysette Cohen to do her devious best, and read everyone's mind. Not a pleasant prospect, I know, but her power has deliberately been concealed from almost everyone at the house. It is a road we do not want to travel, people, but one we may be forced to take."

There were a few murmurs of agreement. It didn't scare

me that Lysette could read my mind. She would sense my doubts, but maybe that was a good thing. I supposed that's one of the reasons I was in this room.

A half-smile ghosted around Myleene's lips. "And now for the good news." she paused.

Ceriden grunted and smiled. "Wait, wait, I know. Clooney's outside?"

Felicia said, "Don't tease us, Myleene. Just get on with it."

"First, Logan and Devon I'd like to inform you that there are more species of Uber than we led you to believe. We did not hide this deliberately, but simply because of time constrictions."

"Time *remains* an issue," Giles growled, checking his watch.

"Relax. A member of Cheyne's coven came up with a wonderful idea. That we should enlist the help of the *Gargoyle.*"

I scratched my head. "As in those ugly concrete statues that stick out from half the buildings in York?" I asked. "How the hell could they help us?"

"They *listen.*" Myleene told me with a wink. "Unmoving, unseeing, they are inhabited by an old, unloved spirit. This spirit was banished in ancient days but allowed to continue existing because he isn't malevolent. Just solitary. So, they gave him a habitat. And built millions of statues in his image to let him roam at will. Now he inhabits all of them, his vast conscience able to pick up any sound at all."

Belinda clapped her hands. "People talk."

Ceriden looked ecstatic. "*Oh!* I could *use* him. Imagine the scandals!"

Myleene held up a finger. "Yes, but the gargoyle

demands a high price in return for his assistance."

"He has already proven his worth," Giles said with satisfaction. "The price is not too high. Our enemies are loose of tongue. What they say, *we hear.* Already we know things about Gorgoth, and the Destroyers. And Kinkade learns more every minute. Every second."

"Kinkade?" I said. "That's the gargoyles name?"

"Yes, Logan."

"And what is the price?"

"When this is all over, providing we win, Kinkade wants to inhabit the body of a female movie star for a year. Without her knowledge," Eleanor shook her head. "We have agreed to his terms."

Ceriden looked interested. "Which one? I know a few. Maybe I could soften her up a little."

"She won't *know,*" Eleanor snapped. "Weren't you listening? And he hasn't decided yet."

Ceriden flapped a wrist. "Well, maybe I could assist right there. Julia's a good bet. Or Nicole. Or maybe he should go for someone who's already pretty vacant," he laughed.

I pursed my lips, waiting for him to run out of steam, then leaned forward with my gaze fixed on Myleene. "So," I said. "What do you know?"

27

HONOLULU, HAWAII

Tanya Jordan had lived in Honolulu her entire life. All the locals knew her. It wasn't a good day if the old men who drifted down to Waikiki Beach to catch the sunrise didn't see her bronzed figure jogging past as the first golden rays graced the horizon. It wasn't a good day if the newspaper-reading businessmen didn't catch sight of her stretching outside her – and, coincidentally, *their* – favorite Starbucks a little after seven in the morning. And it sure as hell wasn't a good day if the construction workers didn't get a saucy *hi* and a wink when she jogged past them as they sat in traffic with their tanned arms resting on their open car windows.

Tanya Jordan was more than an easy-going, familiar figure. She was a local idol, known and talked about by everyone.

Today Tanya did nothing different. She was a creature of habit. The beach run, followed by an exhausting stretch, the three shot, skinny, iced Vanilla Latte with the long straw, the peaceful but brisk stroll home.

The shower. She flicked on the news. Headlines blared at her, shouting about a lethal tsunami in Hong Kong, an earthquake somewhere in the Pacific, unrest in Miami. She flicked the news off. She stood naked in front of the floor-to-ceiling mirror and checked for white spots, for growths, for wrinkles.

After a light lunch she connected to the internet, checked her e-mails, deleted a ton of spam, and logged on to her bank account. Everything was the same. Constant. That meant everything was good. Tanya hated it when things changed. Her $750,000 was still there, conned from the sweating hands of her cornered ex-husband who once thought it a pleasure to beat her senseless two or three times a week. The high point, he used to tell her later, was when she blacked out, because that was when he realized he was more than a man.

Eventually she'd taped him, confronted him, divorced him, and then set him up with half a dozen other women. Together they had trapped him, conned him, and walked away with a million each.

Now, outgoings were constant. Life was good. Tanya walked to the local market and bought fresh fruit and vegetables every day. She walked home. She washed the food, made a pasta meal, and sat in front of the TV.

This was the sum of her day. Every day. Monday to Saturday. On Sundays she threw in an extra evening run around sundown.

Today was Sunday.

Tanya jogged along the beach, feeling the light sand particles between her bare toes. A fresh breeze skipped off the ocean, cooling the sweat on her arms. She concentrated on the cool stretch and flow of her body, on the freedom and perfection of exercise.

She pushed her limits. The exertion made it hard to think, which was good. Her blonde hair fluttered out behind her, its streaks of grey a testament to why she didn't want to think.

But think she did. Her recurring memories were as inevitable as the Hawaiian sunrise.

Her ex-husband had killed the child in her stomach three months before it would have been born. Even then the child had a name – Alyson. Her husband had known what his fists could do, but the knowledge had not stopped him. The man was a monster and deserved so much more than simple extortion.

Tanya lived every day with every hateful detail. And each day she tried to get past it, tried to move on. And live.

But each day she failed.

Now her muscles caught fire, her heart hammered. Images were vanquished by pain as she slammed along the beach, chasing the waves up and down the surf line, chasing the setting sun.

A man was pacing her, she realized. Tall, with eyes the colour of her ex-husband's dead heart, he looked eastern European. He ran beside her, watching her.

She slowed. He jogged a few paces, then turned and ran backwards, still staring. He didn't speak. She stopped, suddenly feeling self-conscious in her Lycra shorts and top, an odd sensation that she, a Hawaiian native, couldn't remember experiencing before.

Perhaps it was the man. The force of his black gaze.

"I am Leo," he said in a desolate voice. "I am Sorcerer."

"That's good," A quick look around confirmed her worst fear, that she was alone on this stretch of beach.

"Good?" Leo echoed. "Just good? Do you know what I endured to receive His power, Tanya Jordan?" The mention of her name chilled her. "Do you know the hell I went through? The people I had to murder? The innocents? No? Let me show you."

The man raised his arms in the air. Tanya backed up a step. Cold waves splashed across her feet. Tanya noticed the man's arms were crisscrossed by deep wounds. She swallowed in fear as several shadows suddenly shot straight up from the sand and began to writhe around him.

"Did you hear about Hong Kong, Ms Jordan? Did you hear about Montreal? About the Louvre? That was me. And now that we know who you are, and what you may become, I have been blessed with a new task."

"Who I am?" Tanya backed away and moved her back foot around to present a slimmer target.

My God, she thought. *Where did that idea come from?*

Something sweeter than terror began to sweep through her body.

"You are one of the pieces of Eight," Leo sneered at her. "Don't you know?"

"What the hell are you talking about?"

But Leo didn't seem to hear. He turned his attention to the darkening ocean, and suddenly sent his shadows flying out over the rippling waves. "And after Hong Kong," he spoke to the ocean. "Comes Honolulu."

Immediately Tanya heard a sound deeper than thunder from beyond the rolling horizon. She tucked a strand of hair around her ear and out of her eyes. What the hell was that noise?

"Time to die," Leo's voice was more terrifying than the deepest cavern of Hades. Tanya flinched as he gestured, then screamed in disbelief as a dozen shadows twisted towards her. Like mini-whirlwinds they ate up the beach, flinging sand everywhere before coalescing into dark figures.

The first punched her in the stomach.

Unimpressed, Tanya felt a surge of absolute adrenalin. She had been punched before. The blow did not hurt, it just made her angry. It was time to fight back

Then power exploded through her, resonating out of every pore, slamming through every nerve ending. She spun and leapt and ducked so fluidly she might have been a ballerina, or a warrior-monk. Without strategy, and without previous knowledge, she put together combination after combination, evading the shadows, punching and kicking hard at the twisting figures, fighting her way towards their controller.

Leo. Self-proclaimed sorcerer.

Just another pig-bastard who punched women.

Hatred fired her blood and made her crazy. But skill and mastery controlled her movements. She fought like a dancer would dance her greatest routine, like a composer would write his perfect symphony, like a painter would create his ultimate work of art.

With grace and fluidity and perfect ease of movement she fought her way to Leo's side. His eyes, closed in ecstasy all this time, suddenly flew open in shock.

"Surprise!" Tanya kicked at his chest, spun and back-kicked his left arm which cracked and made him scream. Her routine never stopped, never changed, but continued with lethal grace, like the flow of a violent but beautiful stream. A sweep cracked his shin, which turned into a side kick that took out a rib that became an elbow to his throat, which turned into a leaping front kick that slammed his head back, which became a standing front kick that made him stagger.

And so on. Nonstop. She was a dancing, fighting force of nature that was as elegant as it was unstoppable. As poised as it was lethal.

"I am...a Destroyer," Leo panted, forced back, his arms hanging limp, his knees shaking. "You cannot beat me. Gorgoth will *annihilate* you!"

Tanya paused for three seconds, studying her adversary. The sudden emergence of this strange power stunned her, but for now she pushed the shock to one side.

"Here it comes!" Leo cackled and pointed past her. Tanya turned to see a tidal wave almost on top of them, about a minute away, a wall of water maybe three feet high, not devastating by any means but enough to cause panic. To create mayhem.

Which is what this *Destroyer* and his cohorts wanted.

They were terrorists. Nothing more than scum in a toilet bowl.

Tanya used her minute well. The dance continued. In only half her time she reduced Leo to a broken, lifeless mass of bleeding flesh.

She used the remaining thirty seconds to get clear of the wave.

28

YORK, ENGLAND

Our training continued mercilessly. It seemed surreal that we six, standing within the walls of a typical English garden, were preparing to save the world. I missed my old life, our home. A hateful inner voice pointed out that I might have missed some contact from Raychel.

"The *link* is still missing," Eleanor said to me. "It will come."

It has to, I thought. A power without aim and purpose is no power at all. I tried to quell thoughts of failure by concentrating on the news Myleene had revealed earlier.

Kinkade the gargoyle was proving himself a fantastic asset. And how could he fail? Everyone talked. How could anyone know that countless three hundred year old stone statues were listening in?

Kinkade was sending constant updates, like a BBC World News ticker. Every time someone somewhere uttered one of countless flagged names or phrases the gargoyles presence would flicker to life, listen and report. Say *Gorgoth,* or *Aegis* or *Destroyer.* We had you. We were like the NSA on steroids.

His reports filtered down through a dedicated witch's coven. Focusing their might through inert metals – a trick of augmentation understood only by those blessed with extremely crooked noses – they had concocted a spell that allowed Kinkade to pass information through them. Spoken words were turned into instant e-mail by cyber-geeks and transmitted to Cheyne at the Library, to

Eldritch in Miami, and here to Myleene.

Loki was old news. Emily Crowe was a major shock since almost all of us respected Supernatural's rock-chick music. To suddenly find out that their lead singer was a Destroyer bent on ending our world was a major mind-blower. Crowe was currently in Paris, close to where the Louvre was burning. The other Destroyers- Jondal and Leo- were so far just names; we knew nothing more about them.

More updates rolled in by the minute. The seventh Destroyer, Trickster, had not yet surfaced, but was held in high regard by his peers, whispered of as being one of the wiliest of Gorgoth's Destroyers.

We learned Ashka was moving steadily through York, asking questions about Dean Logan. About Aegis. We weren't too worried. Look up at any building in the city of York and you are likely to see a gargoyle. We felt confident we knew what she knew.

And Gorgoth? Well, finally, we knew everything. And it all made perfect sense. And it was so far beyond terrible.

It was then I noticed Belinda, watching me from the kitchen doorway. Her t-shirt shouted: *bitchslap me back to Heaven!*

After a few seconds she spoke. "Guys, you'd better wrap it up. Latest from Gargoyle News says that Jondal has hit London, and was responsible for a bomb that went off today. It's bad, guys."

29

YORK, ENGLAND

Imagine the cosmos long before Earth was even a twinkle in God's eye. Imagine nothing but vast, eternal space for untold millennia.

Now something glitters in the limitless black. Life, of a fashion. An immense darkness, slightly lighter than the black nothingness that surrounds it. Vast beyond imagination, it is one being among many.

What is it? It is nothing that can be described.

What is it called? It has no name other than the one we give it.

Where is it from? It came *before existence*. It is from the *outside*.

It rolls in space, it turns, and it glides. The cosmos is its realm, a limitless place outside our universe, but a place that will always exist. The creature has not noticed humanity more than once, fleetingly, because it sees ten thousand years as but the blinking of an eye.

Now, imagine this creature is the first of its kind to visualize a new concept called *evil*. In fact *this creature invents evil*. It brings forth from its immense maw the very concept of wrongdoing and, happening upon a new place called Earth, it plants the first drop of badness in our world. It invents Heaven. And Hell.

For its own amusement.

It is the *creator* of evil. If you can imagine that, you can imagine the being that is Gorgoth.

30

YORK, ENGLAND

I had learned all this last night. We knew now why there were no written texts about this creature. Who could write about a creature that existed in limitless space? Apart from HP Lovecraft, I suppose, but then he was dead.

My grasp of the situation was that this eternal creature, having planted the initial root of evil eons ago, had missed the next few thousand years of our existence. Now it had returned as a *new* creature to us, but one older than our imagining.

Imagine the catastrophic consequences if something so colossal and powerful managed to punch its way through to our world?

Now Belinda turned on the portable TV in the kitchen and balanced it on top of the fridge. We all crowded around to watch.

"Outside the temporary ticket booth at Kings Cross station this is the scene-" the red Sky News banner flickered across the screen. Jeremy Thompson, looking shocked and disheveled, was talking animatedly as the picture cut past him and focused on what I could only describe as utter chaos.

Black and grey smoke billowed into the air. Concrete walls were smashed and battered and blackened behind the smoke. Eager flames licked at everything in sight.

No one spoke. I felt tears spring to my eyes. The people didn't deserve this. It looked like a terrorist attack.

"Jondal," Myleene told us. Belinda flicked off the TV.

"The Destroyer called Spirit. He has the power of invisibility, and the ability to inject hate into people's minds. I have no doubt that they will catch someone for this bombing, but our intelligence says it was Jondal."

"His power turns good people bad?" Lysette said.

"In Barbados he made an entire community consume itself."

Ken, the surfer dude from 'Frisco, was explaining it all to Kisami, using hand signals. His last gesture left no doubt in anyone's mind what he thought of Jondal.

"I need a beer," Ken said, opening the fridge. He pulled out a six-pack, and then offered one to Kisami. "Coming, man?"

"Ah, yis," the little Japanese guy bleated.

Ken smiled around at everyone. "Hear that? Been teaching the little guy some pure American English."

Ken pushed through us. I felt pity for the poor guy. He was only trying to lighten the mood, but didn't have the social skills to appreciate there were times you just simply shouldn't.

"I want only those people from last night," Myleene sounded as overwrought as I felt. "In the conference room. Now."

I found my seat as Myleene's Sony Vaio signaled a newly arrived e-mail.

"Kinkade?" I asked, pouring a glass of water.

"Gargoyle's chattier than a nest of sparrows. It seems like he's enjoying his first contact in five thousand years."

I watched Myleene read the e-mails as the others filed in. I felt absurd, sitting with these people, hiding the knowledge that I was a sure-fire failure, so I sipped my water and stayed quiet.

Belinda spoke up quickly. "Okay, some things *have* started to make sense now guys, but still not the involvement of the Hierarchy of Demons."

"Because they need this world as much as we do?" Devon's question was a mix of sarcasm and understanding.

"Correct."

Felicia held up a small hand. "Didn't I hear Ryan and Ken reporting that they'd already had a run in with the demon, Dementia?"

Myleene nodded. "Yes. It's another one of those things we can't explain, I'm afraid. Dementia is the worst kind of demon. She is devilry incarnate, and crazy to boot."

"Our intelligence," Lysette spoke up next. "Seems very *limited.*"

"Know this, Lysette. Before the witches involved Kinkade we were floundering badly. Without his help, Aegis would be lost. He has furthered our efforts more in the last few days than all the witches and scholars combined in the previous twelve months."

Myleene's laptop bleeped again, as if Kinkade was listening.

"My God," she said. "That's insane!*"*

My heart started to race. "What?" I echoed, along with everyone else.

"We have *Tanya Jordan,*" she said without taking her eyes off the screen. "She's okay. *And she killed a Destroyer!*"

I felt my mouth go dry from the knowledge that yet another one of the so-called Eight had proven themselves.

And I had not.

"I quote," Myleene's eyes were wide. "'Message from Remy. I have met Tanya Jordan. I saw what she did. I have never seen the like of it before, not in all my years. Jordan is *the* Master of her art. And her art is fighting.'"

There was a revered silence. Belinda made a pouty, but good-humoured face. "Coming from Remy, that *is* sheer gold. Bet she's not as cute and feisty as me though."

"*Bonus!*" Felicia struck at the air with both hands. "One Destroyer down, only five to go. Score one to the good guys," her last few words became a long drawl.

"It also says Tanya should be here late tomorrow. And that her powers surfaced as she fought for her life."

That pattern was getting irritating. What the hell did I have to do? Run naked across the Minster grounds shouting: "*Ashka! Ashka! Come find me!*" and then hope my fucking powers decided to kick in?

"It's all coming together," Myleene said. "But not quickly enough. Our enemies' plan has been devised over centuries. We mustn't lose sight of the sort of evil we're dealing with."

"Yes, mother," Belinda said, making me laugh into my water. When I looked up, spluttering, I found her gaze locked on to me. I froze.

Belinda's eyes smoldered at me with barely concealed heat. Jolts of passion shot through me, making me shiver. Nobody but Raychel had ever fired my heart that way. But I didn't want to fuck it all up again.

I barely heard Ceriden rise to his feet to inform us that a *great amount* of Vampire resources were now being focused on the capture of Loki and Emily Crowe- the two Destroyers Kinkade told us had killed Tristran.

Another 'message delivered' chimed out. Using the distraction, Belinda scooted over next to me. The creak of her leather pants made me catch my breath. When she was settled beside me she leaned so close that her lips brushed my earlobe.

"Finally," she whispered. "I got your attention."

"Finally?"

"Finally, honeycake."

"Ah. Well, I have been busy."

"Busy putting me off."

"I didn't realise-"

"Huh. What are you saying? That I haven't dropped enough hints? Is that what you're saying? Well, how big a hint is this?"

My breath stopped as her right hand landed on my thigh and her hot breath tickled my ear.

Then Myleene gave another shocking exclamation.

"*Whoa! Kinkade got the whispers off the street all right! He tracked down the last of the Chosen!*" She slammed the round table.

"Who is it?" Felicia was bouncing in her excitement. "And where?"

"New York," Myleene squinted at the screen. "Someone called Johnny Trevochet. Shit, Trevochet? I know that name. He used to be a soap opera star."

"In *Friends?*" Felicia cried. It was her all-time favourite programme.

"No, something else. Ah," Myleene pulled at her bottom lip in apprehension. "I can't believe it. We have nobody on that side of the United States. Not one single person."

Felicia ventured. "Cleaver?"

Myleene shook her head. "Needed where he is."

All eyes then turned to Belinda and widened in surprise as they realized her proximity to yours truly.

Belinda blinked, then shook her head and said: "That bastard James Bond never has this much trouble when he's trying to get laid."

There was a shocked silence. I didn't dare move a

muscle. Belinda finally relented. "Alright, alright, I'm on my way."

Belinda jumped to her feet. I shrugged and tried to hide my face behind my glass of water.

31

MIAMI, USA

Marian Cleaver got a call from Myleene and left the mall. The local Homeland Security unit was running operations now, and was treating the scene as a terrorist incident. Cleaver thought that was the best way to go.

Cleaver drove through the dark Miami streets, through rundown neighborhoods that bordered on multi-million dollar estates, bypassing ghetto blocks where cops and self-respecting hoes never ventured anymore. He cut through the resplendent Coconut Grove area that catered for the filthy rich and starry-eyed tourists and headed for the famous beach. On the way he crossed over one of the sprawling bridges and slowed to watch the black water churning below. At the beach he parked his old Corvette, locked it, and walked across the sand to the edge of the calm ocean.

Miami, he thought. Diamond city of the States.

The skyline behind him glittered with skyscrapers. Personally, he thought the hotels looked gaudy; places rappers might come to make videos that showcased their ridiculous music, thinking it made them look flash. Or fly. Or whatever.

New Babylon.

Cleaver had lived here his whole life. He had done murder, paid his dues, boxed himself into oblivion, and bettered himself here. In Miami. The name of the place, the beach, the nightlife- spoke of glitz, of glamour. The tourists loved it. So did the rich. But he *lived* here. The other stuff meant nothing to him.

Cleaver waited. At length a tall enigmatic figure approached out of the shadows. "So," Cleaver said. "I left my post for you. I switched my cell off. I'm already at the top of my wonderful boss' shit-list. Again. This is Miami's peak crime hours, Mr. Elf. What can I do for you?"

Eldritch stopped, and then turned in a slow circle. Cleaver watched him, eyes roving across the lightly rolling Pacific, past the breakers as they foamed down the shoreline, over a few groups of tourists lounging and canoodling in the sand, along those fancy hotels that sat in a million-dollar line behind them, and finally returning to the calm, limitless expanse of water.

Cleaver heard movement. From his left, materializing out of the dark, came a few dozen figures. Lycans, judging by their lithe bodies and hungry stares and by the way they just couldn't resist shifting a glance toward the thin sliver of silver floating high above. Cleaver then sensed bodies behind him, turned and gasped. At least fifty Vampires stood there, silent in the night, pale like dying sunlight and as ageless as the shifting ocean. Cleaver's heart started to beat so fast he thought a stoned-out drummer from a heavy metal band had just gone wild in there.

"My name is Eldritch," the Elf said quietly. "I bring you these Ubers. More are coming. And they will arrive in their thousands."

Cleaver gasped. *"Thousands?"*

"This is the place where Ubers and Humans will make their final stand," Eldritch said. "Together, an army united, we will fight as one to save our world."

Cleaver tried to pull himself together, but it wasn't finished yet. Cleaver watched a beautiful woman approach from the right. It was all he could do not to stare at her wildfire eyes and perfect, pouting mouth. The woman's nose though, was hopelessly crooked.

"This is Cheyne," Eldritch indicated her with an open hand turned palm up. "She is the witch Queen, originally out of Key West. Their finest."

"I bring three covens," Cheyne told Cleaver in a high voice. "With more on the way. Are you alright?"

Cleaver breathed deeply. This whole thing was getting impossibly big, real fast. A new meteor-like thought slammed through him.

Why are they all talking to me?

"We are identifying various weak points around Miami-" Cheyne was saying.

"Weak points?" Cleaver managed to blurt out.

"Areas of suppurating evil. Some places are more susceptible than others. It is at these weaker places that the demons will break through."

"Why?"

"Bridges," Cheyne pressed. "Malls. Part of South Beach. Coconut Grove."

"Coconut Grove?"

"Evil is a frequent companion of vanity."

"And what of Gorgoth?" Eldritch spoke up, much to Cleaver's relief. "Has Kinkade learned more?"

"Kinkade is a veritable torrent of information. And he is warming to his task more with every second that passes. He is definitely worth the price."

Cleaver's head was starting to spin with all this information. "What price? And who is Kinkade?"

"Gorgoth will be invoked over the ocean," Cheyne rocked Cleaver with a smoldering glance, then turned to take in the surf. "A place vast and wild and untamed enough to accommodate his presence."

"Here?" Cleaver said, biting his tongue. "You mean right here!"

Cheyne nodded and drew her dark cloak around her as though suddenly cold.

Cleaver stared out over the rolling waves. "This is all I've ever known," he said quietly. "How can Miami be destroyed? *Good* people live here."

Eldritch touched his shoulder. "Worry not, Mr. Cleaver," he said in his rich voice. "It is now that we will start to make a difference. Ubers. And Aegis. Believe it or not, we do have a plan."

Eldritch laid an arm across his shoulders, turned him, and walked him off the beach. He said, "We need your help. Before this is over, you *will* make a difference."

Cleaver couldn't believe his ears. For so long he had tried to do just that.

Now these good people were offering him their help. And they *needed* him.

He looked the King right in the eyes. "Let's get started."

32

YORK, ENGLAND

I sat across from Lucy, a chess board between us. It was my move. I couldn't take my eyes away from her red-rimmed stare.

The chess set forgotten, Lucy said, "I miss her, dad. I miss her so much."

"Lucy-"

"No, dad. Where did she go? What did I do?"

"It wasn't *you*," I told her. "Your mother-" how could I say *I don't know?* How could that ever be good enough?

I hung my head. "I still look for her sometimes. On the internet. I trawl through websites of missing persons."

"I know."

I had feared my confession might upset her, but in an adult way she had simply being waiting for me to open up.

"I failed," I said. "Her, and you," I looked down. "And...and I think I'm going to end up failing *these* people. This power they say that I have? It exists, Luce. I can feel it inside me. But I can't draw it out. I think Kisami, Ken and me are the only ones who've failed."

Since Raychel left I hadn't succeeded at anything.

Why would I start now?

Later that night I got called into the conference room again. Instantly, I knew we had trouble. I had never seen Myleene looking so stressed.

She walked up to me, her eyes glistening with fear. "We don't know the full details, Logan, but Ashka's got Belinda.

And the Trevochet's. She captured them coming back to York from the airport. She's holding them at the old Bonding Warehouse."

I stared at her in horror. "The *Destroyer* Ashka? *How do you know?*"

"Kinkade. That place has been abandoned for years, but the Gargoyles are active. We *must* help Belinda, she is vital to *everything,* but we can't risk everyone."

"I'll go," I said without hesitation. Then I thought of Lucy. "But I made my daughter a promise I wouldn't leave her alone again."

"She won't be alone," Myleene said. "We are only sending Mai, Giles, and Lysette, and you. People we can trust."

Cold. I stared into her hard eyes. "Is...is Belinda alive?"

"No reason why she shouldn't be. Our enemy can't know we're using the Gargoyles yet."

"This means the traitor, if one exists, is almost certainly one of the Eight."

"A fair deduction," Mai looked bright and happy under the circumstances, the darkness of her eyes offset by several diamond studded ear piercings, blood-red lipstick- *at least I hoped it was lipstick-* and even a touch of electric blue eyeliner. And that 'rising-sun' smile. A vampire I hadn't seen before glowered at her side.

"You must go now," Myleene said. "We're being forced to act quickly. We can't find Felicia right now, and Ceriden's too important to risk. Our poodle would be an asset, but we can't waste time checking under every tree and bush."

"They say a female dog is a bitch," said a voice from behind me. "But the more I mix with humans, the more I seem to find among *you.*"

I turned, relief evident in my voice as I said, "Felicia. Thank God."

Felicia winked at me and grinned nastily at Myleene. "Get together soon," she said with a little finger wave and walked out. I followed her at a run.

"Wait, Felicia. We have to round some people up."

"Everyone's in the car, Logan," she said without turning or slowing down. "We're just waiting for you."

And then she *did* turn around with a toothy grin. "Let's go get your girlfriend."

33

YORK, ENGLAND

There was nothing subtle about the way we hit the
Bonding Warehouse. As we approached, Lysette, seated in
the passenger seat of Giles' Chrysler, saw a woman
standing in the shadows outside the long-abandoned
restaurant.

"That is Ashka," Lysette said after a moment. "I just
read her briefly. And, believe me, that's a one-time only
deal."

"Bad vibes?" I ventured.

"Horrific," Lysette shuddered. "Pure evil. She was
human once, and remembers her power was forced upon
her by a demon. But she remembers little of her humanity.
One thing she remembers is going outside for a smoke."

"Our gain," Giles said, and aimed the Chrysler at her.

All hell broke loose. Ashka leapt out of the way, her
angular features hardening and her eyes flashing with
fury. The Chrysler crashed through the half open door of
the Bonding Warehouse, sending planks of wood and
rusty metal flying. The car slewed to a halt halfway across
the rubbish littered floor, having spun back around to face
the way it came.

Ashka stood motionless, framed in the shattered
doorway.

Doors were flung open. We all dived out. Giles left the
motor running. A glance revealed Belinda chained to a far
wall, her head hanging in a way that chilled me to the
marrow. Lying at her feet was a man in a wheelchair, the

chair having been upended. The man's hands scrabbled uselessly as he tried to extricate himself from the chair.

Then- *oh God!* Natalie Trevochet was swinging beside Belinda, but her neck was in a noose. Her legs kicked wildly. Adrenalin surged through my body. She was being strangled to death before her disabled husband's eyes *even as I watched!*

I ran. Nothing had prepared me for this. My feet flew and my heart pounded. As I ran, I shouted, screamed at the woman to hold on, to slip the tips of her bloody fingers under the rope. *Just one more second!*

I got there. I hoisted her legs so that the rope became slack. I looked up into her eyes.

She was alive, and conscious. "Hold on," I mouthed, then looked back to see how the others were faring.

Ashka hadn't moved. She was flinging her arms left and right, unleashing horrifying visions into the hearts and minds of my friends. I staggered as an image beset me, almost losing my hold on Natalie Trevochet's legs.

Belinda, chained as she was now, but not here. Instead, inside a vast underground cavern that dripped with rank water and smelled of blood and death. The centre of the cavern was heaped with bodies. Indeed, it was a mountain *of bodies, all ripped flesh and broken bones. Most of them wore army gear.*

It is your future! Ashka's visage flew at me out of the dark, making me duck and cover. Natalie Trevochet choked as the rope grew taught. I thrust my body back upright, caught her swinging legs and heaved again. *Please,* I thought. *Don't fail now. Please God, I can't fail this poor woman.*

I couldn't move as Ashka flung terrifying visions at my friends. Felicia ran at the Destroyer, blonde-hair flying, then fell to her knees amidst the rubble and started beating at her own body in horror. I saw Mai take up a splinter of wood and try to pierce her own heart. Her friend Vipas saved her by wrestling her to the ground. Both vampires rolled for a second and then, with stunning speed were suddenly up and streaked to within a metre of Ashka. But the Destroyer flung hell at them again, folding them both in an imagined anguish.

And then Ashka reached behind the broken warehouse doors and pulled something out of the shadows.

A fucking broadsword!

Ashka held the weapon high as she advanced upon the helpless Ubers. I screamed their names, trying to penetrate the miasma that clouded their brains. Then I heard a loud noise and saw Lysette dash away from the Chrysler as Giles slammed the boot shut. In one hand Giles held a small pistol, which he handed to Lysette. With the other he loaded a shotgun by jerking it upwards in a smooth, practiced motion.

Come on, Giles.

Behind me I heard a low moan. I turned. Belinda was staring at me, shock and horror etched across her face. If ever we needed the world's best, it was now.

"Can you get free?" I cried.

Belinda wrenched at her bonds. The rope held but slackened. She would free herself, but maybe too late.

I turned back to a sight that filled me with horror. Giles was on his knees. He had turned the shotgun on himself. In another second, he placed the weapon in his mouth and tightened the trigger.

Lysette barreled into him. The shotgun discharged, its blast taking concrete chunks out of the far wall. But Giles wasn't free yet. He was fighting Lysette off and trying to swivel the gun barrel towards her.

What the hell could I do? Feeling inadequate, desperate and desolate I stared up at Natalie Trevochet, asking a question with my eyes. Could I waste her life to try to save seven others?

Natalie Trevochet stared down at me with understanding. It was as if she could read my mind. Then she closed her eyes. A signal of acquiescence.

But her husband was one of the Eight! He was squirming on the floor, screaming now as he saw my dilemma. In a second of indecision I turned back to the other scene.

Just in time to see Ashka swing her heavy sword. In horror I watched it slice through the helpless vampire, Vipas, taking his arm and then his head.

Vipas collapsed in a heap. He was gone. Mai would likely be next, though she did not know it.

It was do-or-die time. Felicia was on her feet, but was merely standing with her head down, as if awaiting the death swing. My heart broke in two. My head spun in horror and terror and despair. The life-loving Lycan had been defeated by empty visions. Ashka now moved towards her, spinning the sword baton style, grinning and snarling and slavering, the true epitome of evil.

Behind me, Belinda freed herself and fell to the concrete floor, groaning. I made a terrible, impossible choice. I took a deep breath, and then prepared to launch myself at this creature as it geared up to take another life.

I heard Johnny Trevochet's tortured voice. *"Please! Don't leave my wife!"*

Belinda crawled up beside me. "Go,"

I dropped Natalie Trevochet's legs, felt the rope go taut and then heard Johnny's scream. I launched myself forward. Natalie's cut-off shriek drove spears into my heart. I covered half the ground between the Destroyer and me in two seconds.

Lysette threw her gun into the air as I barreled past.

I caught it in the perfect firing position.

I fired. The bullet missed Ashka but smashed into her sword and sent it flickering end over end into the wooden door behind her, where it stuck and quivered. Then, Mai grabbed her legs. Felicia blinked away the visions, then screamed and turned lycan in less than a second. I have never seen so much unleashed fury as she morphed from sweet woman to unrecognizable wolf, teeth and jaws gnashing, eyes like molten lava, as she leapt upon the Destroyer.

But Ashka moved frighteningly fast, turning her hips to fling the lycan across the floor. I saw Ashka's eyes darting from side to side now as I lined up a second shot. The evil bitch was looking for a way out.

At that moment another shadow filled the doorway. I paused, unsure.

Lysette blinked at the figure, then cried out, "My God, that's Tanya Jordan. She's here!"

This was the Hawaiian woman who had already killed a Destroyer.

Ashka didn't waste another second. She fired off a barrage of visions, designed, I imagine, to knock us off balance

And again, it worked. A second later, when we all shook our heads and looked around, the Destroyer was gone.

"*Laters,*" a disembodied voice floated around the silent warehouse.

I snapped my head around. How could I have left Natalie Trevochet to die like that? How could I have failed yet another person?

"Oh, God,"

My eyes found Belinda's. And my heart went out to her as I saw her standing, bleeding and crying with the effort it took to hold Natalie Trevochet's frame so that the rope wouldn't choke her to death.

Both women were alive.

But Johnny Trevochet glared at me with undisguised hatred. My gut ached as I realized I had left his wife to die.

I dropped to my knees, letting the gun fall to the cold, hard floor. Everything I did, even the best-intentioned acts, seemed to leave in their wake some dire consequence. Was it my doom to always gain with one hand and lose with the other?

Was that my destiny?

34

YORK, ENGLAND

Ken Hamilton couldn't take it any longer. Sitting around listening to the warbling of Avril Lavigne whilst '*I no Engleesee*' boy, Kisami, tapped away at his handheld video game was not an image Ken wanted to put out there to the *ladies*. He'd made himself a strong chick-magnet already by offering to teach Kisami a bit of Good Ole' American English. Kisami now understood three of the 'all-time great' American words.

Dude- because conversation started with a greeting.

Budweiser- because *everyone* needed fluids.

And *Underworld*. Because every dude should have a hot vampire chick to stare at whilst he downed his Bud. Especially in the current circumstances.

Ken nodded to geek-boy and pointed to the door. "Outta here,"

Geek-boy didn't even look up. "*Bud.*"

"Loser," Ken ran a hand through his hair and headed into the hallway. It was getting on for midnight. Where the hell had Ryan wandered off to? It seemed like all the chicks had retired for the night, which, in truth, was okay by him. If he was being honest he was fine with beach chicks, a Big Ten with college chicks, and a pure stud with most rock chicks.

But put him in a room with someone like Lysette Cohen, all sophistication and chic and Dior parties; or a more-worldly, educated woman like Devon Summers and he was out of his depth.

So, he'd settled on Belinda, or maybe Felicia. Might be cool getting it on with a werewolf. Dangerous. Unfortunately, neither lucky candidate appeared to be home tonight.

Shit, he thought. *You haven't gotten laid since you left frisky 'frisco. Guess its ham instead of beaver tonight, man. Again.*

Ken headed for the kitchen. He'd make a quick cheese-mayo and grab a couple of cans. As he entered, he noticed two people were already there. He paused at the threshold, his hand on the doorknob.

A tall, thin man stood by the fridge, his jet-black eyes narrowing. Before two seconds had passed Ken realized those eyes were wrong. The evil that blasted out of them was palpable.

"Greetings," the tall man said. "I am Jondal."

Jondal? Ken thought. Where had he heard that name before?

"We have come to cause mayhem" Jondal said. "And to kill as many of you as we are able." Jondal executed a perfect bow. The man's frame was thin to the point of emaciation.

"Jondal!" Ken shouted as realization struck. This man was a Destroyer, the one who had forced some people in London to detonate a bomb.

Where the fuck was the panic button?

Then Ken registered the second person in the kitchen. A shockwave of recognition jolted through him.

"Dementia!"

"The demon herself," Jondal hissed in agreement. "For your *dying* pleasure."

Dementia grinned as she unsheathed the sword Ken had seen once before. He found himself transfixed by her white hair, tied and braided with what looked like tiny animal bones wrapped with slivers of flesh; by the double-row of finger-bones that encircled her neck; by the metal that pierced her nose and the larger piece through her *neck.* Her eyes were slits of demonic yellow, glowing as if they were windows that looked upon a sulphuric soul.

"How did you get in here?" he asked needlessly, stupidly. They were here. He should be running.

Jondal extended an arm as thin as a cane. The Destroyer's bloodless lips moved soundlessly. Ken screamed and managed to turn away before the voices in his head told him to stop, to *kneel, to hang his head and just...wait...*

And the worst part, the abominable part, was that as he obeyed the voices in his head and knelt in submission. He was also aware of Dementia moving towards him, and he knew what she was about to do.

He just couldn't help himself.

Hands on your knees. You know its best. Nothing here for you now. Sit straight. Head up. No more struggle. No need to prove yourself. Just...wait...for the salvation of the sword...

The tip of the sword pressed against his neck, at the point where his blonde curls ended.

"I missed you on the Golden Gate," Dementia's voice writhed around him like poisonous snakes. "I don't miss twice."

"Stop!" they were running up the corridor towards him now. The women. *Oh, God!* He had a momentary thought: *Good Lord, I'm already in heaven!* Then Eleanor and Myleene and Devon were sweeping past him, followed by Ceriden and little Kisami, and the compulsion inside his head collapsed.

Ken pitched face first to the floor. All hell broke loose around him. Screams stung the air.

Jondal's voice rose in pitch. A woman's scream rang out. *Oh, no.* Ken thought. *That's Eleanor!*

"No fucking way, man!" Ken leapt to his feet as rage vanquished his fear. Eleanor was pure. She was an elf, one of the great people. She was the Chosen's *teacher.*

Inside the kitchen Dementia was holding everyone at bay, swinging her sword with precision. The boiling yellow slits of her eyes gleamed as if she was having the time of her life.

It appeared Eleanor had dragged open a cutlery drawer. Then, she'd jammed one of the paring knives through her wrist. Even now she was trying to twist the knife so that it hurt her more, even as she screamed in agony and Devon tried to stop her.

Jondal, a tall emaciation of cruelty and vile intent, was leaning against the fridge as if needing its support, and flinging his arms out at people. His power had to be immense, for everyone went down! Ken felt his throat close in horror. The skeletal Destroyer was strong enough to strike everyone at once!

Then from behind Ken came a sleepy voice that made his heart stop.

"What's going on, Ken? Is my dad around?"

Lucy! Logan's daughter!

Ken's heart froze over as Jondal's attention flicked towards him. Powerful, incessant words crept into his brain.

Turn. Smile. Walk up to her. Then throttle her. Watch the life fade from the young one's eyes, smile as her blackening tongue escapes her lifeless lips. Take the life of the young one, but don't take your own. Her father will do that for you later.

Ken's face went slack with anguish. Terror and denial fought Jondal's iron will behind Ken's blue eyes.

Lucy stepped towards him.

Please, he prayed. *Please someone stop him. Or me. Don't let me do this.*

Ken lurched forward. Lucy stared at him in confusion, then smiled. "Are you having a laugh?"

Please...

Lucy must have seen the massive conflict in his eyes. For at that moment she paused and stepped back. She brought a protective hand up to her throat. "Ken?"

Ken collapsed to his knees as Jondal's will left him. He hit the carpeted floor hard, banging his head and seeing stars. Then he sensed someone step past him.

On his knees, on the carpet, he blew the hair out of his eyes and looked up.

NOOO!

Jondal himself now confronted Lucy. Logan's daughter was gazing up at the Destroyer through vacant eyes.

Jondal struck her with an open palm. Lucy's head snapped sideways. Jondal hit her again, and Lucy staggered. But after a second, she regained her balance and went back to staring blankly into the Destroyer's hell-scorched eyes.

Jondal grinned with malice and handed Lucy the paring knife. Ken squeezed his fists into the carpet. He willed his limbs to obey. Jondal nodded at Lucy. There was a moment, a still second in time when Ken struggled so hard he felt his heart might burst, when Lucy hesitated to turn the blade on herself, when Jondal backed up in surprise as if he thought she might resist him.

Then Lucy cut her left arm, deep, so that the blood welled up. Without a sound she switched the knife and cut into her other arm. Jondal's terrible laughter made Ken want to commit murder, and to cry. He stared helplessly at Lucy, who stood with her arms held at her sides, dripping streams of blood onto the floor.

Ken strained with every fibre of his being, exerting so much pressure he thought his head would explode. He couldn't do it. Couldn't move. Tears of despair sprang from his eyes.

He could not save Dean Logan's fifteen-year-old daughter.

Lucy brought the paring knife up towards her throat.

"No!"

Someone used Ken as a springboard. Someone athletic and confident leapt onto his back and then launched himself at Jondal. *Whoa, man, that's Ceriden!* Ken planted his forearms. *This time.* Trumpets blared as he gained his feet. Where were the dancing girls? Late, as per fucking usual.

Ken saw Ceriden strike Jondal with every ounce of his impressive bulk, knocking the Destroyer almost through the wall. The thin man struck hard, his bony frame doing nothing to protect him. Plasterboard cracked amidst plumes of dust. Jondal gasped and stumbled, pointing fingers at Ceriden, but the vampire King grabbed his wrist, jerked it high and leapt three feet off the ground to deliver two rib-cracking kicks to Jondal's sternum.

Jondal collapsed, writhing in agony. Ceriden bent down and delivered a palm strike to his neck, rendering him unconscious.

"Step back, my darling" Ceriden said to Lucy. Lucy backed up slowly, her mouth set in a perfect 'o' of surprise and shock. Ken thought the pain hadn't registered yet. Ceriden ripped off his shirt and started to bind her wounds.

"My dad," Ken heard her saying. "Where's my dad, Ceriden? He said he would never leave me again."

Ken climbed to one knee and twisted his head around, almost too terrified to look. Dementia stood with her back to the kitchen door, the wicked blade held steady in front of her. Outnumbered, she practically *hummed* with confidence.

"It isss sssstaylemaaate," Ken winced at the sibilant tones that trickled across her crooked lips like venom. "You willll not take me without blood and painnn, little onesssss. *You might not take me at allll.*"

No one gave ground. Not an inch.

"Sssstand back," Dementia hissed. "Sssstand down. Keep Sssspirit. He is of no con-ssss-equense to meee," The demon woman shook her white hair defiantly and the finger bones rattled around her neck.

"Agreed," Myleene said very quickly.

Nothing changed. Ken knew everyone in that room wanted to take the demon bitch out.

Myleene grated her words more forcefully. "Now is not the time."

Ken sensed the tensions slacken. In a second Dementia had opened the door; in another second she was gone.

35

YORK, ENGLAND

Do you ever think that you'd give anything, *anything at all,* for a particular event never to have happened? Picture the event now. Can you see how your entire life might have turned on that one inconsequential or devastating incident?

Sometimes we never see it. Sometimes we see it only in retrospect and wonder what might have been.

Me, I knew this was it. When I came home from rescuing Belinda and almost getting Natalie Trevochet killed, I read the utter devastation in my daughter's eyes. I read the betrayal. I walked into her bedroom, but stopped inside the doorway, stunned.

Lucy was sitting on the bed, alone and looking so vulnerable and despondent.

"Lucy. I-"

"Don't you say you're sorry," she said. "You don't get to apologise."

"But-" I stopped talking. No excuses. She was right. Did it matter that I'd thought she would be safer here than anywhere else in the world, protected by elves and a vampire King and so many capable people?

Did it matter?

No. Because I'd sworn I would never leave her again.

I felt breathless, and I had to sit down on the vanity chair. I watched my daughter, my eyes desolate.

Lucy held up freshly bandaged arms. "Do you see this?" her voice raised. *"Do you?"*

I stared at her, speechless. I don't think I'd ever felt so hollow and wretched. Even after Raychel vanished.

"Please leave me alone," Lucy stared at the door, at the wall, at the floor, anywhere but at me.

"Please," she said, and I turned away so she wouldn't see my anguish. I left her room, and closed the door.

That was the moment.

A conversation was occurring in the big conference room when I walked in. The whole household was there, save Lucy, Belinda, and the Trevochet's. I took a seat next to Holly and tried to ignore her sympathetic stare.

A few moments earlier my mobile had started ringing. The call was from Lucy's school. Real life was intruding, making everything more complicated. I threw the mobile against the nearest wall, then spent five minutes picking up the pieces and fixing them back together.

Now, I caught the tail-end of what Myleene was explaining – how Belinda had been hit out of nowhere by a veritable Molotov Cocktail of images. Whilst she struggled to recover, Ashka had injected her with some heady concoction of drugs, and then driven her and the Trevochet's over to the abandoned Bonding Warehouse.

"Thank God for Kinkade," Felicia was studying the bruises that covered her arms, the results of her own bespelled actions.

"It was Ashka's chance to hurt us badly," Myleene said. "So badly that we might never have recovered. If she had killed Belinda, and then the Trevochet's I can't imagine what we would have lost."

But evil is evil for a reason. And that means a simple killing is out of the question. Ashka had been hoping to draw their deaths out all night.

"Kinkade saved them. And our efforts." Myleene smiled.

Mai, the vampire girl, cleared her throat. "Vipas died out there tonight."

I looked down and pinched the bridge of my nose.

I missed the next ten or fifteen minutes. Despair played havoc with my heart. I realized I was ready to walk away from all this if it meant I could save my relationship with Lucy. I wanted the controlled chaos of our normal life back. Our Victory Wall. The 'old man-hopeless child' jesting sessions. Our father-daughter night's out. I mean, why the hell had I been chosen anyway?

I drifted back. A disheveled Giles was explaining how Jondal and Dementia had broken into their house. "Call it complacency. Call it lack of foresight. We thought Ashka was our only enemy in York. Gorgoth's followers are spread so thin, we didn't think there'd be more here. However," he paused. "Their finding us raises that terrible issue. Again."

I tried to focus.

"Ashka knew where Belinda would be and at what time. Jondal and Dementia knew our location..." Giles let it hang.

Felicia whispered. *"How?"*

Mai's normally placid face was twisted with hate. "A *betrayer*," she hissed, her voice filled more venom than a Viper. "One I will find and *kill*."

Undoubtedly now, there was a traitor among us. Someone we trusted worked for an evil so extreme it made Satan look like a naughty schoolboy. Of course, we already suspected this but had done nothing to flush the traitor out.

Jondal might tell us.

Jondal. I wanted to tear him apart.

It was agreed that Ken, Ceriden, Felicia and Eleanor would interrogate the Destroyer known as Spirit. One representative from each race. As they walked out and the meeting broke up, I turned to Holly.

"She won't talk to me," I said. "My own daughter won't talk to me. And I can't blame her."

At that moment a hand touched my shoulder. I looked up to see Ken standing beside me, an odd kind of hurt filling his eyes. "I tried *everything* to help her, man. I'm so sorry."

I let respect show in my face. "I know, Ken. Thanks."

"Give her time," Holly said to me after Ken had moved off. "She's *fifteen*. Impressionable and hormonal as hell. Christ, when I was fifteen I *loved* being Queen Bitch of the world. I married Bastard Face to spite my mother. How's that for a harsh lesson in life?"

I grimaced at my friend. "I think Lucy's learned too many harsh lessons recently, don't you?"

"I really do. But Dean, I know you want to shield her from life. I guess every parent wants to protect their child from the *real world-*" She shrugged. "It's not gonna happen."

"I know that," I said. "But I can't figure out this bloody *power* inside me. It's there, but I don't know what it *does*."

I looked at my friend, really *looked* at her for the first time in days. She'd put her life on hold because I asked her to trust me. Her presence here had nothing to do with Aegis, or vampires, or Destroyers.

I took a deep breath and said, "Do you believe all this?" I indicated the room, the house, the situation.

"I'm here aren't I?"

Yeah, I thought. *Someone else to let down.*

***

I was informed later that it was actually a simple matter to interrogate a man with Jondal's capabilities. He may be the master of coercion, but he couldn't see in the dark. So the only illumination in the interrogation room was a light aimed at his body tied to the bed. In the darkness pooled around him an unknown number of people aimed cattle-prods at various parts of his body. If he tried a mind-strike he would get a jolt. He got the message quickly.

Felicia later told me that Jondal didn't even try to hold anything back. The guy gave up all he knew, which amounted to little more than nothing. When 'pushed', however, he gave an extra snippet of information, one we couldn't start to wrap our heads around.

Whilst babbling rubbish he said: "*I cleared the way for Black Chapter to operate. It was I who cleared away the buildings above the sacred ground. My bomb-*"

Jondal had masterminded the London bombing. Black Chapter was an unknown group set on invoking the Hierarchy of Demons- an incomprehensible act still mostly below our radar.

"What do demons and Black Chapter have to do with any of this?" Felicia asked.

"Will any of that help us stop Gorgoth?" I asked Felicia.

She shrugged. "Not a clue. But it's a step in the right direction."

That sounded like politician-talk for *no* to me.

By now it was after four in the morning, so I headed upstairs to bed. I looked in on Lucy. My daughter was entangled among the bed sheets in a way that made me smile, though the darkness hid my face. Lucy, from an early age, had a habit of using every inch of the duvet. She was facing away from me, her body arranged under the sheet like a bumpy Chinese puzzle.

I retreated and closed the door. I leaned my forehead against the hard wood for a second. Lucy was sixteen in two days.

What next?

Sleep eluded me that night. I repaired my mobile with strong tape. Then I checked my bank balance and business balance by Wi-Fi. The wolves were closing in, so close to the door now I could hear their expensive black suits rustling.

I stood by my window and watched the dawn rise through the trees. I watched it send glowing fronds through swaying tree limbs.

What now?

36

THE LIBRARY OF AEGIS, NEAR SEATTLE

The man called Loki crept through the damp forest as the first rays of sunlight filtered through the heavy boughs. At his back, making no sound at all, were sixty six Wayclearer demons. Leo – Sorcerer – should have been here too, but Leo was dead. Taken out by one of the Eight, a woman called Tanya Jordan.

Intelligence suggested that Tanya was the best of her kind. And her kind was Loki's kind. They were both world-warriors. Loki looked forward to pitting his talents against hers, probably in Miami, at the end of all things.

The trees began to thin out. Loki held up a hand. Behind him there came a cacophony of snuffles and low growls, the pure anticipation of violence.

He had summoned the Wayclearer demons himself. They were the facilitators of the summoning of Gorgoth, sacrificial spawn to shine the light.

Beyond the tree-line he saw a house. Huge and old, four-storied, fronted by clapboard-covered windows and chipped and weathered brick. Dilapidated. Run down. The garden was weed-strewn and overgrown, and concealed one of the most sophisticated early-warning systems known to man.

The frontage was a lie, of course. Behind that decrepit exterior was the fabled Library of Aegis, the greatest source of historical knowledge. Loki felt great privilege at being the one chosen to destroy it.

Last night, he had prepared himself by assuaging all

three vices. This place was changing him, this so-called Land of the Free, with its sweet offerings, its lifestyle of temptation, and its struggling yet insanely upbeat inhabitants.

Already, he looked forward to his victory reward.

Now he assessed his hastily arranged army. Short, with gnarled faces and skin that looked like old tree-bark. Stubby horns protruded from bald heads. Powerful claws and cloven hooves turned limbs into lethal weapons. Terrible racks of teeth protruded from bloody jaws.

He said, "Kill everyone. In particular their leaders."

A body could not function without its head.

"And then raze this whole place from the face of the earth."

The attack happened before dawn. Loki should have waited to annul the vampiric defence, but he'd never been blessed with much foresight. He was a warrior, not a strategist. And Vices beckoned, both old and new. He called the charge and, as they ran across overgrown lawns towards the ramshackle mansion, Loki thrilled to see vampires start running from the shadows towards them. *At last,* he thought. A true running battle.

They pounded towards each other across the grass, meeting with a clash of blood and breaking bones. Demons fell upon vampires. Loki bounced a flying kick off the chest of a vampire, breaking its ribs like so many cracking twigs; landed and pivoted to catch another full in the face as it leapt at him. His power was devastating. The high grass all around the mansion became a blur of struggling bodies.

From the left, outflanking them, Loki saw a pack of lycans start to charge. That was probably Hugo's pack.

And the vampires were led by one named Eliza- the so-called 'perfect' vampire. His inside-intelligence was top notch, and transmitted from the inner circles of Aegis, from their soon-to-be-destroyed headquarters in Northern England.

He flicked an arm. Twenty demons peeled off to meet the charging lycans. The sound of their meeting rang out like thunder among the trees, a detonation of animal violence and aggression.

A vampire, tall and white and bony, reared up in front of him. Loki struck quickly, pleased when the thing blocked his strikes and came back with a combination of its own. This was more like it. This was what he'd been born to do. Sweet pleasure crept through him as he broke his adversary down, blow by blow, and ended up ripping its pale head off with a sound like old parchment tearing.

Loki raised his arms, roared, and threw the head away.

They'd cleared a route to the house. A quick tally told him he had lost twenty demons, and that his enemies body count was in the low teens, four of which he had dispatched himself. His demon-brood was weak. This would cut his fun short.

He turned again towards the mansion.

To see a row of humans in black body armor lining up on the crumbling steps outside, machine-pistols at the ready.

Loki cried, *"Tabular!"*

Every demon suddenly made a break for the house. The harsh sound of gunfire rent the air as the humans opened fire, but their bullets bounced off toughened demon hide like they were rubber balls.

Loki hung back. He was *not* immune to a bullet or two. The demon attack shielded him as precious seconds went by, and then the demons were among the humans, tearing at them with claws and hooves and jagged teeth.

Vampires and growling lycans were a split second behind, pouncing on the demons' exposed backs.

Loki could see how this was going to go.

"Not this time, Loki," a voice said.

He turned to see a female vampire, tall and ethereally beautiful. Something about this being said Vice Number One to the nth power.

"Eliza," he purred delightedly. At last someone worth fighting. He had to admit, she was a sight, this Eliza, clad in body-hugging shiny leather and facing him with flawless poise and balance.

"We could tangle, you and I," Eliza's voice was warm honey ladled over ice-cream. "And one of us will die. But both of us will come to great harm, I promise you that."

"Or?" Loki was always open to suggestion. It was how he'd lived this long.

"You can go. And take what's left of your pathetic army with you."

Loki studied her flawless face as he thought about it. She offered a good bargain. Extra time for him. They were badly outnumbered here. Even more important, it saved face and gave him the chance to try again.

A veiled challenge. He liked that.

"Agreed," he told her. "I hope to meet you again, Eliza. And soon."

He gave her the smile he usually reserved for the procurement of Vice Number One and turned away. He strode through the long grass, letting his fingers brush the tops of the highest stalks, and headed towards the woods, calling whatever remained of the weak and pathetic demon brethren to follow him.

37

YORK, ENGLAND

All I wanted out of the next few days was a chance to talk to Lucy, but life prevented me.

When I entered the kitchen Felicia was there, along with Giles, Lysette, Mai and Ceriden. Not surprisingly, Mai had barely spoken two words since Ashka murdered her friend, Vipas. I poured myself a mug, relieved that Johnny Trevochet wasn't around.

I sat next to Felicia, hoping to get a little lift from the playful lycan. But Ceriden had her attention.

"Big day today, poodle," the vampire was saying. "*Jade* arrived last night. *What* a luscious head of hair that girls got! So today there will be *two* elves training the Eight," Ceriden fixed a long-faced stare on me, eyes full of appraisal. "Jade is a *huge* asset, my fashion-challenged friend. Today will be very interesting for everyone, I think. A day to be marked in history."

Felicia nodded, her expression as serious as I'd ever seen. "One of the greatest."

And that was it. Soon I met the newcomer, Jade, a striking elf with sharp emerald-hued eyes and medium length hair the tips of which were dyed dark green. I was left gawping as she walked past me and into the garden, her every movement a fluid dance.

The training grew in intensity until we were being bombarded with visions and advice on how to mould our thought processes, intentions and reactions. Two elves faced seven chosen humans, along with Felicia and a tired looking Belinda. Then, even Myleene came to join us. I heard Belinda whisper to Felicia that *'there will never be another training session of this magnitude in my lifetime'* and when I heard this woman, who I totally respected, say something so humbling I really started to throw myself into the moment, into the day, and into my future.

Sometime towards late morning Lucy joined in, and I have never seen such concentration on my daughter's face. I think we all knew that we were part of something special, something that might never be repeated. Even Holly came out, drawn to the wondrous atmosphere that rose and spread through the garden. I wanted this day to live on in my memory as one of the greatest days of my life.

Eleanor and Jade worked their magic. Ken drew slowly upon his inner power until it seemed a barrier gave way. Light filled his eyes and lit his face, and the strength and poise of a great warrior lifted him. Tanya, already the best of the best, honed and sculpted her talent until even the elves applauded her movement. Lysette stood in silence – her great power was still being kept secret for her own protection – but I could tell by the sudden brightness that filled her usually lonesome eyes that her inner strength had increased tenfold. Devon Summers sat in perfect concentration, legs crossed and arms resting upon her knees. The soft glow in her bright eyes fanned out, emitting a healing power that steadily washed away our fatigue. I stood for hours. I concentrated my entire being and fought against my inner damnation, and I never tired for one second.

Devon Summers held us all together, surprising everybody when – for one shocking moment – she sheltered us even as Jade hurled dark visions our way.

"Now I see! You are the Healer *and* the Shield!"

Eleanor exclaimed, her small frame practically shaking with excitement. "The blanket we have been hoping for. Your healing power helps protect our minds. You will defend us against mind attacks, suggestion, and even compulsion." Eleanor's own self-inflicted wounds were still raw. "Thank the Heavens for you."

Her words, I guessed, were meant to reassure us that Ashka and Jondal had now been neutered.

Kisami, our Japanese friend, found that he was what Eleanor called an 'elemental.' This was a supreme power. The little guy could manipulate certain factors of the four elements

Everything was coming together. That pretty much left Johnny Trevochet and me. Throughout that tremendous day I felt something gathering inside me, a feeling that gave me fleeting victory over doubt. By the time the afternoon sun began to wane, and even the curious vampires were standing around observing in the shade, a final rush of power sent me over the top and I stumbled into Trevochet's wheelchair.

"Crap!" I cried as a flood of power washed through me and clearly through him and expanded to form a simmering effervescence in the air above our heads

More power than I'd ever imagined shimmered around me. Through the faint haze I could see everyone watching us. I moved closer to Johnny so we stayed in contact, blatantly ignoring each other but staying close, staring wide-eyed at those who would stare back at us.

I heard Eleanor say, "Hit them with images. *Try* to invoke their power!"

Something struck at our power curtain. Something black, like weaponised midnight. I staggered but held it together. Terrible visions collided inside me. My daughter draped across the steps that led up to the Empire State Building, bled dry, not yet dead but dying alone. Felicia, lost in some infernal forest, at last giving up and lying down to die as hungry flames surrounded her, and Belinda, flayed and burned and tortured by demons, the last hope of mankind passing in agony and signifying the fall of our world.

A passing thought struck me. *These visions were of Hierarchy demons! Not Gorgoth...*

Sunlight returned as, with the merest thought, I banished Eleanor's attack. In another second, I swatted Jade's powerfully thrown and well-aimed tennis ball from the air with nothing more than a flick of thought.

I saw Johnny rattle all the house windows with a nod of his head.

I heard his wife, Natalie, slapping out her applause like an enthusiastic seal. Thank God she was sounding better.

In a simultaneous movement I tangled Belinda's blonde hair and knocked Myleene to the ground.

"Stop!" I heard Eleanor say. "You are still green, both of you. You have no mastery yet." I cocked my head at her. She said, "It seems your power, your *combined* power, is the ability to do *anything*. By the King, we have it!"

I shrugged at Myleene. "I was trying to stroke Belinda's cheek," I said.

"The power could be omnipotent," Eleanor explained. "And somewhat lively. It will need an iron will to contain it. But its ultimate strength will come with supreme *focus*. Both of you together, concentrating on the same outcome."

"A perfect fusion of thought," I heard Jade say.

"Focusing on *what*, though?" Johnny shifted painfully in his wheelchair.

"On Gorgoth," Eleanor told him. "On his destruction. When he is summoned, you two will be the front line. All else will be but well-placed distractions. *They* will save countless lives but you two will send the World-Ender back to oblivion."

My jaw practically hit the floor. When I cast around, I saw everyone regarding us with something akin to awe. More pressure. The impact of my failure, if it happened, had just increased exponentially.

"With him?" Johnny said darkly. "Don't count on it."

Great, I thought. *Just bloody great.*

Belinda was regarding me with a smile, as if she'd expected something like this all along. Wow, there was faith for you. I'd harboured the belief that my power was fake and would doom us all in the end.

And it still might, of course. Natalie Trevochet was living proof. And she still lived *despite* me, not because of me. If there was a real God, a supreme being for Good, I wondered at his judgment.

Or maybe God was on holiday and the Devil was standing in. A fiendish jest.

I saved a longer look for Lucy. I just wanted my daughter to look away from the shadows, away from the approaching dark, and see my eyes fixed on her. I just wanted to smile at her and see her smile in return.

She didn't.

Jondal, the Destroyer, listened intently as he heard the discreet rattle of a doorknob. He had long since given up testing his bonds. He knew there was no way he could escape Aegis' house without help.

But he also knew there was one inside who *would* help him.

And now, as he lay there in the teeming dark, dreaming his unspeakable dreams, he heard someone tiptoeing towards him. The person was small, but the shadow they cast on the wall was long, tall, and warped.

With no sound the shadow reached down and unclipped Jondal's bonds.

"You must leave now," the shadow said in perfect, clipped English. "Do not linger, Whisperer. Go straight to New Babylon, to Loki. You will complete your duty there."

Jondal nodded and slid to the ground. He followed the fleeting shadow into the dimly lit corridor. The shadow pointed ahead, then drifted away into deeper cover. Jondal opened a door and entered a darkened room.

He could smell the girl instantly. Beyond her, the window was wide open, providing the perfect escape route.

He paused by the bed. With trembling hands, he reached down and touched the girl's damp forehead. She was restless tonight.

Lucy, they had called her.

He recalled how she'd bled. How she ripped open her skin at his bequest. And how he had coveted the sight of that blood.

Jondal bent over the sleeping girl and brushed her forehead with his dry, chapped lips. Her taste was softness and salt on his tongue. And one other thing, the one added ingredient that attracted him to her.

Innocence lost. The taste of youth blighted before its time.

"You are mine," he whispered as he straightened. "At New Babylon, you will kill yourself, little one. And that will *not* be a part of my duty.

"It will be my greatest masterpiece."

***

Later, Myleene summoned everyone to the house library. It was the first time I'd ever ventured in there. The place was immense. Built on three floors with no ceilings and only the exposed rafters of the roof high above gave the impression of great space. Each floor had a balcony running around it, made safe by a glass barrier. I spent the first five minutes gawping at endless rows of books until my neck ached and my eyes hurt.

"I wanted to show you this place," Myleene raised her hands for attention. "I hope that you will see it is a gift." she paused. "A sanctuary for some of you. A haven. Everyone here, and everyone who has ever helped Aegis, is always welcome."

I watched as Myleene perched herself on the edge of a table and started smoothing down her skirt. I was still elated with my breakthrough, worried about Johnny's reaction, but trying to dampen the conflicting emotions.

"Our ancient Library was recently attacked, as you know," she said. "Eliza and Hugo helped our house guard fight off the attack," she paused. "They were led by the Destroyer called Loki, who, Kinkade reports, is ranked first under Gorgoth."

We all listened. I got the impression Myleene was skirting around something.

"And speaking of Kinkade. Our friendly gargoyle has come up with a shortlist of actresses he wants to vacation *inside*. And when I say 'shortlist', I mean it. There's a choice of three."

"Don't tell me, dear," Ceriden scrunched his face in thought. "Nicole. Evangeline. And Cameron."

"I'd pick Cameron," Ken smiled. "She's *frisky!*"

"Couldn't be Angelina," Ceriden murmured. "She's already taken."

Someone, I think it was Mai, said, "Myleene, stop stalling. What's going on?"

I don't know how many of us were stood waiting in that room, but Myleene, I'm sure, eyeballed every one of us.

"It has been decided," she said. "By various leaders around the world... that humanity should be made aware of the existence of Ubers."

I stared. Shock, clear and palpable and laced with anxiety, descended over the room. I wondered if I'd heard correctly.

"*What?*"

"*My God,*" I heard Johnny Trevochet say. "I only just found out myself. Don't you realise how hard it will hit 'em? It'll be like breaking into the President's Thanksgiving speech and saying: *hey, the Mayor of New York's an alien. Just thought everyone should know.*"

"Dude," Ken shook his head and let out a guffaw. "That's some line, dude. I mean, you should know. *Is* he?"

"It will cause outrage," Ceriden told us with uncharacteristic restraint. "And mass hysteria. There will be attempts at genocide. Vigilante groups will emerge. Humanity will finally discover that it is not, in fact, master of this universe, and that it no longer resides at the top of the food chain. Moreover, *it is a part of it.*"

"Why?" Trevochet persisted and banged his fist on the arm of his wheelchair. "Why risk this now?" I saw Natalie lean over and try to soothe him.

"Because of Miami," Myleene said. "This approaching *New Babylon* event. What will happen in Miami is unstoppable. Imagine the panic if Gorgoth's *summoning* is when the people of this world learn *other species exist.* Imagine the chaos then, Mr. Trevochet."

"World leaders and people of influence have known for generations," Ceriden said. "Those few who previously wanted to unmask us were...dissuaded. And all are agreed. In a few days we go public."

I pondered the word *dissuaded* and saw new conspiracy theories cropping up everywhere. Was Kennedy *dissuaded?* Reagan? John Lennon? Thinking back to my own recent astonishment I imagined a world in disbelief, then in denial, and finally in turmoil.

But then, as if we didn't have enough to take in, Geoffrey Giles came running into the library, looking horror-stricken.

"That bloody Destroyer," he cried. "Jondal. *He's gone!*"

Myleene gaped. "What? How-"

Giles said, "Somebody freed him."

Felicia stood up instantly. "Who *isn't* in this room?"

I got it. Whoever wasn't in the room was the traitor.

"Lucy!" I shouted, jumping to my feet so fast the blood rushed to my head.

"She's fine," Giles waved a hand at me. "We checked the house. No casualties."

"How long has he been gone?" I asked.

"About twenty minutes," Giles wiped sweat from his temples.

Belinda pulled a face. "Not good, Gilesy old boy, we've been in this room about ten."

I realized she was right. My eyes flicked unbidden towards Lysette. Maybe it was time to let the girl from Monaco sift through our innermost thoughts.

"This can't go on," Myleene said in a strained voice. "Aegis is *not* this incompetent."

I stayed silent and raised my eyebrows at Belinda. I realized I hand't had chance to talk to her since she left to pick up the Trevochet's.

I banged my head hard against my seat back

Why was life always dealing us the Death card?

38

YORK, ENGLAND

When the meeting broke Belinda made her way over to me and stood so close my nostrils were filled with the heavy smell of leather. Her t-shirt read: *'I'll be even naughtier if you give me chocolate.'*

"Hey."

"How's it going?"

I grinned at the sparkle in her eyes. This was the real Belinda. Thank God Ashka's drugs hand't hurt her too much.

"Been better," I said, thinking of Lucy. "And, hey, aren't I good enough to warrant the sweet nickname anymore?"

"Saving the best ones for later."

"Later," I widened my eyes. Maybe that t-shirt offered a clue. "Would you like a Twix? Or, wow, what would a King Size Mars bar get me? What was it you said before? Something about James Bond..."

Belinda stepped forward, now so close that I had to open my knees. "How's this?"

I swallowed hard. "Not bad, actually." I'd never known anyone so forward. My own confidence had taken a hit when Raychel left and had laid low ever since. But Belinda had confidence for two, well *twenty* actually. I guessed that knowing her would be like riding a roller coaster – fun and adrenalin-fuelled, an endless series of highs with not many lows, and with the added spice that somewhere along the way a track or two might be missing.

"That's fine," I croaked.

"Logan?" a voice interrupted us.

Lysette appeared behind Belinda, a faint smile on her flawless face.

"Hi."

"I'm sorry to interrupt, but I really need to talk to you, Logan," Lysette said to me.

I rolled my eyes at her. "Can't it wait?"

"Yes," Belinda breathed. "After all, he's not going anywhere."

"Sorry, Belinda, but no it can't wait," Lysette persisted, keeping her face neutral. "Logan. It's about Lucy."

A shadow fell over my heart. "Lucy?"

Belinda moved backwards without saying another word. I opened my mouth to speak but she shook her head. She made a noise of frustration and left the room, leaving me red-faced and bothered.

"Sorry," Lysette took the seat beside me. "Looks like you and Leathercrotch are hitting it off."

"Leathercrotch?"

"Everyone gets a nickname. It helps me remember who they are."

"I see. I'm not even gonna ask."

"You mean what's yours?" Lysette fingered the dainty gold necklace that hung around her neck. No matter what time of day, or where she was, this woman cried wealth.

"I would never mock you," something old and hidden and best left alone shifted behind her eyes.

"So," I sighed. "What's Lucy done now?"

"You shouldn't be so negative about her."

"I know. It's just *hard*. It gets better, and then it fucks up again. Every damn day."

"Well, you need to hear this." Lysette glanced around. "But not here. Let's walk in the garden."

We rose. We walked down the corridor, through the kitchen and out into the garden. The air was cold out here, but the night was completely still. Not a breath of wind stirred the immaculate hedges, nor shifted through the high trees. I steered Lysette off to the left, following a hand-laid path. From experience I knew if we followed it to its end, we would complete one circuit of the garden.

I said, "Okay, Lysette, let's hear it."

Lysette cleared her throat lightly. "I'm guilty, Logan," she said, taking me aback. "My gift is sometimes wonderful, more often a curse."

"A curse? How's that?"

Lysette sighed. "I'll tell you a story. Don't worry; it'll be the abbreviated version. But, before I tell you what I know about Lucy, you need to know *why* I know."

"Okay."

"Once upon a time there was a married woman," she said without emotion. "This woman lived in a little house with a nasty man who kept her so downtrodden she began to forget who she really was. Not only that, she forgot to *care* who she really was."

As Lysette paused for breath I thought of Holly. This sounded like her story, too.

"Anyway, the little man got angry and the woman got wise, but only because she found something like a blessing from God rattling around inside her head. Was it a gift from God? A boon from some Angel who cares for abused women? No matter. It saved her life. But an inner Joker then questioned the power inside her, whispering his dark magic, and ever after, when the woman would meet someone new, she dealt the loaded deck of cards in her mind and used her ace. Or rather, her 'so-called' ace. She can read minds, this lucky woman. Can you imagine her horror, Logan? Imagine being able to discern everyone's innermost thoughts and feelings."

I didn't even try to pretend otherwise. I simply said, "Yes."

"Isolation," Lysette said, keeping her eyes on the meandering path. "That's the worst of it. Knowing that everyone, everywhere, has some dark secret. The nicest woman. The loveliest groom. And knowing that if I don't check – say, *this* person," she waved a well-manicured hand. "That person...I could be befriending a mass murderer. And knowing that if I *do* check-"

"Even a truly wonderful person sometimes dances with darkness," I finished for her.

"Exactly," she stopped to stare at me. "Where'd that line come from?"

I shrugged. "Dunno. Maybe it's the setting."

We continued walking and I let Lysette think. I guessed we were coming to what she really wanted to say. Ironically, we were walking past the part of the garden that Lucy's window overlooked.

"I read Lucy," Lysette said, and I sensed the weight of that responsibility crushing her. "Against all my vows, I pushed. You have to understand-" she turned to me, eyes pleading. "I did it only to be helpful. When that evil man, Jondal, hurt her I wanted to help. Lucy was terrified. I thought if I knew the source of her terror..."

"It's okay, Lysette," I said. "You wanted to help."

"Your Lucy," Lysette said. "She is a lovely person, but she has known hurt more times than a fifteen-year-old should."

I heard a noise ahead. A grunt. I stopped, listened, but the gardens were blanched silver, and silent.

"Her mother practically tore us apart when she

vanished. You talk about that Joker dealing you a loaded deck. Well, he's in my dreams too. He's in my house at night. He keeps Raychel's memory alive there. He never bloody leaves."

"Lucy toys with the idea of becoming a shade."

"A shade? What, as in a *vampire's* shade?"

"She sees the chance of eternal love. Romance. Passion. Security..."

"She's *really* considering this?"

"Yes. It is the foremost thought in her head. And she *will do it,* Logan. Unless you can help her."

Great choice of words, I thought. Lysette could have said *unless you can* stop *her.* But she knew Lucy. She knew my daughter's mind and how she made her choices.

"Why?" I managed, as my world fell away. "*Why?*"

"A way out. She sees it as a chance to stop the hurt and guarantee eternal love. It is darkly romantic, and she is changing, Logan. Changing like you can't imagine. She may see this as the only way."

"No."

We stopped. The cool night air raised goose bumps on my arms. I kicked at the stepping-stones, at the grass. I felt my eyes grow shiny as I faced Lysette.

"I failed her."

Lysette grabbed me. "*No!* Nothing is set in stone. Go to her, Logan. She needs help. Talk it through. Have that talk about her mother you've been putting off for so long. Get it out there. You may save her."

I was about to say: *may?* But then heard another faint noise. A whisper maybe, a groan?

I put a finger to my lips and tried to bury the big pile of hurt. Slowly I sneaked along the hedges, hugging them, with Lysette close behind me.

I parted a bunch of leaves and saw the clearing beyond.

Shock hit me like a cruise missile. Now I did fall to my knees, and the rest of my world collapsed.

"Belinda."

She was on her feet, facing away from a garden bench. Her tight leather trousers were bunched around her ankles. I could see the pale half-moon of her flat stomach, a smooth curve of hips, and the thin line of her black thong stretched over her thighs. When I spoke, she turned her head towards me, and a mess of blonde hair fell across her cheek.

Good ol' Ken Hamilton was sitting behind her, getting the lap dance of his life.

"Dammit, Logan," Belinda's voice was choked with emotion.

"It's nothing," she said to my back.

I felt weak. I stared at Lucy's window. I couldn't look at Lysette. How much more could I take?

The answer came immediately.

The house alarms went off. Hoarse shouts of warning came from the front and side gardens. Someone in the kitchen shouted out:

"We're under attack!"

Fuck.

39

YORK, ENGLAND

"Move!" I said, and then tried to stem my panic. One thing was certain – we Chosen had trained together. We'd be better fighting together.

I saw Mai fall through the kitchen door, out into the garden. I cast around quickly. Lysette stayed behind me, as she'd been taught. Her power wasn't combative. Ken stumbled around, his lack of trousers and guilty expression making him look decidedly un-cool. Belinda tugged her leather trousers over her hips, then buttoned them together over her crotch, before zipping up with a little leap.

"Lysette, stay back!" Belinda cried, becoming the leader we needed. "Ken, at my side. Logan, behind us. Don't panic, Logan, just focus."

I nodded. I hadn't yet learned to harness my power. Indeed, I'd barely had time to adjust to its existence. I might attack a single enemy and accidentally knock the house down.

As she passed me, Belinda whispered, "We must talk later. *Please.*"

I managed a half-hearted nod. Alfresco lap dance aside, she hadn't changed. We walked towards the house. At that moment two ugly looking beasts stepped into the garden, presumably hunting Mai, who lay dazed on the ground.

My jaw dropped. *Demons.*

"Wayclearers," Belinda said without breaking stride.

"Remember what Eliza told us. They are weak."

Weak, I thought, and bloody ugly. Both demons were about five-five, with stubby cloven hooves that kicked up divots from the garden as they walked, and wicked looking curved claws that ended in scimitar-like nails. Their heads were large in proportion to their chunky bodies, and their faces twisted maliciously in the half-dark. Yellow light seeped from slitted eyes and reflected off racks of dripping fangs. When one snarled it tore away half its own cheek.

Mai scrabbled away from them. Belinda stepped in, waited for one of the demons to move, then ducked under its attack and struck into its soft belly. This was followed by a strike to the neck and a chop that sounded like a tree being felled. The demon collapsed, unconscious.

"We need weapons," she said, not even breathing hard as she broke the demon's neck with her boot. When she turned and saw Lysette and me regarding her in outright shock, she smiled.

"Get real Chosen," she said. "Training is over. It's kill or be killed from here on in."

Ken ran and leapt at the second demon, catching it under the chin with a mid-air uppercut. Its snarl was cut off by a choked gurgle as it landed hard, already dead.

"Dude," he whispered in respect of his own skill.

Belinda helped Mai to her feet. I glanced up towards Lucy's window. Call it luck or instinct or a paternal sixth-sense, I don't know, but I saw my daughter standing at the window, staring down at us.

"Lucy!" I cried. "Wait there! I'm coming!"

Another demon blocked our path. Without breaking stride, I called on my power until it shimmered around me. That took half a second. A moment later I flung it with all my will, thinking: *punch!*

My power struck the demon like an F15. Even Belinda cringed when the beast barreled backwards and impacted the side of the house in a cloud of mortar and pulverized bone and brick fragment.

The demon disintegrated. Bricks cascaded from the wall, leaving a demon-sized hole. When I sprinted into the kitchen, I saw that several blocks had exploded *inside* as well, one of them striking another demon full in the face and destroying its tusks and fangs.

Score two to Logan! The demon was down on its knees, making a horrible gurgling noise. Mai seemed to float across the floor, moving with incredible speed to its side. A second later she had broken its neck. I hadn't even had time to draw breath.

"Control it!" Belinda hissed at me.

The kitchen was a melee. A pitch battle. I saw a guard yank open the fridge door and slam it into the face of a lunging demon. I saw Myleene throw our prized coffee machine at the crazy Hierarchy demon – Dementia. I saw Jade pinned to the floor by two demons suddenly pivot and rise up into a handstand, kicking out at both demons and sending them crashing into kitchen furniture.

Only winner here's IKEA! I thought crazily.

Belinda said, "We four stick together. We get Lucy first. If the crisis preparations were followed then Giles should have Devon and the Trevochet's already hidden away. They should be using their powers to help us from concealment. Now, go."

She turned quickly to Lysette. "Sorry, but you'll have to stick with us."

I skirted the chaotic struggle, but as I slipped out the kitchen and into the corridor, I heard a scream. I whipped around just as Dementia leaped upon Myleene.

Dementia's white hair flicked and whipped like it had a mind of its own, its braids of flesh and bone slicing into the demon-bitch's own hatred-filled face.

"Nowwwwww, Myleeeeeneee," I heard her slur. "Dieeeeee."

I gathered power, but in less than a split second Dementia wrenched Myleene's right arm from its socket and threw it across the floor. Blood fountained and flowed, and Myleene's screech was so high we barely heard it. I threw my power at Dementia, but the bitch was fast, hellishly fast, ripping open Myleene's throat with switchblade nails and twisting away from my blast in a movement that defied the eye.

Myleene lay face up, unseeing, already dead.

We stared at the scene, aghast.

"Go!" Belinda recovered, making the Commander's decision in a flash. She chose, and we followed, up the dimly lit corridor and the stairs at its end, my face strained and white with horror. Mai and Belinda dispatched three demons along the way. Mai said they were probably searching for Devon Summers, our shield.

"We risk getting trapped along here," Mai pointed out as we ran.

"There's a way out through the library," Belinda said, over her shoulder.

"The library's *downstairs.*"

"We'll make it," Belinda started to slow.

We moved along the second floor corridor, stopping outside Lucy's room. Belinda shouted her name, then pushed the door open. My daughter rushed out into my arms, tearful and shaking.

"Lucy!" I held her and stroked her hair and thought *God, why can't we just be allowed some time together!*

Mai cried, "Look out!"

I looked over the top of Lucy's head to see a demon rushing towards us. Ken stepped forward to meet it without fear, rushing it with a shoulder charge. It fell to the floor, snarling, and Ken stumbled too, tangled up in its flailing limbs. The demon made a noise like a pressure hose as it turned on him, fangs and jaws gnashing, drools of acid slowly dribbling from its mouth and chin. Within a second Mai was beside Ken. She took hold of the demon's skull and smashed it three times into the wall until I heard the sound of destroyed bones.

Mai flung the body away, and then held out a hand to Ken.

Belinda was looking calmly back the way we'd come. "I wish I knew where everyone was," she said with a calculating frown.

Ken said, "I feel naked without a weapon."

Everyone blinked at him. To our knowledge he'd never *used* a weapon.

"Poor Myleene," Lysette began, but Belinda cut her off. "Don't," the blonde girl said. "First we survive, then we grieve. Let's get through this night first."

She led the way back. I draped an arm over Lucy's shoulder and held her close, comforting her as best I could. I was desperate to say something, desperate to talk, but not now. Not like this.

Once downstairs we heard ongoing sounds of combat from the kitchen. A demon came tearing down the corridor, brandishing a sword which it swung at Ken, our rear guard. It was then I realized just how dumb these beasts were as its sword got stuck in the plaster wall. The thing stared up at its jammed sword, then looked back at us. You could almost hear it going *oops!*

Ken kicked and punched and finished the thing off. Then he wrenched the sword free. From beneath curly blonde locks he eyed Belinda.

"Suddenly...I feel better." He swung the weapon as if he'd been a sword master even before he'd learned to surf.

"Keep it then," Belinda hurried towards the back of the house, heading, I presumed, for the library. As we drew closer, however, we heard more sounds of combat.

"Bastards are in the library," Belinda hissed in anger. She closed her eyes for a few seconds, then decided. "No choice. We go on."

And we did. We followed her because she was our leader. We followed her because, even having witnessed the unmatched skills of Tanya Jordan and the elves, we still trusted her with our lives.

The library was ten times more frantic than the kitchen. Dozens of demons fought against Kisami, Eleanor, Jade and Tanya Jordan. With disbelief I watched Jade perform a literal dance of death, weaving in and out of the enemy, punching and kicking with decisive strikes and leaving a pile of dead in her wake. I saw Jondal gesturing and Ashka jabbing her fingers, but their opponents did little more than flinch. Thank God for Devon Summers, our shield. Undaunted though, both destroyers unsheathed swords and attacked with infernal precision.

Kisami slipped and fell, falling luckily beyond Ashka's swing. The deadly blade sliced so close it took a slither off his hair. Transfixed, I watched as the slither separated and drifted up through the air, fluttering apart like a shattered dream. Kisami's luck ended there though. Ashka stepped onto his thigh, pinning him to the spot with her vicious weight. Then she upended the sword over his heaving chest.

The Destroyer plunged the sword down. I almost cried when I saw Eleanor throw herself across Kisami's chest and take the sword in her own body. The elf reared up in agony, eyes wide, then slumped lifelessly.

"*No!*"

I flung a blast at Ashka. The impact knocked her back, but only a few feet. Somehow, she'd absorbed most of the energy.

A thought struck me. Our crisis plan was flawed. If Johnny was here now, together we could stop this.

I cast around. Bodies fought and struggled and slipped and leapt from one wall of the library to the next. Demons and humans used chairs and sofas to gain advantage and even climbed the bookcase walls to fight. Tanya Jordan performed a lethal ballet right in the thick of it, sending demons sprawling to left and right, and leaving none alive as she danced right back over them, a dripping stiletto in her hand.

I pushed Lucy behind me and backed right up to the wall. A scream sent my eyes searching and I saw two of our house guards torn apart. Jondal struck at Tanya using magic as well as metal, but all his strength combined barely kept him alive. I think that Tanya would have killed him right then if not for the death of Eleanor, which had shredded everyone's concentration.

Then, suddenly, Ashka was there! Coming straight at us. Belinda stepped in front of me, Ken at her side. I moved to the centre. This was our formation. When Ashka struck we all flinched. I got the faintest mental image of the world in ruin, but I recovered immediately.

"Fuck you, bitch," I heard Ken say. He poised to leap at her, but then several things happened at once. Dementia came barging through the library door, covered in blood.

The vampire, Mai, reacted instantly and leapt onto the demon's back. Mai sunk her teeth into Dementia's neck and bit down. Blood welled up in torrents. Dementia squealed and barreled through us, twisting and turning, trying to throw Mai off, but the vampire hung on, even digging her nails deep into her enemy's arms to stay in place.

Vengeful strength from Mai, desperate strength, heroic and stupid and everything we needed right now.

Ken, distracted, only managed to evade Ashka's sword when Belinda shoved him aside. But Belinda was suddenly exposed as the sword came down on her skull.

I almost screamed. Power exploded from me. But I was a second late. The sword struck.

But Belinda caught the blade between her hands! The room seemed to stop and stare in awe. Almost in the praying position, Belinda smiled right back into Ashka's blazing eyes.

"Not this time, *bitch.*"

My power, reckless, slammed into everyone, and I mean *everyone*. Those nearest me staggered to their knees, those further away were rocked and buffeted as if caught in a strong wind. I gritted my teeth and tried to focus. Yes, I had been reckless, but I had been trying to save Belinda's life.

Ashka leapt away, leaving her sword behind.

Dementia screamed, and then, still with Mai on her back, managed to *flip* herself over, landing heavily on the floor with Mai trapped underneath.

Mai struggled weakly, the breath crushed out of her. Dementia spun and kicked and clawed, now lying atop the vampire.

Ken jabbed the sword at the demon's ribs, but she

twisted and rolled away, disappearing among a tangle of legs and bodies.

This time, Ken helped a grateful Mai to her feet. "Just needed a big weapon," he said with a cheeky grin.

Ashka rose slowly to her feet. I braced myself, fighting off the whisper of fear that crept through my brain.

There was a moment when the room stilled. A breathless, timeless instant when we all took stock. I saw the chance of death and the fast-approaching moment when I would stand and fight and live or die alongside my new friends, together.

Then something seemed to pass among what remained of our enemies. Four demons, plus Dementia, Jondal, and Ashka. Suddenly, with snarls of hatred, all the demons broke a far window. Two of them sacrificed themselves by distracting Tanya and Ken. A third died on jagged shards of reinforced glass as it leapt through the opening. The fourth cut itself to pieces widening the gap.

Dementia and then both Destroyers stepped over its still twitching body out into the dark, boundless night.

"Until New Babylon!" Ashka cried out as they departed.

We were left bleeding and disheveled, stunned survivors, standing uncertainly and staring at each other with haunted expressions.

Belinda, our leader, took charge, rallying us into the conference room before we started dwelling on the bodies of the dead.

Lucy laid her head on my shoulder as Ceriden, Felicia and Giles brought in the people they had been guarding – the Trevochet's, Devon, and Holly.

"We lost Myleene," Ken said, his voice strangled with grief. "And most of the house guard."

"Myleene," Giles' face fell apart, and tears welled up in his eyes.

"Eleanor died," Lucy said in a small voice that wrenched at my heart.

Desolation filled the room.

"You know who's to blame for this!" Ken slammed a fist onto the table, his eyes crazy. "That fucking traitorous *bastard*." He turned around fiercely. "The one who gave away our location and released Jondal."

Giles cast a murderous glance around the room. "Lock the doors," he said. "No one leaves. I don't care how long this takes."

His eyes came to rest upon the person to my right.

"Lysette?"

40

YORK, ENGLAND

Giles opened Myleene's laptop and, after a respectful moment, logged onto the website that would give him Kinkade's latest updates.

I turned to Lysette. "I'll go first, Lysette. No worries."

She smiled. "Thanks, Logan. You won't feel a thing."

As Lysette worked I allowed my eyes to wander. I saw tension and fear in many faces, confusion in a few, and disinterest in others. I didn't envy Lysette's task, not after what she'd told me earlier about herself.

"Done," Lysette murmured. "You're okay."

"Thanks."

"Next?"

Whilst Lysette worked I fought my inner warning system that told me to remain alert because something *had* to happen and took a moment to focus on Lucy. Gently, I put a finger under her chin and lifted her head.

"Hey, kiddo."

"I'm not a kid," she said. "You're a ..." she blinked. "Hey, I'm..." She pulled away from me and looked her watch. "Dad, I'm *sixteen!*"

It took me a second to understand. It was getting on for five in the morning. Today was Lucy's sixteenth birthday.

"Not *that's* old," I laughed. "How do you feel about a bus pass?"

I heard Lysette speak as she moved on to someone else.

"Never be as old as you, *wrinkly,*" she mock punched me, and it was like before. Me teasing her. She haranguing me about my 'old' age. I felt a sudden urge to take her away, to celebrate her birthday properly, just to let her *live* once more in this teetering old world.

"I've come of age," Lucy said, and a veil fell over her eyes. I felt my heart pause. It was an off turn of phrase for a sixteen year old.

"Time to let yourself *live*," I said.

"I...I want to, dad. I feel. . . different."

I tried to ignore the tension that continued to thicken around us.

I noticed Tanya Jordan sitting forward in her chair. "I overheard," she said with a smile. "But then I *was* listening," she shrugged at me. "Sixteen is big. One of the biggest. We wrinkleys tend to forget."

Lucy turned a smile on her that was reminiscent of a sunrise illuminating a dark valley. "*See.* Tanya knows."

"Big changes," Tanya spoke mainly to me. "You think this Gorgoth guy's hard to handle; you wait 'til Lucy turns *eighteen.*"

Lucy looked at me and laughed, her eyes twinkling.

"When this is over," I said. "We'll go away somewhere, just you and me, Luce. For as long as you want. Or until the money runs out. Hell, Logan's Tours has probably gone under by now anyway."

"What about school?"

Lysette said, "Next."

"We're about to save the world. We'll get you schooling later."

I saw a brief opening in those iron shutters. "Promise?"

"With all my heart, darling."

I held her, taking care not to graze her fresh wounds. "You came for me tonight," she whispered against my chest. "You did."

"Yes."

I glanced up as Lysette stiffened next to me. "You okay?"

"Got him-" Lysette started to whisper but then a gunshot rang out.

And then the greatest shock. *Kisami stood up, brandishing a small firearm.*

And in perfect, clipped English tones he said, "May I just say that I am looking forward to testing you all at New Babylon," before turning on a smart heal and striding out of the conference room.

Devon had weaved her shield an instant before Kisami fired at us. It had taken immediate effect, slinking over us like a giant bullet-proof tarpaulin.

I sucked in a huge lungful of air. I rubbed Lucy's back until she stopped shaking.

"Waiting for us," Giles spat. "The bloody bastard was just waiting for us." He started to go after Kisami, but Jade restrained him with a shake of her head. *Not worth it. Not yet.*

I noticed Lysette was trembling. "You okay?"

"His mind was not evil, not broken," she sobbed. "It was just *gone*. A great black hole. But when I probed, when I pressed the *nothing,* I felt myself being sucked in. Oh, God, I almost lost my mind."

Giles walked over to comfort her.

"You mean the little fucker could speak English all along?" Ken was fuming. "I spent *hours* teaching him..."

"And Eleanor died saving *his* life," Jade spat with as much vehemence as I'd ever seen. "It now seems she was set up... to die."

"Yes."

We stared at each other, bowed by the knowledge that Eleanor had died for nothing.

"He fooled everyone," Ceriden stepped to the centre of the room to grab our attention. "All this time. But here's the kicker, you guys; here's the real mind-blower...*we thought Kisami was one of the Eight.* The location spell identified him as such. So, if Kisami is in fact allied with our enemy, then who is the other Chosen. . ?"

He left the sentence dangling, a big, attention-grabbing carrot poised over our heads.

I watched the leaders of Aegis sink into confusion.

Who is the last of the Chosen?

And just as important: *how had the search spell failed to identify them?*

41

YORK, ENGLAND

We couldn't risk staying at the house, so we decided to move to a new location. Before the sun came up Ceriden had left. Shortly after that the rest of us rode out in convoy, Lucy, Holly and I riding in Belinda's Audi, following Giles' Chrysler 300 and tailed by Jade driving Eleanor's gleaming Lexus.

I knew the route. Belinda had taken Lucy and I to this place just a few days ago. I wondered how much money had been drained from my bank account in that time by those circling sharks that masqueraded as the government. And when would Lucy's headmaster decide to call me in person? Did any of it matter?

We were trying to save the world here.

The yawning black hole that was my fear of failure sent a snapping beast into my brain. It reminded me that I couldn't take all this. It said the power inside me was not my friend, promised I would fail them all at the end of days.

When we all went down to Miami for our Last Supper.

And Lucy? My daughter entertained thoughts about becoming a shade. She saw the romantic side of it, the sweet, dark pain. How had it come to this? I wondered when events would drive her to the point of decision.

When we all went down to Miami...

Why the hell had I been chosen anyway?

Gravel crunched under the slow-moving wheels as Belinda brought the car to a stop outside Ceriden's front door.

"We'll catch up," Belinda put a hand on my arm and then spoke directly to the other two. "Go straight inside. Ceriden will be waiting."

I breathed deeply to calm my nerves. Holly gave me a concerned look as she exited the car but said nothing. Lucy practically flew into the mansion.

"I wanted to talk," Belinda said into the resulting silence.

"I get that." I noticed her t-shirt was simply black today. No legend.

"It's not easy for me. This, I mean," she pointed at me and then at her. "Us," the cars leather seats creaked as she changed position. "I'm usually pretty flighty. . .a fickle bird, unreliable, but never forgotten."

"And the knowing will forever ruin the person that met you." I said.

"Something like that," Belinda exhaled. "What I mean is I don't usually hang around."

"Why?"

"It's the rule I live by. *The* rule – no ties, no relationships. Because I'm not gonna live forever."

"I don't understand."

"Don't you, Logan? I'm a *fighter*. I face off with monsters nine days a week. Sooner or later I'm gonna come up against something I can't beat," she paused and looked at me sadly. "I won't make anyone grieve for me."

I saw an unattainable desire for companionship crush the light out of her eyes.

"Grieve?" I repeated. "So you don't want the responsibility of *knowing* that you have to survive."

"I don't want to leave anyone behind."

I held her sad gaze. "You don't want to *care*."

"Logan, I *will* die young. It is inevitable. I've known

that for years. It's why I live my life to the full. Every hour of every day. It's why I made that mistake..." she faltered. "With Ken."

It wrung my heart to see Belinda, of all people, diminished like this. And now I understood, or thought I understood, the motive behind it. "I get it," I said. "You live. You have fun. You move on. It saves you from knowing that someone's gonna cry for you when you're gone. I get it."

"Until now."

"Sorry?"

"Until I met *you*, Logan. Sounds corny, doesn't it? Crazy mad. But I guess you're the exception to *The Rule*."

I nodded, not trusting myself to speak.

"Ken was meaningless," Belinda said. "You are not."

"Ah, Belinda," I said, leaning forward so I could frame her perfect face with my hands. "What the hell am I letting myself in for?"

In the end I went to bed around nine a.m. I dozed restlessly for a few hours in my new bed and started awake early in the afternoon. I explored Ceriden's mansion, a warren of over-decorated, extensively modernized, rooms. It must have cost millions to convert. Through the open door of one room I thought I saw Kate Moss and Bridget Hall, draped across a velvet chaise-longue, laughing and sipping champagne. When they beckoned to me I turned tail and ran. In another room I saw a set of ethereal twins with jet-black hair that reached their hips. They were laughing and running feathers up and down each other's semi-naked bodies. Shades, maybe. Servants of vampires. It made me think about Mai, who seemed a likeable girl despite her obvious undead flaw, and about her relationship to Lucy.

Was Mai courting Lucy?

Or was Ceriden?

I thought about the Maseratis, the Lamborghini I'd spied in the three-car garage. The sparkling Tiffany collection. The Bvlgari wall clocks. What was the salary for this 'save the world' gig anyway? I mean, one of those wall clocks could probably save my business.

Around another corner I came across Tanya. I smiled. "Thanks for helping out the other day."

"Your daughter is sweet. But mixed up, I'm afraid."

I rolled my eyes. "Long story."

"I guess. Well, we seem to have some time-"

I felt my stomach clench. "Not yet."

"That's okay, Logan. Just- don't take too long about it. She needs to hear what you have to say."

I nodded and turned away, unable to say more. I felt Tanya's eyes follow me until I turned the corridor, but it didn't feel like the weighty stare of judgment. It felt more like, what?. . . Sorrow? *Loss?* I wondered what Tanya Jordan regretted.

I ended up in Lucy's room. I thought about visiting Belinda's, but Lucy came first and although my daughter and I were almost back on speaking terms, I still hadn't tackled her in depth about the 'Shade' issue.

I locked Lucy's door behind me. I perched on the edge of her bed, watching her sleep.

"I love you, baby." I whispered. She would always be my baby. How could a father ever truly express the depthless love he felt for his daughter?

Tears shone in my eyes as Lucy came awake.

"Dad?"

"Hi."

Lucy rubbed her eyes and sat up. "Everything okay?"

"Yes," I reached out and stroked her hair. "Don't worry. We're safe here."

"No more Kisamis?"

"No more," I agreed.

I saw her face cloud over. "What will happen to Myleene and the others?"

The house in York was being 'cleaned up' even as we spoke. I didn't go into detail. "They'll be buried," I said. "After."

"You mean if we survive."

"*When.* Look, Lucy," I couldn't hold back any longer, nor think of an easy way to say it. "A Shade is not a person. After the consummation, they cease to feel. They cease to care."

Lucy looked at me for a long time. "That's not true," she said at last. "A Shade is loved by its Master, and loves in return. It is a lifelong bond, and once made the Shade will never feel loss or despair or loneliness ever again."

"That's not *living*."

"Living's overrated."

I wondered where she was getting this from. Nights of conversation, perhaps. With Mai. How long had it been going on? And what was Ceriden's agenda?

I wondered again if a vampire courted its Shade. "Oh, Lucy, if living is overrated," I said. "Then why the hell are all these good people putting their lives at risk to save the world? Tell me that."

"Dad?" Lucy said then. "Why are you saying this?"

I was being shut out. "Is Mai filling your head with this...this shit? Is Ceriden? God, I love you, Lucy, you're my daughter. Please don't push me away. It can be fun again."

"I'm tired," Lucy turned away from me and pulled the sheets over her head.

I watched her a while longer, unaware I was crying until tears began to sting my eyes.

Help me be a better father.

I held a sacred image in my mind of a much younger Lucy dancing around the kitchen table with her mum, aping every movement Raychel made, both of them clowning around to some old pop tune- *Video killed the radio star,* I think it was.

I smiled in memory now as I entered Ceriden's kitchen. Younger days, older days, awesome days.

Days of happiness.

Long gone.

My eyes sought the whisky bottle. *Hello, darkness, my old friend.* Another old song. My life in poetry, measured and defined by music.

The bottle gleamed at me, an amber charm. It had been a while. I walked over to the shelf. I picked up the bottle, contemplated the lure.

"Your future lies in that bottle," a voice said behind me. Holly.

"I don't have a future," I said, and right then I believed it. Avert Armageddon or not, my life was over. I was heading back down to the Yawning Cave where monsters dwelled.

When we all went down to Miami...

Hello, darkness-

Then a voice said, "But *we* do...I hope." and I turned.

Belinda stood behind Holly in the doorway, looking afraid, unsure whether to smile or frown.

My friends, I thought. My friends were always saving me.

Sooner or later, I was going to have to return the favor.

42

YORK, ENGLAND

That night, Ceriden had his house staff cook a six-course meal. I took my seat between Lucy and Belinda, and straight opposite Felicia, and held up my glass of Barefoot Merlot.

"To meeting new friends," I said. There was a bond that joined us now, and when Felicia saluted me back with the same toast others around the table heard and raised their glasses.

"To new friends," it was a poised moment, sad and heartfelt. I locked eyes with people I barely knew, people I would soon be fighting alongside and trusting my life to, and I felt faith flow through me.

The waitresses came out. Conversation struck up, glasses clinked and cutlery scraped away at plates. The laughter rose and fell and people like Ceriden, Jade and Lysette showed themselves confident enough to regale the entire table with stories, whilst those of us who were less outgoing sat back, satisfied with chatting to our neighbours or just soaking up the atmosphere.

It was one of those nights that come along rarely. Something unplanned and unexpected that turns out to be one of the best times of your life. I was with Lucy and others who mattered to me.

Life had turned on a dime for me, a dime that turned into a silver dollar. Since the night of the treasure hunt, I had become close to people who cared and were more focused than anyone I had ever met. Raychel and all the shitty baggage that came with her memory had regressed further into the past. I had the *now* to worry about. I had my daughter to worry about. I had new friends and millions of people to worry about.

The night went on and the courses kept coming. We all applauded Milo, the Head Chef- an absolute man-mountain of a vampire. Kate Moss wandered in and shared a toast with us and told a few catwalk stories; the wine flowed and the conversation turned, and all the time, through the merriment and the camaraderie and the bonding, there wasn't a person in that room who wasn't just a bit sad, voices husky and emotions a little bit shaky, because we all knew that no matter what happened in the approaching final battle, not everyone would survive.

The next few days were a dangerous mix of boredom and chaos. Humanity was informed of the existence of Ubers. Every news outlet cried indignity and tried to milk the chaos for circulation, every so-called 'expert' jumped on the band-wagon. There were speeches by the President, by the British Prime Minister, by the Pope. You name it; if you appeared credible you were courted by the press, or by the government, to share.

We watched it all unfold from the safety of Ceriden's mansion. It was expected that the world would react with disbelief, then with amazement and fear, and then with some violence and curiosity. Our expectations were pretty much met.

Lucy continued to act cool around me. Tanya helped by lightening the mood, and by distracting my daughter from the attentions of Mai. I wanted to confront the vampire woman, but now felt fearful of how Lucy would react if I did. Belinda stayed close and supportive but didn't push it.

Ken avoided me like the plague. Johnny Trevochet and I agreed to bury our differences for the greater good.

I took great pleasure in refining my new power on my various housemates.

Meaning *Ken.*

For example, as Ken started up the stairs, I thought *shove,* and sent a little gust of power that sent him sprawling against the wooden risers.

And another: as Ken opened a can of Bud, I thought *fizz,* and shook it so violently that foam and beer spurted out, leaving him dripping and red-faced.

"Focusing," I explained. "Just focusing."

He took it well, though. Later, Johnny and I raised him three feet off the ground. It took all our concentration and growing finesse to move him against his will out the front door and into a heavy rainstorm. But we managed it.

After that I gave him a break. I concentrated on rearranging bottles and mugs on shelves and artistically billowing the curtains.

Kinkade kept up a steady flow of stunning information. Unbelievably, at New Babylon, Loki was planning to open the Gates of Hell. Lesser fiends would spew forth. We would then be in the fight of our lives. Earth would be on the brink.

Kinkade explained how the Destroyers would have to invoke lesser Gods first, Gods like Coyote- the God of Mischief- and Abominata- the God of Corruption-themselves beings of immense evil and unutterable power that, when summoned alone, could raze a small country. The Destroyer's would then bind these Gods and coerce them into helping summon forth the world-killer – Gorgoth.

Troops were being deployed to Miami. The army. The

marines. You name the acronym – FBI, NSA, SWAT, CIA, it was on its way there.

The endgame, magical, lethal, cruel and terrifying, was coming.

I was sitting on the sofa with my feet stretched out, watching Sky's new daily segment of 'Uber News', and trying to hone my power to the point where I could tickle Lysette's bare feet, when a pair of bronzed arms slapped the cushion beside my head.

Tanya leaned over. "News from the kitchen," she said. "We're going to Miami. Tomorrow."

I felt my heart twist. "Miami? Are you sure?"

"That's what they said. It's time. Kinkade says the remaining Destroyers are already there. So we have to go too."

"You *overheard* all this?"

"Well, yeah," Tanya tried and failed to look sheepish. "Anyway, the point is – Belinda saw me. Then asked me to tell you something. She wants to see you. Upstairs."

I grinned, then wiped it away, but couldn't keep the smile out of my eyes. "Right."

Tanya gave me a knowing look. "Something about this last night not being meaningless."

43

YORK, ENGLAND

She was wearing her leather trousers and a t-shirt that read 'If It Wears A Skirt- You Can't Afford It.' She stood by the window, a heady vision with moonlight framing her figure. Her eyes sparkled when I closed the door.

"Lock it, honey cake."

I felt a rush of anticipation, a shiver of fear. This was the first woman who'd stirred me since Raychel left. I wanted to know what drove her, and why she laughed and cried and did what she did.

I walked over to her. "God, I'm nervous." I laughed.

She leaned forward and hugged me. Tingles shot down my spine when she trailed a finger across the nape of my neck.

"Does that help?" her lips brushed my right ear. "Or this?"

I rubbed her back softly, then slipped my hands under her t-shirt and started to graze my nails gently across her skin. She shuddered, pressed herself against me. The heat of her body made my heart race. She locked her hands behind my neck and kissed me on the mouth.

I hesitated for only a second and then kissed her back, hard. Her mouth was cool and slightly sweet. I put a hand behind her head and let her hair fall between my fingers. She lifted my t-shirt up and I felt her nails on my back. We were both breathing heavily.

She unzipped my jeans and pushed them below my hips. I said, "Wait." and shuffled back a little.

"New party trick," I said.

And, feeling a little foolish standing there in the puddle of my jeans, I concentrated my power and motioned for Belinda to retreat towards the window. The night pressed into the glass behind her, occasionally shot by a riot of white as the outside lights flashed on and off.

In a moment, without touching, I had tousled her beautiful blonde hair, raised her t-shirt, and started to inch down the zipper on her pants. Belinda stared at me with a mixture of mischief and disbelief. I focused on the silver zipper, slipping it down a centimetre at a time until it came to a stop.

Belinda put her hands on her hips and pouted. *"Now whatcha gonna do?"*

With an effort that popped out droplets of sweat across my forehead I snicked open the button that held her pants together. Now the two halves fell apart.

"Sweet," I said.

Belinda wriggled until the trousers slid down to her ankles. "I can be, but not tonight, Logan."

I pressed her up against the glass. Our passion, restrained, yet deep and meaningful, fired my adrenalin and brought my heart to life again.

For a while the Yawning Cave retreated, and all the dark things gnashed their teeth and crawled away from a new light.

Oh, Christ, I thought later. *I've gone and fallen again.*

How ironic. On the night before we all went down to Miami to start a confrontation none of us might survive.

I woke in the dead of night, staring up at the ceiling where violent shadows flickered in harmony with the swaying trees outside the window. For a moment I blinked in confusion, not recognizing my room. I sensed the weight of someone beside me, something I hadn't known for years, and was transported back to a past where Raychel and the dark things that kept her memory lived.

I squeezed my eyes shut, battling the memories away. I sat up in bed and gazed down at Belinda. She was a vision, a well-turned corner, a light in the dark. In sleep, her face smoothed out and took on an innocent, sheltered look that I guessed not many people had ever seen. A curl of blonde hair had fallen across her brow. I reached out to tuck it away, making her stir gently, and a faint smile turned up the corners of her mouth.

I slid out of bed, wrapped a dressing gown around me and walked over to the window. The night outside was windswept and violent and black. I glanced back towards the bed, seeing the alternative.

I heard noises in the corridor outside my room. A footfall. A whisper.

I paused for a second to cover Belinda's naked form with the duvet, then cracked open the door and peered through the gap.

"*I want it!*" Hushed, furious tones. A girl's tones.

Lucy.

My heartbeat suddenly tripled. I stepped out into the hallway. Three doors down stood Lucy, clad in her nightie, facing an open door. Her hair was wild and her face was scrunched up with anger. Her body language was confrontational.

"No," I heard Ceriden's squeaky voice say. "The answer is no, my dear. Or rather – not yet."

"The answer to what?" I asked, my voice cutting through the atmosphere of tension and anger that filled the corridor.

Lucy jumped and turned towards me. Someone stepped out of the room and, surprisingly, it was not Ceriden, but a black-haired, blue-eyed woman with a lithe body and the most striking way of staring at you that I'd ever seen. One look and I couldn't look away.

"Hello," she said. "I am Eliza. I have just arrived."

Eliza was steel and silk, leather and lace. She was all things sweet and all things wicked and every temptation under the sun. But for us, I sensed, for the people of Aegis, she was a welcome light in the dark.

I struggled to find my voice. "What's going on here?"

"Nothing," Lucy said quickly. "Absolutely nothing."

I walked forward. "I said- what the *hell* is going on here?"

Eliza came out into the corridor to face me. Her black bodysuit absorbed all the light in the corridor and gleamed like polished obsidian. She said, "Your daughter needs you, Mr. Logan. That is all. You would do well to focus on that."

"What do you mean? What have you bastards been doing with her?"

Eliza appeared to come to a decision. She walked towards me, blocking my view of Lucy. This woman's presence, right next to me, inspired a sense of awe. It also blunted my anger. I noticed her full lips were redder than they should be, probably coated with a sheen of fresh blood. She moved until our bodies touched, and her lips were right next to my ear.

She murmured, "Lucy came to *us* tonight. She wants the life of a Shade. She begged us, Logan. But, for you, we refused. You have only one chance left now. Don't fail her again."

My stomach turned to acid. I locked eyes with my

daughter as Eliza turned away and walked back into Ceriden's room, closing the door. Lucy stared at me, haunted, lost, alone.

What could *I* do? I was a man who had lost everything.

"Lucy?" I said, and my daughter crumbled, collapsing in a heap right there in the corridor, not reaching for me but hugging herself, curling up fetus-like, almost as if she was trying to disappear by sinking right through the floorboards.

"Lucy?"

My daughter looked up at me through tumbles of dark hair, her eyes glistening. "It's *her,* dad. It's mum. I can't let her go. The only way I can make her go away is to become *something else*. A Shade. *They don't feel*. What did I do to make her leave us? *What?*"

Tears rolled down my face as I sprinted to her side. I put my forehead against her own, staring straight into her haunted eyes.

My mouth opened but nothing came out. What could I say that hadn't been said already?

44

MIAMI, US.A.

The one and only meeting of Gorgoth's Destroyers took place in Coconut Grove, in an old gargoyle-encrusted building that used to be a bank but was now a shiny Starbucks. Loki ordered muffins and Caramel Macchiato's all round. They could have been five ordinary friends gathered for a weekly natter at the coffee shop. All they needed, Loki reflected, was the arrival of Jennifer Anniston.

That would give him ultimate proof that there *was* a God. Didn't happen, of course.

Whatever, he thought. That was a great American word wasn't it?

I killed your mom last night. *Whatever*...I fucked your wife, your sister, your secretary, and your dog...*whateverrrr*...

We're gonna end the world tomorrow...*whatever, man, whatever*...

Loki studied his companions. Ashka, with her hard European features and startlingly red eyes. Earlier, a Barista had sauntered over, wiping his hands on his fetching green pinny and asked her to put out her cigarette. Ashka had leaned back and smiled. The Barista's eyes had bugged, and then he'd gone down fast, banging his head on the table as he went.

"Whatever," Ashka said as his colleagues dragged him away. "Must have really hurt his head." Her smile was like deep, biting winter.

Jondal was virtually a skeleton covered in thin, almost translucent, flesh. Loki thought he appeared on the verge of croaking, and watched him closely just in case. Though entertaining, Jondal's expiration now would hurt their cause. Mena Gaines, on the other hand, was a fighter, and looked the part. Everything about her caused a stir in Loki's blood – from the way she sipped her drink to the way she studied him with unabashed confidence.

An hour wasted with Mena, he thought, would not be wasted at all.

Finally, his gaze lit upon Emily Crowe, the rockstar.

"Everything ready?" Loki sipped his drink.

"Buckets filled with blood," Gaines flicked her tongue across her lower lip in search of caramel left there by her drink. "Tarpaulins filled with freshly severed human limbs. Burning pikes topped with heads. It's all in place. They have no idea that the mall is nothing but a diversion."

"The authorities have not interfered?" Loki pressed.

"Recent losses were not acceptable, it seems. These last few days they have withdrawn further." Gaines shrugged.

"The world has been informed of Ubers," Jondal hissed. Even his voice sounded fragile. "Miami is on alert. Army, Navy, Air Force, Special Forces. They're all here."

"Good," Loki clacked his teeth together. "They'll make a fine feast for our Master."

"His first beach barbecue," Gaines grinned.

"Doom of the world," Jondal whispered.

"Miami Beach then," Loki said, mainly for Jondal's benefit. "Opposite the Shore Club, at dusk tomorrow. We will teach this sorry world the meaning of misery."

He looked at the three women.

"Right," he said. "I've reserved a hotel room for us."

45

MIAMI, U.S.A

Kinkade was an eager sixth attendant at the Destroyers' meeting. The conversation he overheard, the *final* revelations of Loki's plan, would give us the thinnest of edges. It also concluded his part in proceedings.

Cheyne relayed a transcript of the meeting and Kinkade's final message via Wi-Fi.

One day after the saving of the world, I will claim my reward.

Cheyne looked up at us all, her crooked witch's nose twitching. "Well, at least *he's* confident."

I was standing close to her. I cleared my throat. "Do we know the Gargoyles ...umm...final decision?" Lucy had commanded me to ask.

Cheyne's mouth quirked up in half a smile. "Was it ever in any doubt?"

Ceriden, to my left, said, "Has to be Nicole."

"I'll tell you *after* we win."

A few hours ago, we had landed at Miami International, then taken over a hotel on South Beach. Ceriden had arranged it, evicting staff and guests alike, using his lofty connections and his inexhaustible wad of greenbacks.

Now, we were gathered together in the hotel's biggest conference room. How many did we number? I don't know. But count everyone from York- *and I mean everyone, even Ceriden's Head Chef, the hulking vampire called Milo-* Eliza and the dozen or so clans under her control; Felicia and maybe thirty Lycan packs; Marian

Cleaver – the man I'd heard so much about and who Lysette mischievously nicknamed *'OMFG'* much to Giles' chagrin – leading members of SWAT, the FBI, and other acronyms I didn't even recognize, police chiefs from all over Florida, army personnel, marine commanders, navy SEALS, air-force fly-boys, a bevy of Witches, more Elves than anyone had *ever* seen together in one place, and the *vampires?*- well, let's just say the cold emanating from their collective bodies was enough to air-condition the entire room.

To my annoyance I hadn't had time to talk to Belinda or Lucy since we left York. There had been a glorious waking moment when Belinda lay beside me, her golden body painted by a stroke of dawn, and then a few more glorious minutes in the shower, but since then she had kept herself aloof, always involved in something. I remembered how she didn't want anyone to cry or care for her. I guessed this was how she kept herself focused.

And Lucy tolerated me, for now. I was still seeking inspiration.

On a raised dais, before us were Giles, Ceriden, Eldritch, and several official-looking humans. Cheyne sat among them, tapping away at her laptop, relaying proceedings to the Library of Aegis and passing replies on.

Surprisingly, or perhaps commendably, there wasn't a hint of skepticism in the room.

I noted other recognizable faces scattered about the room. Mai stood close to Eliza, the two conversing quietly. Jade sat in one of the few seats, her green-tipped hair marking her amongst the crowd. Cheyne's personal witch coven filed in at one point, and found a spot behind her, their metal talismans gleaming around their necks. They didn't remove their deep, black hoods though. I felt uncomfortable; it was as if they were watching me, these faceless, nameless beings of great power. Maybe Cheyne was using them to intimidate the armed forces and senators present.

Over the course of a few hours two separate groups were assigned: one for the beach defence and one to assault the mall. Names were named. Some of the people I cared about were with me, others were not. It made my heart sink. Reality dug in hard. Training was over. The endgame had arrived, and not everyone was going to make it.

I squeezed Lucy's hand. "Don't worry, kiddo. We'll stick together."

Her vague smile made me understand the hopelessness of my words. I was the supposed *vanguard*. How could I keep an eye on my daughter *and* save the world?

"I'm not a kid," I heard, but the traditional refrain was weak, and lacked her usual gusto. There wasn't even an *old man* to top it off and when I turned, I saw the sadness in her eyes.

"My mother's a *bitch*," she spat the last word out.

And suddenly, in that crowd of hundreds, it was just the two of us.

Lucy's lips trembled.

I laughed. "Oh, yeah," I drawled. "What a *bitch!*"

"*Bitch* of the century!" Lucy choked back a laugh, or a sob.

"*Miss Bitch, USA!*" I laughed out loud.

"*Uber Bitch!*" Lucy cracked and laughed and wiped away tears. "*The Vampire Bitch From Hell!*"

I hugged her and winced over her shoulder at Eliza. "No offence intended."

I framed my daughter's head with both my hands and smiled into her stormy eyes.

"After tomorrow," I said. "We start again." And I meant

it with every single ounce of will left in my body.

"Yes," she replied.

Ignoring the world-shaping events occurring around us I closed my eyes and hugged my daughter. Sometime later I looked up. People were filing out, chatting, and forming rows in the aisles. I saw Tanya Jordan standing patiently to Lucy's left.

"Hi," I smiled.

"Hey," her American drawl was somehow comforting. I liked this woman. She had that *lived-in* look, enhanced by her glorious blonde hair with its streaks of grey that she never tried to hide, and by the crows-feet around her eyes that crinkled when she smiled. When you saw Tanya Jordan, your day got better.

"I'm part of the beach-crew too," she smiled. "Whaddya say we stick together, we three? Hmm? And when *you're* needed," she winked at me. "*I'll* take care of the munchkin here."

Lucy gazed at her happily. So did I.

"Munchkin?" Lucy said, after a minute.

46

NEW BABYLON, U.S.A .- THE MALL

Marian Cleaver returned to Coconut Grove just after sunset. He had never seen the streets of Miami so deserted. The evening skies hung heavy and low, brooding, pregnant with the promise of disaster. Cleaver found it ironic that the human trash who spent their worthless existence buying the streets one life at a time had already blown town, leaving their so-called territories in the hands of the law officers they despised. The Haitian gangbangers, the Columbian drug runners, where were they now? Why weren't they standing side-by-side with the cops, determined to defend Miami?

Not likely, Cleaver thought. They'd probably slithered away along the gutters like the pieces of shit they were. He stared out the window as the mall came into view, his vision crisscrossed by fire and shadow. Dark palm trees swayed in a stifling breeze. When Cleaver exited the car, his nostrils caught the stench of burning. The mall was still ablaze, its façade a fiery spectacle.

The command post was buzzing when he got there. No helicopters, because of the missile threat. Cleaver paused on the sidewalk as Cheyne and Ceriden walked by, then followed Felicia. Now there was one wolf he would like to get howling. Cleaver blinked when a guy who looked like a Californian surfer blocked his path.

"Cleaver, right?" the man held out a hand, and pumped wildly when Cleaver took it. "Or maybe Cleave? I'm Ken Hamilton. Good to meet you, man."

"Ah. You're one of the Eight? Surfer Boy, I presume."

"I guess you've been talking to Lysette."

"She's an engaging woman. It appears that you're the only one of the chosen sent to the mall."

"Yeah," Ken said. "Surfer Boy is *expendable*, it seems."

Cleaver hadn't agreed with the separation of forces either. "I guess they know what they're doing."

"*Aegis?*" Ken looked incredulous. "Been living with them for over a week, dude. They haven't got a clue."

"Let's not cast aspersions, Ken."

"Who's casting? The only reason Giles can find his own ass is because he keeps landing on it."

"That's good to know," Cleaver turned as the noise level ramped up a notch. "Looks like they're ready at the operations centre."

Ken also turned, his blonde locks flying, and faced the mall. "Time to start the assault."

Cleaver walked over to Cheyne, who was conversing with members of her coven in the parking lot. It was the first time Cleaver had seen them without their cloaks. Witchcraft, he decided, agreed with the fairer sex. Save the odd crooked nose there wasn't an ogre among them.

"What do you want me to do, Cheyne?"

Cheyne gave him a wanton smile. He noticed how her nose stayed pointing towards the mall when she turned. "Aside from the obvious?" she said after a moment of eye contact. "Kill anything that moves."

"Are you're sure this preplanned chaos isn't just a diversion?"

"My amulet is *tingling,* Cleaver. What do you think that means?"

Cleaver shrugged. "You're attracted to me?"

"My *amulet*. I said my *amulet,*" Cheyne looked around

at members of her coven "I did say my amulet, didn't I?"

"Something's in there," a blonde spoke up in an English accent. "Something we don't know anything about. I sense an ancient and powerful invocation has already begun."

"*Invocation?*" Ken gasped. "Why would they do that if it's all a diversion?"

"Authenticity, I guess" Cleaver glanced at him then said: "Cheyne, are there any innocent people inside?" He couldn't let it go unasked.

"None," Cheyne gestured to her coven. "In our casting we saw that the mall is *infested* with evil."

"And we're the Raid!" Ken slapped Cleaver on the back. "Hey, dude, you ready to go save the world?"

Cleaver threaded through more Kevlar-clad police and SWAT guys than he could count. They stood in rows, in ranks. Not a man among them knew what to expect. Did it provoke their quaking fear, or hone it to a keener edge? Cleaver moved through them with Ken at his back. Most of these men knew him; some had traded sweat and blood with him at the gym. Some remembered his past and gave him dead eyes.

It was Miami. It was home. This was how it always was.

He stopped next to the bubbly lycan, Felicia. She'd told him earlier how she'd consistently fought his cause back in stuffy old York, and that she wanted to strip naked and rub herself all over him like he was her favourite tree.

First things first, he'd told her.

"You ready?" he bent down to whisper in her ear.

Felicia turned those big blue saucer-eyes on him. "My kind is always ready," she said. "We are hunters. It is worrying, though-" she trailed off.

"Not knowing how our friends are faring at the beach?"

Felicia nodded and repeated "My *friends*," as if she

clung to the word like a treasured locket.

"So we focus," Cleaver thought about the gym, the training, the protracted hour before you climbed into that ring. "Compartmentalize it. Because there's nothing you can do to change it."

Beside them, Ken was almost hopping with impatience. He drew two short, hardwood staffs from inside his coat, letting them hang at his side as he limbered up. Weapons, Jade and he had decided, were the icing on the cake of his special talent.

And then a figure appeared in the entranceway to the mall.

"That's Mena Gaines." Cleaver said.

The Destroyer came forward, spreading her arms wide. "Tonight will be the greatest reckoning in human history!" she cried. "Your ultimate arrogance is that you think you *own* this planet. But you have pillaged it. You have plundered it. Tonight, the Hierarchy will come, the Gates of Hell will open, and the World-ender shall be summoned forth! Cry *havoc!* Humans, and let loose all Hell!"

Cleaver glanced to his right as one of the SWAT guys laughed. "Is this woman for real? She's nuts."

"Nuts she is," Cleaver told him. "But unfortunately, she's also telling the truth."

Ken shrugged. "Go figure."

They didn't notice Cheyne's face and body language express first shock and then raw terror at the mention of the Hierarchy.

Then a second figure stepped out of the mall. There was a communal intake of breath from the gathered ranks.

Someone said, "I know her. Is that Miley Cyrus?"

"No," someone answered. "No. It's *Avril,* I think. Or Amy Lee."

"It's *Emily Crowe,*" Ken withered them all with a glance. "Don't you Florida guys know your rock chicks?"

"So what now?" One of the cops said. "We gonna have to pay to get in there?"

Crowe came forward and pointed something at the sky that looked horribly like a human arm. Cheyne cried. "The time is now! Before they can gather!"

At that moment the mall entrance spewed out a raving mass of demonic bodies. They charged at the gathered ranks of marines and cops, wielding a variety of sharp weapons, their faces twisted in hate.

Cleaver swept his duster aside and unsheathed his shotgun. He heard Felicia growl low in her throat, saw Ken raise his weapons and take a deep breath whilst adopting a fighting stance. The rows of marines shot forward, running straight at the charging demons and voicing their own shouts of defiance.

There was a breathless moment as the opposing forces rushed together. The sound of bullets rent the air along with the dying expletives of men and demons alike. Cleaver could still see Emily Crowe, gesturing at the skies with her ghastly wishbone. It seemed the escalating fear and violence helped make her stronger.

"Astoroth!" She shrieked. *"I summon you!"* It sounded like a highly convincing invocation for nothing more than a diversion.

And Gaines stood before Crowe, a formidable bodyguard.

It's the Destroyers we need to kill, Cleaver thought. *Take them out, and we-*

A demon leapt over the backs of two marines and lunged at Cleaver, snarling and tearing at the air between them. Cleaver stepped back to make room, lowered the shotgun, and then gave it a blast at point blank range. The headless body collapsed at his feet.

By his side Ken kicked, then spun into a meaty uppercut, easily taking out his opponent. Felicia pounced onto a demon's back, tearing its muscles deep, making it rear up and howl in agony. She snapped its neck with an efficient twist. Beyond her, Cleaver saw Ceriden involved in a deadly tussle.

The world was chaos.

Bullets slammed into the mall's concrete walls, sending sharp slivers in every direction. Windows shattered, glass rained down in jagged shards. In another second Cleaver saw a figure appear in a ruined window, a bulky object balanced over its shoulder.

"*Missile!*" Someone shouted. There was a boiling hiss like a thousand angry rattlesnakes, a muffled explosion, and everyone hit the deck. A demon that decided to remain standing was struck head-on by the missile and accelerated from zero to 200 mph in less than a second. The missile, with demon still attached, impacted with a truck in the parking lot, its explosion blasting through the turbulent darkness.

"*Up!*"

The marines ran again, Cleaver following, struggling to keep up. Violence and death filled the night around him.

Crowe was giving the performance of her life. "By the power of the Almighty Lucifer, by Astoroth, by a thousand Fallen Angels, I bid you to *appear!*"

Lucifer? Cleaver thought. Now *that* didn't make any sense at all.

Time was running out.

Step by bloody step they advanced towards the mall.

47

NEW BABYLON - THE MALL AND BAY BRIDGE

Ken Hamilton fought with an economy of movement. When a demon popped up, he marked it, studied its bearing, its lean and drag- the way it moved back and forth, and exterminated it. After the first two went down he stopped pointing out to anyone who would listen how gross they were.

Anyway, he'd woken up next to far uglier specimens after nights of beer, endless viewings of Point Break, and a little marijuana.

He stayed close to Cleaver and tried to keep sight of Felicia. His heart told him it was important to keep the Aegis members together. Was it a companionship thing? It was new to him, an alien emotion. But he had to admit he liked it.

Ceriden was suddenly at his side, pale face glowing like a beacon, and far too jittery for a vampire King. "Problem!" he cried.

Ken teased his hair back into place with a well-trained finger. "How so? Armani Exchange been looted?"

"God forbid!" Ceriden cried, then pointed at Cheyne and her coven. "They want you."

"Now! Me? Why?"

"Too many questions," Ceriden was all authority, something Ken hated. "Just *go.*"

Ken turned away. "I used to like you, man," he mumbled.

Cheyne beckoned him over. "Our first random element

has surfaced," she said in her light voice. Then she paused, seeming reluctant to elaborate.

"Which is?"

"Dementia."

Ken felt a chill fall through him like a tonne of bricks.

"Where is she?"

"Bay Bridge, for some reason. Destroying everything and everyone sent against her. You are one of the Eight. The battle is being lost there. You have to go."

Ken couldn't even croak a reply. *Dementia!* The craziest demon bitch that ever walked the earth.

"To...to fight her?"

"I will be going with you," Cheyne said, then raised her eyebrows. "I am able to conjure up a few surprises of my own, you know."

"And I'll go too," Ken turned to see Ryan, the man who'd recruited him in San Francisco not so long ago, standing behind him. "At least, I might distract her with my rugged good looks."

Ken found his voice at last. "So let's go wax that bitch's ass." His voice, he thought, sounded far more confident than it had any right to.

Ryan drove this time. Ken sat in the back next to Cheyne. At first, he felt intimidated, but one sidelong glance at that huge wonky conk tickled the child in him and calmed his nerves.

Ryan said, "I have never seen the streets of Miami this deserted."

"It's a blessing," Cheyne said. "Do you know how to get to the Bay Bridge?"

"Yeah. Somewhere off the South Dixie. Tell me, Cheyne, why would Dementia ally itself with a being bent on destroying the world she feeds off? As in Gorgoth, I mean."

"The entire northern hemisphere's been chewing on that one for months," Cheyne stared out at the empty streets. Ken noticed her stroking the platinum talisman that dangled around her neck. The sign of her rank? Her coven? The source of her power?

"Best guess?" Ken asked.

Cheyne shrugged, not looking at him. "Our focus has been on Gorgoth so we are at a loss. Gorgoth and the Hierarchy are entirely different entities, with entirely different agendas. It doesn't make sense. Maybe someone summoned her before all this got started and she found a way to stay. Maybe she was *sent here,* by Astoroth or even Lucifer Himself. Or maybe she was cast out of Hell, for deeds unspeakable."

"Whoa," Ken gasped. "Cast out of *Hell?* How could anyone be *that* evil?"

"Gorgoth hates the hierarchy and vice versa," Cheyne mused. "And yet here, tonight, they're both being summoned at the same time. Truly, I don't understand. And keep this in mind," she turned towards Ken now. "Whatever evil we face today, Dementia may yet prove to be the worst of it."

Ryan pointed ahead. "Bay Bridge," he said. "There it is. My God."

Ken leaned forward for a better look. Before them the Bay Bridge stretched in an S-curve over Biscayne Bay, terminating on a narrow spit of land that was an aquatic preserve. The stretch of road that formed the bridge was called the Rickenbacker Causeway. Ken could see dozens of flashing blue and red lights strewn along the road. To his surprise he could also see many figures ducked down behind cars and trucks and concrete walls.

As they drew nearer Ken saw their terrified faces. He saw cops, marines and FBI agents, shivering in the heat, scared half to death.

"What are they doing?" Ryan's growl betrayed his disgust.

"Steady," Cheyne told him. "Don't forget, their world is in upheaval. For them, Ubers were a myth until last week. Now they are being asked to go up against one of the worst. Slow down."

Beyond the cops, a massive struggle was underway. Dozens of men surrounded a very vague figure, something wrapped in darkness and light, something that moved faster than a bullet, deadlier than a blade, and with more menace than a serial killer on his first anniversary.

Then the figure leapt out of the crowd. Intuitively, Ryan slammed on the brakes. There was a sound like two monster trucks clashing as something landed on the hood of their car, crushing the steel and causing the entire vehicle to buckle.

Ken stared with horror into eyes that seemed to fill the windshield - the eyes of Dementia, all blood and yellow-shine, slanted and gleaming with death and hate. He had seen her this way before but this time there would be no running away.

Dementia screamed, a note higher than the squeal of a slaughtered pig. She thrust her sword through the windscreen, straight at Ryan's face, but he managed to duck and fling himself out of the car door onto the asphalt.

Ken jumped out, letting his short staffs slide into his hands. He stepped away from the car to draw Dementia's attention, a voice inside screaming *what the fuck are you doing?* But his head and his heart told him that Ryan and

Cheyne needed time to prepare themselves.

Dementia snarled and drooled at him, as if sensing a meal.

"*I ssssmellled you,*" words fell from the demon's mouth like venomous snakes. "*I have missssed you beforrre. Twicccce. Thissss time, you are minnnne.*"

Ken thought about everything that had ever meant anything in his life. Didn't take long. Before now, it had all been fantasy. But now danger stood snarling before him in its most heinous guise, and if it meant saving his friends, he would meet it head on.

He started to spin the staffs in rhythm, setting up a constant swirl of hardwood. His arms lashed out fast, faster, gaining speed and continuance. His eyes never left those of his adversary.

"Dementia," he hissed. "Come get yours."

The mad demon leapt off the car faster than blinking, but Ken was trained. And he was one of the Chosen. He tracked her through the air and when she landed, feet first, he struck at that point. His left staff struck her skull, his right staff chopped across her neck, and she retreated from the deadly symmetry. Again and again he moved forward, his arms a blur and Dementia was forced to catch the blows on her forearms or take them full in the face. Ken didn't give her a chance to raise her sword.

Pressing forward was his only advantage. He was faster with the lightweight staffs than she was with her sword. He was vaguely aware of Ryan flitting behind her and Cheyne at his own back. He thought Cheyne was holding something large but didn't have time to check.

Dementia's gasps of pain were music to his ears. Her demonic eyes blazed with undiluted hate.

Behind her, ranks of marines and Special Forces were

gathering to watch as he forced her back towards the edge of the bridge. He noticed with satisfaction that her arms were already bruised black, and that her face was starting to swell. He made those areas the focus of his redoubled efforts.

Dementia took four quick strikes in the face, then snarled and kicked out. Her foot caught him in the sternum, making him jerk forward. Dementia's swiftly uplifted sword almost cleaved his head in two, but he dodged, and she succeeded only in drawing a thin line of blood from his right cheek.

Ken paused, catching his breath. He had been stupid to think he could press on and finish her there. Dementia was a thousand year old demon, well versed in the art of fighting and subterfuge.

Ken kept up the whirl of wood whilst taking a breather. Dementia regarded him with curiosity, no doubt the same hungry curiosity she would afford a slap-up meal of bloody, raw human.

Then, without warning, Ryan struck at her from behind. Dementia must have caught the movement in Ken's eyes for she jabbed an elbow back at the precise moment, an elbow that Ryan ran into.

Ryan!

Ken launched himself forward again. Ryan crawled off to one side, face pouring with blood.

Ken struck again and again, and then realization hit him. The crazy bitch was *enjoying* this. She loved the feel of the wood striking her flesh, the assault of a worthy opponent. She was drawing it out.

He paused and stepped back. Dementia grinned at him, her mouth dripping blood mixed with thick drool. Her fervent yellow eyes blazed.

"Now you undersssssstand. . ." she hissed.

Gunshots rang out. Some of the army guys were trying their luck. Thick darkness immediately flowed up around Dementia's form, absorbed the bullets before dissipating. The entire process took less than a second.

"Great body armour," Ken heard himself say.

Dementia attacked, but he was more than ready. His words had been calculated to force her into a mistake like this. So when she leapt he side-stepped, and brought the staffs down on her face and neck and shoulders.

For a second, she floundered. Her sword crashed against a railing, slicing off chips of metal and causing sparks. Dementia staggered.

Ken's entire being rejoiced. *Yes!*

Cheyne stepped into Ken's line of vision. The object she held in her hand gleamed brightly in the lights that shone from nearby buildings.

A sword.

But not just any sword.

"This sword helped subdue the Devil in ancient times," Cheyne whispered. "And has been stored reverently ever since. Waiting for one worthy-"

Dementia cursed and swung around, swiping blindly with her heavy blade.

Cheyne threw the sword towards Ken – its blade flickered through the light and the dark as it tumbled, throwing off shards of brilliance. There was a collective gasp from watching cops. Ken let both staffs fall to the ground and caught the sword by the hilt a split second later. He retreated a bit, now on the causeway proper, on the Bay Bridge itself.

Dementia leapt towards him, hissing like a serpent caught in a trap. Ken deflected her attack, slipped aside, and struck back.

The clash of swords echoed across the Bay Bridge and out across the ocean. Miami's warm night air resounded to the clang of tempered metal. Dementia struck again and again. Ken defended for a time, letting her blows take a toll on her strength, deflecting carefully and precisely so that every blow she threw sapped her muscles that little bit more.

Another volley of gunfire sounded. Once more Dementia defended it with a dark rush of that mystical armour.

She *had* to be tiring!

Ken heard the chop-chop of helicopter rotors above him. He attacked now, sword swirling in his hands like molten metal, every swift arc leaving a blur in the air that melded with the next and the next and the next. Dementia backed towards the side of the bridge, trapped against the railings and the concrete curvature.

The fight was his!

Ken pulled himself out of the zone, stopped and smiled. "This one's for Myleene, you crazy bitch."

He struck, but Dementia was faster. That second, that *split second,* when he had exited the zone, undid him.

Dementia ducked under his thrust and slid her sword into him, into his stomach. The swiftness of it took him by surprise. He paused, and stared into her suddenly grinning face, and then a white heat blossomed from his belly to his brain.

He staggered. Dementia growled, let out an evil hyena-like laugh and raised her sword. Ken stumbled. Worse than the pain was the very *thought* of being beaten by an enemy he'd already defeated.

Then Ryan was at his side, breaking Dementia's nose with a palm strike, spinning and back-kicking her in the ribs. Ken used the respite to take a deep breath. He didn't feel too bad, under the circumstances. Maybe he'd gotten lucky and the steel had only penetrated a few inches, missing his vitals.

Cheyne fell beside him. "It's still there," the witch whispered. "The victory, I mean. Use the pain." She supported him with her shoulders.

"My side is on fire," he spat.

"It's nothing. A scratch. Use the pain. Use it to focus."

Ken slowed his breathing, allowing the pain to rise and then forced it steadily away. He hefted his sword with a grunt and then started to slice it through the air. He watched as Ryan moved in and out of Dementia's range, striking warily, aiming to do no more than keep her busy. But Ryan was tiring, and the blood on his face and arms attested to the accuracy of Dementia's aim.

Ken gathered his wits and focused on the power that Eleanor and Jade had nurtured and moulded and sharpened. The zone snapped into being. He stepped to one side of Ryan just as Dementia's sword came up and flicked out at the Englishman.

The blade pierced Ryan's neck, sliding straight through.

Ryan folded, his body hitting the asphalt with a sickening smack at the same instant that he died.

"NO!"

Ken charged with all the ferocity of the damned, of a man who realizes he must live or die right now, at this very moment. It was his time of reckoning.

Dementia staggered back. Ken saw his sword slice through her shoulder; he saw it take a chunk from her hip. He ignored the sticky ichor that spurted from both wounds.

He sidestepped Ryan's body, ignored the grief that

threatened to snap him out of the zone, and assailed Dementia so powerfully that she was forced to climb onto the guardrail. Her dirty white hair flowed behind her in the sea breeze. She teetered, trying to keep her balance.

Ken didn't stand on ceremony. He slammed his sword through her chest, twisted it in the wound and wrenched it out at a different angle to inflict maximum damage. He danced aside to avoid the sticky black substance that poured out.

Dementia looked down at her wound and giggled. *"The Hierarchy issss comingg,"* she hissed between manic snorts of laughter and pain. *"You have noooo idea. And after them-"*

"Gorgoth will be stopped!" Cheyne rushed forward. The witches face was a mask of sorrow and hatred.

Dementia laughed wildly as her life-blood drained from her. *"Who iss Gorgoth? He isss of no consssequence to usss-"* she whispered. *"For after the Hierarchy comes...comesssss-, comessssssssssssss-"*

Ken stared as the maniacal demon finally fell off the bridge, free-falling to the churning waters below. After a long moment he tore his gaze away and turned in utter confusion towards Cheyne.

They had both heard Dementia's last, low, sibilant gasp of breath as she plummeted towards the calm waters.

"Lucccccciferrrrrrrrrr-"

48

NEW BABYLON- THE BEACH

I climbed out of the car halfway along Ocean Drive, one man amidst hundreds, and turned to study, along with everyone else, the wide beach and rolling seas that that would soon become our battleground. The beach looked pretty, lit by a silver moon that rose by tiny degrees above the ocean, throwing the darkness into stark relief.

Lucy stood by my shoulder, pressed so close I could feel her shivering. Despite the danger, I figured she was better off with us than alone.

Belinda stood beside my other shoulder. "Ten years," she pondered. "Ten years of training and trying. Does it really all come down to this?"

I looked further along our line. Beyond Belinda stood Eliza, hair caught by the breeze, her face a study in tension. A glint of pure white fangs showed between her full red lips. Devon Summers and the Trevochet's were next, Natalie rubbing Johnny's shoulders as he sat rigid in his wheelchair, and beyond them were the Elves- Eldritch, and Jade with her green-tipped hair. I turned my head in the other direction. Tanya Jordan stood beside Lucy, her blonde-grey hair falling over her eyes. Lysette and Giles were next, close enough to be touching and I could only wonder if they had allowed themselves to fall in love, or if they were waiting to see what tomorrow would bring.

I hoped all would go well for Lysette. Earlier, she had told me how surplus she felt. Who needed a mind reader in a battle, right? But I had shared with her a smidgen of my own fears, and she had been gracious enough not to let on that she already knew.

What a legendary team, I thought. How could we lose?

Belinda spoke softly in my ear. "Just so you know, Logan, fighting makes me horny."

I pulled a face at her. "Is there anything that *doesn't?*"

"Not the *act* of fighting," she amended. "More- the *heat.*"

"I'll be here." I shook my head in mock disgust at today's laugh-out-loud t-shirt. It read: *Bite Me!* Obviously picked for the occasion. I couldn't keep the smile off my face. "No one's going to die young today, Belinda. Least of all, you."

Our ranks started to move into formation. Devon and the Trevochet's, Lysette, Giles and an honour-guard of marines stepped back to where those three chosen could bring their powers to bear in relative safety. Holly was with them, and she gave me a last look that said everything.

"Dad," Lucy nudged me and pointed to a spot on the beach where the sand met the sea. "I see shadows."

I squinted. Her eyes were younger and sharper than mine. But, amidst a dense patch of palm trees I thought I saw an insinuation of shadow. Several people, moving slowly. When the next gust of wind reached us it carried the sound of chanting.

"GO!"

Belinda's shout, taut with tension and commitment, almost gave me heart failure. I leapt out of my skin, panting as the rest of the line shot forward, leaving me behind. A thought struck me: *typical.*

Lucy looked up at me, her eyes wide. "We going, Grandad?"

I decided it was time to face my fears. And maybe kick the shit out of them.

Cries rang out from the charging throng. Ranks of vampires shot ahead, fleet of foot. Lycans, changing into wolf form in mid-flight, came next, their rapidly readjusting bone-structure crackling and popping as they ran. The Ubers snarled as they smelled blood. The humans among us slowed a little, perhaps realizing our place was not at the head of this primeval charge.

From the shadows ahead appeared Ashka and Jondal. Both Destroyers flung their arms in the air.

Visions hit us like a blade-filled hurricane. I fell to my knees, my momentum sending me crashing face first into the sand. Lucy writhed at my side, her gasps of fear driving white-hot spears of pain into my heart.

But then the visions withered away to nothing. I sensed another strike aimed towards us dissipate ineffectually. Devon, it seemed, had taken a longer than expected to cast her healer's net, but now her power had come into play.

I struggled to my feet and put an arm around Lucy. Several divisions of cops were moving past us, looking scared behind their face masks and riot-shields.

I walked forward, only now noticing that Tanya had stayed by our side. She nodded at me, and I remembered that I ought to be gathering my power. The battle was on. What the hell was I doing?

By the moon's glow I began to make out the scene ahead. A broad, hard-faced man with skin like old parchment stood at the centre of a grisly circle, the circle's boundaries being made up of rows of headless and limbless bodies, placed trunk against neck against trunk. Standing just outside that circle were Ashka and Jondal.

The lead vamps and lycans were now only twenty feet away from the Destroyers.

Ashka drew her sword. Jondal took out a pair of deadly-looking tridents. Both Destroyers stood ready. It struck me as wrong. Two people waiting patiently for so many and no sign of them backing down. No matter how skillful they were, they weren't *that* skillful.

"It's wrong-" Tanya began, then gasped as the hard-faced man at the centre of the circle cried out. *"Crack the Earth and Open! Crack the Seals and Open! Break the Lock of the Netherworld and the emptiness between, and Open! I, Loki, beseech you!"*

I walked up to Eldritch. "What the hell's going on?"

There was a deafening crash like a terrible traffic accident. I looked in terror at the ground, saw nothing, but up ahead, near the water line, the very air was starting to liquefy. My heart began to hammer. It seemed the air was *melting,* dripping like a length of metal being subjected to intense heat. Even the darkness recoiled in disgust, and a keening, otherworldly wind started to howl.

The hard-faced man was shouting at the top of his voice. *"Crack the Air and open! O, Charon, Gatekeeper of All Worlds, hear me! Heed me! Crack the Gates, and open!"*

"That is Loki," Eldritch answered me at last. "And he has just opened the Gates of Hell."

"My God," I breathed, falling to my knees in the sand. Any idea of summoning my power fled my mind. The significance of that statement stunned me. How could we ever close the Gates of Hell?

"Attack!" Eldritch cried. "Be quick! Before-"

Vampires lurched forward. Lycans leapt on four feet and two. I saw Eliza lunge at Ashka, and the two mighty opponents went down brawling. I saw Jade strike at Jondal and force him back to the very edge of the circle of bodies, his skill no match for the dexterous elf.

Then, out of the newly-formed dripping darkness, straight out of its oozing maw, burst a horde of demons. Some had tusks, others horns, some had horrific-looking claws, whilst still others clacked away with huge improbable mandibles. Many had wide slanted eyes that shone furnace bright whilst others had orbs that waved on thick, bristly stalks.

The demons caused havoc in our ranks, their sudden appearance stunning the Ubers. I heard cops and marines screaming in terror. This was the stuff of human nightmare, never before revealed. In a few seconds the demons had surrounded the circle where Loki continued his invocations.

"Loki is the key," I heard Eldritch say. "The powerful one. Slay him, and they will wither to nothing."

Ahead I saw Jade parted from Jondal, most likely hearing Eldritch's words through elvish telepathy. And then Eliza rushed towards Loki too, as if she had also heard the elf's words.

We were getting stretched. The demons were among us now. Biting. Hacking. Ripping. I refused to panic. I spent a second summoning my power, then aimed a portion of it at the demon nearest to me, thinking *punch*. My blast struck it like a fireball and sent the demon tumbling end over end until it impacted against the trunk of a palm tree so hard that its arms sheared off.

I looked away. Tanya leapt into action beside me, her deadly ballet dispatching two demons with a minimum of effort. She was back in a few seconds, blood-soaked stiletto in her hand.

"Any suggestions?" I shouted.

My voice was swept away by the overwhelming din of

battle. Snarls and screams and the sound of gunfire assaulted my ears. Belinda lunged and leapt amongst the blackened palm trees and the bloodied sand, a bright light of hope surrounded by cackling black creatures from the abyss. Next to me Lucy sobbed and tried to hide her face in my side. I staggered back, suddenly beset with indecision.

I couldn't do this. *I couldn't.* My daughter came first, and to hell with the world. I had to get Lucy to safety. But how? *Where?*

Safe inside his appalling circle Loki's chanting continued, *"O, Abominata, I call on you. God of Loathing, virus of Love. I summon you! And Kahana! God of Lust and Depravity. God of Humiliation! I call you and so bind you now!"*

I hugged Lucy closer. Loki was calling on the lesser Gods that would be sacrificed to summon Gorgoth.

I'd never imagined it would be like this.

Demons snarled and stomped all around. Tanya broke bones as if they were winter-worn twigs beside me. Belinda fought at her side, her efforts both wild and calculating, leaving demon after demon writhing or dead on the gore-soaked beach. Elves fought just ahead in perfect unison, and in their wake the pile of mortally wounded demons grew and grew.

Lucy clutched at me and pointed, uttering a keening cry of terror. I followed her finger and my stomach dropped through a thousand floors of dread. Above Loki's circle, above his upraised arms, above the tops of the palm trees, a swirling darkness had appeared in the sky. I craned my neck and saw the darkness writhe. Within its formless maw I thought I saw racks of glittering teeth and twisted, faceless flesh. A fetid, cloying stench like dead, rotting fish reached my nostrils.

Then something like a gigantic arm came down from the sky. Horrendous, it swayed back and forth. Thick slime dripped off its tapered end, hitting the surface of the ocean and fizzling. The arm was suddenly joined by another. I realized they were tentacles, belonging to some immense, squid-like God, and my stomach began to heave.

Thunder rocked the sky. Lightning struck at the sea beyond the horizon. A rolling, creaking boom struck the earth, sending quakes of shock across the beach. I saw the sand undulating and rippling as if endless waves flowed beneath it.

The shockwave hit us. Lucy screamed, making my heart jackhammer. Demons ran amok. I threw a hand up to shield my face as a cloven hoof smashed into the sand beside me. I sent a blast at its owner, obliterating him into the night.

I rolled over. Lucy was gone. My eyes, at ground level, searched across the sand and saw her not far away, but nearer the water.

Tanya Jordan was at her side.

But so was Ashka.

Tanya rolled towards the surf, flinging out her legs and striking Ashka in the shins. Most adversaries would have folded then, or at least hopped about in agony, but Ashka only laughed, her scarlet, hell-born eyes gleaming with murder.

"I will make you wish Leo finished you in Hawaii," Ashka spat at her.

Tanya danced forward, kicking and punching with economy of movement, but at the same time conscious that she had to force Ashka away from Logan's daughter. The knowledge blunted her edge.

"Behind me," she pushed Lucy into the foamy surf. She pulled her stiletto free and pointed it at Ashka's throat.

"My husband killed my baby," she hissed through consuming pain that constricted her heart. "*That* is evil, you pathetic whore! Do you really think you can scare me after all I've lived through?"

Tanya leapt, kicked at Ashka's neck, then landed and dropped into a crouch, swinging her legs around and taking Ashka's legs away. The Destroyer landed heavily in the wet sand, her body thudding down, breath forced out of her.

Tanya was already on her feet. She aimed a heel at Ashka's throat, but the woman rolled away. Tanya's mind clouded when Ashka threw a vision at her, but Devon's healing net held and Tanya experienced only mild discomfort.

As she stepped forward, she saw the knot of sky that roiled above the beach suddenly split in two. Now another tentacle dropped down, and still another grappled with the edge of the swirling, black hole as if trying to widen it.

At the edges of her concentration she heard Loki's droning voice summoning the third and final lesser God.

The whole place was rapidly going to shit. Forked lightning marched across the horizon, coming closer with every passing minute. Thunder pealed and crashed constantly all around them. Demons hacked and slashed and died amongst the hundreds of vampires and werewolves.

For a moment Tanya wished she was back in Honolulu. Just starting her morning jog on Waikiki Beach. But fate had called, and for a good reason. She was one of the Chosen.

She let Ashka rise then kicked sand at her and struck

with the stiletto. The blade sliced through Ashka's flesh, giving Tanya grim satisfaction.

Then there was a shout, a terrified, desperate shout, from where they had left their transport.

"Help! Help us!"

Tanya couldn't stop herself glancing that way. Fear dropped into the pit of her stomach. Demons were among the marines they had left guarding Devon and Lysette. She saw Johnny Trevochet flung from his wheelchair and sent sprawling to the ground. A demon landed on top of him. Tanya saw Devon, their healer and their shield, duck as a demon struck at her, tearing strips of flesh from her arm. Devon was allowed a moments respite as the demon began to stuff the dripping flesh into its mouth.

Tanya knew what it meant. Devon's concentration had been razed.

Ashka's grin sent daggers through Tanya's heart. *"At last."*

A devastating mental assault sent Tanya lurching. The attack on the rear guard had destroyed Devon's shield. Tanya buckled as a fist slammed into her neck. She fell to her knees.

She heard Lucy scream.

"No," Tanya struggled against terrifying visions to raise her head. Ashka stood right before her. A hateful apparition struck Tanya's brain with such force that it caused her to black out for a second.

When she looked up again Ashka had an arm wrapped tightly around Lucy's waist and was holding Tanya's own stiletto at the girl's throat. Ashka grinned malevolently.

"You ready for this?"

Lucy screamed. Tanya pushed with superhuman strength and managed to gain her feet. She stumbled forward, almost fell.

Ashka smiled and drew the blade across Lucy's throat. Tanya shrieked, seeing the scene in slow motion, watching the blood start to flow.

The world stopped. Miami, the beach, the boiling sky, it all receded. Tanya saw the death of another innocent, the death of a young girl, and she felt a deep-rooted, maternal anger like nothing she had ever felt before.

And suddenly her strength surged back, the terrible vision withered away, and she leapt forward from a crouched position, determined to save Lucy or die trying.

But then something hit her, flinging her haphazardly across the beach. It was a wall of water. *A wall of water had hit them!*

What?

Baffled, Tanya spit out wet sand and looked up from the ground. The sight she beheld was awe-inspiring.

Lucy stood before Ashka, staring point bank into the Destroyer's hellfire eyes. Not a hint of fear showed in Lucy's expression. A thin line of blood red ran across her throat, but not a drop of blood flowed. As Tanya watched a small spark of fire leapt across the open wound, cauterizing its edges, effectively closing it. Lucy emitted no sound, not a grunt, not a whimper of pain.

But that wasn't even the real wonder. What truly blew Tanya's mind was that Ashka was suspended two feet off the ground, struggling and trapped in a solid cocoon of water. The Destroyer was being drowned before Tanya's disbelieving eyes, in mid-air, and on land!

Tanya watched as Lucy gestured. Water-jets started striking Ashka's pain-filled eyes within the cocoon. Liquid forced its insipid way down her throat. With a last gurgling cry the Destroyers eyes went black, her face dropped towards her chest, and then she just hung in the air, supported only by Lucy's will.

Tanya stared at Lucy in amazement. "You are one of the Eight!" She cried. "The one we couldn't find. Lucy, you have been chosen too."

Lucy's face showed shock, delight, and then mortal fear. And finally, absolute confusion. She slumped, collapsing at Tanya's feet, the display of power having drained her to the core.

Tanya caught her, trying to make sense of this new twist. Kisami, originally thought to be one of the Eight, had been an impostor. And despite Ceriden and Myleene's best efforts they had never found the eighth member of their little group. Lucy must not have shown up on the Witches search because she was so close to Logan at the time. *That* was how they had missed her.

And Lucy controlled at the very least water and fire.

She was Kisami's alternate. She was an elemental!

49

NEW BABYLON- THE BEACH

I'd been five seconds from my daughter's side when Ashka slit her throat.

I would have failed to reach her.

You fucking ten-time failure!

Now, I went up to Lucy, stopped, and reached out a hand. She smiled.

I met Tanya's shocked eyes.

For once, neither of us could think of anything to say.

After a few seconds respite I surveyed the hellish situation. Loki continued to bellow his ruinous incantation. A deadly struggle, ten bodies deep, was taking place around his circle. Vampires and lycans and elves endeavored to reach him, only to be beaten back by the sheer number of demons defending him. The Gates of Hell continued to belch forth abominations. Over by the road the Trevochet's and Devon had been rescued and saved by Belinda and a company of Delta force. Lysette was attempting to read the minds of the wounded to determine how best to heal them. Devon was trying to hear her advice above the pandemonium. Belinda was shouting and directing the assault on Loki's circle even as she checked Johnny Trevochet's vitals and spoke reassuringly to Devon. She was truly our leader, a shining jewel, and she was entirely focused.

Above us the skies sparked with magic. Thunder splintered our ears; lightning dazzled the air leaving a burning stench in its wake. Every now and again that rotting fish stench struck us anew and made us gag.

As the battle ebbed and flowed Jade pulled herself away from the general melee and came over to us. "Loki," she panted. "is now summoning Gorgoth. He seems powerful enough to attempt anything he wants."

"Eleanor said something similar about Johnny and I." I reminded her.

It was time to go on faith and accept that Lucy could defend herself. *My daughter? One of the Chosen?* Her newfound abilities lifted a massive burden from my heart. I could now focus on saving the world.

I ventured as close as I dared to the chaotic struggle around Loki's circle. Tanya and Jade walked at my side, dispatching the occasional demon that spotted us and tried its luck.

I concentrated my power, gathering it as I went, making Loki my target.

But in that ironic instant the grotesque circle that surrounded him was finally broken. I heard Loki's chant cut short. I saw a fearless, leather-clad figure stand up to him.

And I heard Loki's words. "Ah, Eliza. I hoped we would meet again."

The vampire didn't waste time, just leapt forward and sent a series of jabs and flurries at his body. And I saw now why Loki was their best, maybe the best of all of us, as he parried her every strike without losing ground, and connected solidly with quick jabs of his own.

I watched as he wore even Eliza down. The battle quieted it seemed, as we all watched. I dared not strike at him because my power wasn't that accurate. Or maybe it was. I had honed it pretty well back home. But, the truth is, I didn't have the confidence to risk it.

In another moment Eliza, realizing her predicament, launched a stunning volley of blows at Loki, and even the great Destroyer stumbled backwards. I watched in awe. Beside me I heard Tanya catch her breath, and that single act, coming from her, was the highest accolade I could imagine.

Then Eliza stumbled over a half-dead demon. Loki leapt upon her, fists lashing out with deadly precision. I unleashed my power strike, but nearly cried as it smashed against Loki and rolled harmlessly away.

The evil bastard was protected by a demonic shield. I saw him straighten, a triumphant grin splitting his face. And then with one hand he hauled up Eliza's slumped body by the neck.

He cried, *"It is over! Your best has perished! The summoning is complete. There is nothing you can do to stop the coming of Gorgoth – the World-Ender. You will all die!"* With that Loki flung Eliza's body aside and regarded the desperate heaving fray around him.

A blood-curdling grin twisted his face. "And now, it is my time!"

Loki leapt into the battle.

I looked away, sickened. I couldn't see Loki anymore, but I could see Eliza's unmoving body. Loki had exploited a millisecond of weakness by killing her in less time than it takes to speak his name.

How could we stand against something that ruthless? How could we fight alongside our loved ones and hope to compete with that?

I looked beyond the circle and its pitched battle. Belinda was guarding the Trevochet's now, along with a phalanx of marines. Johnny Trevochet beckoned me over.

"It's about time," he said. "That we work together. To end all this," he pointed at the skies.

I nodded, distracted as, at that moment, there was a whoosh like the scream of a jet engine and pillars of fire flashed among us. I cried out as the hairs on my arms were singed. I saw Lucy pull a face and hit everything with a curtain of water. Including us.

The fire died away. I wiped water from my eyes, spluttering. "What the fu-"

And then I saw Kisami, the traitor, rushing straight at Lysette Cohen. Her back was to him. She had no time. I panicked by shouting a warning when I should have launched a power strike.

Lysette spun around straight into a bolt of fire, but Giles tackled her to the ground. The bolt passed overhead, splitting the air between our two groups with a sound like a missile.

"Traitor!" I heard the cry, and other expletives go up around us. Kisami just stood there laughing, moulding fire like putty in his hands.

I caught Johnny's eye. He nodded. I crouched so that our shoulders touched. We gathered our power and flung out a savage surge as he threw fire at us.

Our combined power overwhelmed his and sent the fire straight back at him. An expression of horror flitted across his face as he saw his clothes burst aflame. In another moment he had collapsed to the ground, smothered by the searing heat. Then, from out of nowhere, a bloated cloud formed over his body and burst in a deluge of water that doused the flames.

Johnny and I stared at each other in shock. When we turned back Kisami was struggling to his feet. Once upright he glared, face blackened and seared by flame, a shattered vessel brimful of sin.

I flinched when I heard the rifle report. Kisami spun to

the left, and I saw that the back of his head was missing. A second report rang out and Kisami slumped amidst his own spraying blood, landing heavily in the sand.

There were several snipers stationed on the roofs of nearby hotels and lying prone atop the vans, all waiting to take pot shots. It had been the local Mayor's idea, and a good one. Kisami's mistake was presenting a target.

I met Johnny's eyes and my whole fear of failure showed in my expression like a sickly-lit beacon.

"We will try," Johnny touched my shoulder. "Us two. Together."

Belinda grazed my left ear with her lips. "Make it count, sweetcakes."

Make it count.

When we all went down to. . .

It was time. I was in Miami, at the end of the world. I had a chance to dictate the outcome of events. I looked up, studying the roiling skies. I saw a mass of noxious cloud, simmering with evil intent. Tentacles beyond count now lashed the ocean surface and the beach, as if scouring for life. I joined hands with Johnny and concentrated my gaze up into that black, unspeakable maw.

"Now!"

We flung power strikes at it. When they hit, the cloud mass shrunk inward and then snapped back. I heard a repugnant whine, something so vile I had to press my hands over my ears. I struggled to focus. Johnnny's hand on my shoulder helped.

I mustered my reserves again. Belinda stood beside me to lend support. Then, Johnny and I unleashed a blast more powerful than I could have imagined possible, something with feral and primordial strength, and at the same time I thought *mend!*

Our power struck the lesser Gods and forced their emerging bodies back into whatever Hell they occupied. Tentacles swung wildly. I fell to my knees but managed to maintain my bond with Johnny as we sent yet another blast into the skies.

We made the Gods flinch. The holes in the sky that were their wombs, the birth-tunnel between our world and theirs, contracted almost to closing point.

I heard Lucy's inspiring war-cry. *"Slam it to 'em, dad!"*

I nodded at Johnny. "One more."

We lifted our heads to send out a final colossal strike, but at that moment I saw a flash to my left and suddenly Jondal was among us. The Destroyer struck out with a razor-edged staff, killing two marines, and then striking at Johnny. Belinda thrust Johnny away, and our bond was lost.

Above us the lesser Gods shrieked like hordes of the damned and expanded even more. Huge tentacles slithered out of the clouds, smashing into the facades of the nearby hotels. Concrete was ripped away in destructive swathes. Glass and metal smashed and shrieked. I tried to shrug away a sudden feeling of weariness. This was Hell on earth, in all its apocalyptic anguish. Devon nodded at me and sent a rush of pure strength through my veins.

Damn Jondal! We had almost won the day there.

I turned around, looking for Johnny. Maybe we could try again. But then a horde of new demons attacked us, fresh from the gates of Hell, and it was all I could do to help keep myself, my daughter and my companions alive.

50

NEW BABYLON- THE MALL

Marian Cleaver strode forward, firing left and right, blasting Wayclearer demons until the percussion of his shotgun and the shocking cadence of his enemies' screams blended into a single sound in his mind – the sound of Josh Walker's dying scream. His world shattered and shattered again with an endless series of explosions – pulverized concrete, breaking glass, the tortured wrench and squeal of tearing metal.

He advanced at a steady pace, face set hard, but always keeping one eye on the progress of his colleagues.

He heard Ceriden swearing off to his left, more drama queen than vampire, but the man certainly could fight. He watched Felicia tear her way through demons and foul humans alike, not yet adopting her lycan form.

They were metres away from Mena Gaines and the mall entrance. The façade that fronted the mall had been shredded by gunfire. Blood was splashed over the walls like the work of a psychotic graffiti artist.

Cleaver saw Mena Gaines take stock of the situation. Emily Crowe inclined her head in Gaines' direction. "It is done," he heard Crowe say.

In that moment Gaines' eyes locked onto his own.

"Ah, Marian. I thought my battle might be against you."

Cleaver hesitated, looking beyond her into the mall where he saw twelve strange, robed figures. Crowe was striding towards the figures, her pace swift and purposeful. Around her the mall blazed and burned. A brand-new yellow Hummer, raised on a dais, listed onto its side with a crash as its support collapsed. Crowe fairly danced through the inferno.

He needed to hurry. What would happen if Crowe raised this mysterious Hierarchy? Moot question, really. Cheyne didn't even know what the hell the Hierarchy was up to.

Either way, Cleaver thought, his duty was to stop Gaines and Crowe.

Delta boys dropped to one knee, took aim with their weapons, and fired a volley. Crazed bodies jerked and fell backwards, sprawling on the mall's marble floor. The shots echoed and played havoc with the building's acoustics, repeating again until even Cleaver ducked instinctively.

Emily Crowe was down amongst the bodies. Cleaver couldn't tell whether she was dead or alive.

They penetrated further inside the mall, entering through the food court. Metal chairs and tables were scattered around in disarray. A row of barricaded eateries circled the court.

Cleaver saw bodies dotted here and there, some tied to the barriers that separated the food court from the restaurants, a few hung from the rafters above, others sprawling over the cushioned seating. For some, this mall truly had been Hell.

Cleaver ached with guilt. Innocents *had* died here, even as the cops and the feds and *Aegis* dithered around outside.

For a long second everyone just stood there, wiping their brows and taking stock. Cleaver even managed to return Felicia's grim smile.

"Looks like-" he began, but a sound cut him off.

Behind him he heard Mena Gaines start to laugh, a corrupt sound that set his nerves on edge. When he turned, she was standing in the entrance way, her right foot resting atop the lifeless body of a cop, her left hand constricting the throat of another. Cleaver flinched away from the hate that glowed from her ashen eyes.

"Fight me!" she screamed at him. *"Your cowardice owns you, Marian! Just like the dictators you work for!"*

Cleaver leveled his shotgun. "Fuck you."

He fired. She danced aside, and the blast missed her right cheek by a millimetre, so close he saw sparks chewing and burning her flesh in the shell's wake.

Beside him, Felicia fell to her knees. At first he thought the lycan had given up and a searing horror gripped him, but then he saw her scrabbling for a cop's discarded gun.

Felicia fired three successive shots at Gaines. The Destroyer danced aside and then, with supernatural speed, was close to him. Her elbow caught him across the cheek and sent him reeling. Her front kick slammed into his ribcage with crushing strength. He fell back, gasping for breath, barely avoiding her follow up.

At that moment a sight greeted his eyes that *stunned* him into immobility.

A *tank* was trundling through the mall entrance behind Gaines, grinding away plaster and concrete as it went. Its gun turret swiveled a few notches – towards the Destroyer.

Cleaver moved just in time as Gaines spun and leapt towards him, executing perfect strikes that he barely managed to evade. In one moment of do or die decision-making he let her get near him, close enough to smell her fetid breath.

"Weak," she hissed, spittle flying from bloodless lips.

"There's a tank behind you," he hissed back, reveling in the fear that crossed her face.

Cleaver unloosened the cattle prod from beneath his duster and pressed it against her heart.

"I'll always be better than you, Gaines," he said and pressed the button.

Mena Gaines's eyes widened into pools of agony. Cleaver shoved her body away as it shook with epileptic convulsions.

And suddenly Cleaver gave a double-take as Ken Hamilton strode past him, gleaming sword held in one hand, closely followed by Cheyne and the members of her coven.

Cheyne said, "We have wasted enough time here."

Mena Gaines groaned at his feet. Cleaver looked down at her and felt a moment's pity. Here was a human woman, corrupted beyond recognition or repair, writhing in agony but seeking a way to destroy him.

Cleaver hardened his heart, took out a Glock, and aimed it at her skull.

"You could...never...kill," she spat up at him. "Not in cold...blood."

Cleaver thought back through his life. At every turn he'd tried to nudge the wanderers back on the right path.

Was she *truly* beyond help?

Gaines stared up into his eyes, holding his gaze, his attention.

The cynical part of him thought *why?*

He heard Ceriden's yell and jumped back, more through years of well-honed instinct than anything else, not even sure he was the object of the vampires warning.

But Mena Gaines' dagger still sliced through his shin. If he hadn't stepped back it would have crippled him.

Gaines squeal of glee sounded like knives grating over bone. She rose to her feet like a demonic phoenix, daggers flashing. Cleaver then saw a fantastical sight: Felicia, sprinting gracefully- wild, blonde hair streaming out behind her, arms and legs thrusting like the pistons in a V8 Camaro- suddenly dropping into a four-legged sprint without missing a beat. As she dropped, her body moulded seamlessly into a wolfs, gaining powerful hind legs and a strong, muscular back, front paws with razor-like claws and a lycan's pronounced skull. Her cry became a snarl and then a howl of joyful bloodlust.

She struck Gaines in the chest, then used her ripping claws to gain purchase and wrap herself around the Destroyer's hard body, scrambling around her back, and then reappearing with her fangs bared right at Gaines' exposed throat.

In that explosive moment Gaines hadn't even moved an inch. Felicia ripped out Gaines' throat in a tearing mess of flesh and blood. The Destroyer staggered, dropped to a knee, and then collapsed with a soft sigh, unable to give vent to her dying agonies because her vocal chords had been shredded.

Felicia, still in wolf form, snarled up towards the heights of the mall.

Cheyne sighed. "The Hierarchy were not summoned then," she said almost to herself. "I do not understand this diversion at all." Her voice sounded hollow, defeated.

Ken rested the tip of his sword on the floor and turned to her. "You don't sound very happy about that. Isn't it *good* news?"

Cheyne scratched her nose. "Let's be honest, the question is right in our faces- *why* would a demon want to ruin this world?"

"Pointless," a member of Cheyne's coven put in helpfully. Cleaver peered into the depths of her cowl but saw only a hint of blonde hair, blue eyes, and her platinum talisman.

"Their plan either runs deeper," Cheyne said. "or this is the most elaborate diversion of all time."

"So," Ceriden regarded Cheyne with wide eyes. "What *is* their plan?"

"We're missing something. And I bet my broomstick Crowe's in on it."

"I saw her," Cleaver said. "Walking towards a group of robed figures."

"Black Chapter," Cheyne said. "They would have summoned the hierarchy."

"Why?" Ken asked.

"Crowe was *here*," Cheyne said. "Orchestrating everything. Now, that bitch has vanished."

"There were a dozen robed figures chanting," Cleaver told them.

"Didn't Crowe go to Egypt, then Paris?" Ken recalled from Kinkade's bulletins. "Didn't she steal something from the Louvre?"

"Yes. The Louvre text," Cheyne said, then spun towards her coven. "Look into it," she said urgently. "We need to know everything about that text. *Now*."

In the silence that followed Cleaver shook his head and surveyed the chaos around him. Oddly, he felt good. At the end of the day they *had* re-taken the mall.

"So," he said. "Who fancies a trip to the beach?"

51

NEW BABYLON - THE BEACH

The lesser Gods tore at the skies.

I fell back as Jondal hurled his staff at my head. I sensed Tanya dancing in from my left, kicking the sand into tiny whorls under her bare feet, and watched her engage the Destroyer, effortlessly spinning and ducking under Jondal's precise swings, pirouetting to avoid one blow, then striking savagely with a lunge that almost broke the skeletal man's arm.

I gathered some power. Beside me I sensed Lucy doing the same. I was aware that Gorgoth- the World Ender- was on his way, but I took a moment to glance sideways.

"So now you're chosen too?" I had a hundred questions, a thousand.

Lucy shrugged. "Always knew I was, dad, didn't you?"

I grinned and pretended to reach out to ruffle her hair.

"No *way*," she cried in mock-anger. Then she raised a finger. "I'll soak you."

I watched as Tanya drove Jondal back. A demon breached our lines. I used my power to thrust it into the sand, forcing it feet first until it was buried up to its neck and unable to move. Then Lucy fireballed it's head.

"Go team!" Lucy shrieked. Father and daughter working together. Quaint.

At that moment there was a massive commotion in our front line. Several vampires fell at once, writhing in agony. Then, horribly, Loki was there. With unbelievable skill he cleared a space around him- an unstoppable, deadly dervish. The deadliest warrior our world had ever known.

Loki cut through our ranks, his stony face crinkling into the most malicious expression I'd ever seen. He craved all this death and destruction, worshipped at its altar and drank from its poisoned chalice. Above us the Gods trumpeted and then there was an ear-splitting crack as if the heavens had been ripped wide open.

Lightning sheared through the dark, illuminating everything in relentless sparkling incandescence. Thunderclaps pealed in constant succession, a thousand bombs detonating one after another without end.

A vast spinning darkness appeared over the ocean, a darkness that dwarfed even the skies into insignificance. In disbelief, I saw the pale grey arms that belonged to the lesser Gods start waving uncontrollably as if in pure terror.

The great darkness expanded once more. Lightning struck the rolling oceans, hissing like molten steel plunged in ice water.

"This is it," Johnny, in his wheelchair, was at my side. "This is everything we have trained for."

Loki leapt our way. *"My Master has arrived!"*

I tried to collect my power, but the warrior was too quick. In a second, he was among us and I remembered the speed with which he'd punished Eliza's single mistake.

This was our death. I cast around desperately for Lucy.

Loki hacked at my neck, but I stumbled away. He had hold of Johnny's elbow with his other hand.

All of a sudden Eldritch was there; the King of the elves struck at Loki, forcing him to focus on his own defence.

"I knew we would meet again, Eldritch-" Loki's sibilant taunt slipped past my ears.

With Loki and Eldritch locked in deadly combat next to

us, Johnny, Lucy, and I turned our full attention once more to the boiling oceans.

"This is our last chance," Belinda positioned herself before us, a magnificent guardian. Tanya Jordan moved to her side. In another second Jade, looking battle-torn and speckled with blood came to stand with them.

Guardians among guardians.

"We will make this our line," Belinda said to the amazing warriors around her. "Our line of death. Nothing gets past it, nothing gets past us. Or we die trying."

And now *Ken* walked past me, looking somehow changed in the silvery light. The surfer dude looked harder. Gone was the flippant smile. Gone was the trademark slouch. Here was a man who had found his calling.

"Last stand time is it?" he smiled. "Right where I wanna be."

Ceriden came to my other side, and helped make a second line with Felicia, Cheyne and Marian Cleaver.

In the next few minutes I saw some of the greatest feats of combat our world had ever known. I felt privileged, breathless, to be a part of it. It all started when the Gates of Hell belched forth dozens of shrieking fiends brandishing weapons, and among them ran Emily Crowe, fresh from Hell. She saw us and sent the whole infernal group at us with a hissed command. And among us they fell. Ripping. Snarling. Possessed of a bloodlust beyond anything I had ever seen, fired by brimstone and sulphur. But, like I said, we stood firm. Those warriors like Belinda and Tanya, Jade and Ken and Felicia punched and kicked left and right, they slashed with weapons and feet and claws, they made their stand and retreated not one inch. And the fiends of Hell fell dying and dead on the ground, shattered apart, painting the sand with their leaking life-blood, their ranks falling on the unbreakable steel of our iron defence like mere waves smashing upon a mountain of unyielding rock.

Only Crowe remained alive, and simply because her cowardly, black heart told her to flee.

Hundreds of feet above us the skies churned. With a grinding, cracking sound the heavens literally *tore apart*. The new black hole overwhelmed everything else. The agonized trumpeting of the lesser Gods spoke reams to us of what was happening up there.

It was Gorgoth. The World-ender. He was here. And he was feasting on the very gods that had summoned him.

Half-chewed tentacles splashed into the ocean. Chunks of pallid, slimy flesh tumbled down from the skies, a terrible solid rain that made me want to retch.

I touched Johnny's hand. Together we expanded our power until it was just visible in the night air, a faint sheen of light pulsing with energy.

Above us something immense, probably *immeasurable*, began to force its way through. There was a mind-numbing noise that accompanied it, like a thousand whispers running through my head all at once.

Pain exploded behind my eyes. I turned around, grimacing. I saw Devon struggling to contain this new attack. Lysette had collapsed to her knees. I hoped to God she hadn't gotten a glimpse of Gorgoth's mind. Giles was bent over beside her.

"Do it *now!*" I heard Belinda scream and saw from my periphery another great phalanx of demons crashing into our ranks. Suddenly humans and Ubers were battling everywhere. Loki was still locked in a deadly struggle with Eldritch. Emily Crowe was wearing our forces down on the left flank.

Cheyne raised her arms as the members of her coven

assembled. After a moments murmuring, I saw a blur form in the air around the dark-cloaked coven, shimmering like St Elmo's fire, then portions of the blur shot off in several directions.

Demons were struck but they did not fall. Instead they stopped moving, seemingly mesmerized. Cheyne and her brethren had unleashed a glamour on them, one that robbed them of all volition.

Vampires and lycans fell upon them.

I looked up. A miniscule portion of Gorgoth had already slipped through into our world, a portion that dwarfed the ocean.

Gorgoth was the original evil, the root of everything we feared – from the darkness that crawls under your bed to the shadow stalking you in the night. He was the pale white hand that falls on your shoulder in a locked, empty room; the light footfall from downstairs that drags you out of sleep. Gorgoth spawned the very *idea* of badness, of evil, of the existence of the Devil. It was he who planted that seed in our minds and left us to nurture it.

Loki flung elbows and punches and spin kicks. Eldritch blocked well for a time, but then his regal bearing started to diminish.

At that moment Emily Crowe distracted Eldritch with a staff strike. Loki struck a stiffened finger into Eldritch's neck and even from my position I heard cartilage snap. Eldritch went down clutching his neck. Loki stomped on his head, then growled like a rabid dog.

"I win!" he cried. *"Your best of best cannot defeat me! No one will ever beat me!"*

My heart and mind choked as now, finally, I saw Belinda step up to him, a beautiful reed standing before the mighty storm, catching his full attention. Even as I prepared to let loose the power Johnny and I had gathered I saw on Belinda's face an acceptance at having to engage this deadly opponent. I knew she expected to die for us.

There was no more time. Behind me Devon Summers' voice strained and cracked with the effort of keeping us strong. I squeezed Johnny's hand and we hurled our sheet of force at Gorgoth's maw like a shrieking comet.

It struck true and the God screamed. I watched in awe as the cloud contracted and then expanded further. Gorgoth's voice slid through our brains again, sibilant and eerie, the voice that tells psychopathic murderers to commit atrocity. I caught Johnny's eye.

"What the hell are we supposed to do now?"

Johnny shook his head. "We keep trying," he said. "We never stop."

Lucy screamed then, terrifying me. *What now?* I glanced to see that the Destroyer, Jondal, had crept up to her side. Still emaciated and as repulsive as a den of maggots he leered at her and reached for her with veiny hands.

"NO!" Lucy screamed and stumbled into my arms.

"I knew I would get my chance with you," the vile words dripped from his lips like drops of venom. "I promised you, little one."

Lucy screamed again and buried her head against my chest. In her terror she had forgotten her power. Jondal lurched forward with an insane giggle. I saw the trident in his right hand, sharp and deadly.

Jondal struck. The trident's gleaming points arced down towards Lucy's back. I dragged her aside, making myself the target. But when the daggers were an inch away Tanya Jordan inserted herself between us, effecting an impossible deflection and sending the weapon a millimetre past her waist.

"Pick on me," she said, her voice a blast of arctic ice. "If you can."

I hugged Lucy close as Jondal struck. Tanya calmly turned his wrist around twice, breaking it two ways in less than a second and making him squeal as the bones grated. Jondal tried to kick out but Tanya caught his foot on her instep, then stomped once on his knee and once on his shins, breaking two more bones.

Jondal collapsed in a writhing heap. His squeals were the sounds of eels being burned alive.

Tanya broke his other arm at the shoulder. "Harm a young girl would you?"

Lucy peered out from the safety of my chest.

Tanya met her eyes, then nodded at Jondal. "Fry him."

I turned away as Lucy acted and Jondal's screams intensified to the power of ten.

No one bothered to put him out of his misery.

I smiled at Tanya. With a wink she was gone, leaping back into fray, already headed to confront Emily Crowe.

"We must finish this!" Johnny cried. "Before Gorgoth destroys everything we love!"

Incredibly, there was a scream of jet engines and suddenly a formation of F-16 Fighting Falcons sped over the nearby hotels straight at the black hole that was Gorgoth. I nodded at Johnny. Here was the diversion we needed.

The F-16's banked and circled, sleek streaks of hot metal in the sky, and let loose a volley of missiles into Gorgoth's midst. At the same time Johnny and I unleashed our own arsenal. At the same time, from the beach away to our left I saw two dozen white streaks sear the air as mobile missile launchers let loose their own payloads.

All this earth-born power *shattered* into Gorgoth's core. The whispers in our heads died away and the gargantuan cloud *pulsed*. But then Gorgoth appeared to fight back, maybe in desperation I will never know, but from out of his boiling darkness exploded a mass of pale, writhing arms. Thick grey tentacles struck out at the passing jets. One was struck a glancing blow and flew end over end until it crashed into the sea with a tremendous burst of steam and fire and exploding metal. I saw two more destroyed in the skies, their wings shorn off, their cockpits crushed. Another veered away, only to be struck from behind, and went spinning down into Miami's streets. There was a colossal explosion and a rolling ball of black smoke plumed over the city. The rumbling crash of a collapsing building momentarily stilled the battle-cries around me.

I closed my eyes in despair. *What could we do against this? Did we have anything left?*

I looked up at the menacing cloud that was Gorgoth.

It was horrendous. A cloud of foamy horror, scintillating with flashes of lightning and dripping with noxious gases from outer space. Tentacles swayed and struck with startling anticipation and intelligence. And now, even as we gaped in wordless awe, dozens of hairy, spindly legs like those of a gigantic spider dropped down from the cloud.

Dread choked me as I imagined the creature those legs belonged too. A score of tentacles lashed out and played havoc among the mobile missile carriers arrayed just down the beach. I saw men and vehicles lifted high into the air, torn apart, and dropped into the heaving seas.

Tentacles strafed the hotels behind us, destroying the frontages. Concrete and glass crashed into the street. Palm trees were uprooted and flung like missiles over the hotels and into the city.

"I don't know what to do-" I turned to Johnny.

My confidence bottomed out about then.

"A miracle," Johnny was muttering, his eyes glistening. "We need a miracle."

Now I noticed that worse things than demons were starting to emerge through the Gates of Hell. A beast over ten feet tall with scimitar-like talons and a face like a boar stepped out. And somewhere behind it, faint for now, came a hungry bellow that could only belong to something bigger than a T-Rex and probably twice as ravenous.

It was falling apart.

"We need to get out of here," I fixed on Lucy. I thought about failure. I wouldn't let Lucy die here.

"No!" Johnny cried. "Look," he pointed ahead but I did not lift my eyes.

Johnny grabbed my arm and shouted, *"Look!"*

I glanced up and there, in my sights, was Belinda, striking and leaping back and forth under Loki's vicious onslaught. The Destroyer caught her in the ribs, but Belinda barely flinched, just came back with a lightning fast combination that connected solidly with Loki's shoulders and face. I saw him step back, shock registering on his features, and then I saw him wilt under Belinda's devastating attack.

Yes!

She had always been our best. But I had never imagined she could beat Loki. And neither had she. I shouted encouragement, raising my fists. I flashed a manic grin to my right and saw something similar lighting up Lucy's face.

We could win this. All we had to do was win our

individual battles, and the prize was ours.

Tanya Jordan danced across the sand – a lethal ballerina, rolling and ducking and evading Emily Crowe's attacks with jaw-dropping skill and grace. In one frenzied blitz Crowe didn't land a single blow on Tanya, but I saw the Destroyer struck a dozen times.

Spidery legs swept down from the sky, lowering towards the land. Lightning struck them and deflected in a score of directions, demolishing trees and the sides of buildings. To add to the feel of being in a war zone I saw the fifth F-16 dog-fighting up there, ducking and diving between tentacles and legs and seeping grey flesh. It was beyond heroic. It was one small jet against the most monstrous creature imaginable, and one air-force pilot's immense courage against unspeakable evil.

My jaw dropped. The jet weaved in and out of certain death, chasing his own vapour trail, firing off missile after missile and then switching to guns, racing to cling on to life.

Before us Loki flicked a wrist and Belinda fell to one knee. I saw the dull glint of a blade in her ribcage.

"Belinda!" the cry tore from my heart like a living thing.

Loki leapt at her, a flying kick that caught her full in the face. I could tell by the way she went down that she wasn't getting back up.

"NO!" this time it was Ken's scream and now he leapt at Loki without hesitation. Marian Cleaver jumped in too and both men were against Loki, striking in unison to wear their enemy down.

Devon Summers rushed past me, unmindful of her own peril, dropping to Belinda's side.

I couldn't think straight. "No, oh no."

Devon bent over Belinda's body. Their foreheads

touched and I saw both girl's heads enveloped in the green glow that emanated from Devon's eyes.

Belinda turned her head towards Devon, and I saw life there.

Ken struck at Loki, his sword slicing the Destroyers arm off at the shoulder, and then Cleaver touched him in the chest with a thin stick that made him jerk in a mad frenzy. Loki went down, spraying blood and convulsing in agony.

But he managed to perform one final duty.

Even as he fell to his death his good arm flicked out a blade. It flew fast and accurate and true, embedding itself in Devon Summers' brain. Our healer fell backwards. Dead. Not even she could heal instant death.

Johnny grabbed my shoulders. I read the pleading in his eyes that said *concentrate, oh, please concentrate.*

I dug deeper than at any time in my life, deep into my very core where race memory and raw courage and primordial violence struggled to stay contained.

I looked up, my face covered in tears, my eyes blazing, screaming Belinda's name.

Beside me I felt Lucy stiffen. Out on the ocean a water spout exploded into life. Its swirling waters caused mayhem as it swept around Gorgoth's hateful limbs, making the God bellow in confusion.

I linked with Johnny and, together, we sent out the strongest surge of pure power we could ever muster. Lucy's typhoon and our power blast struck simultaneously, hitting the God with more destructive might than the world had ever known.

Radiant white light splashed across Gorgoth's loathsome cloud. Even the *lightning* exploded up there, painting the vast tear with sparkling incandescence, blinding and healing as it swept the skies with brilliance.

I screamed "BELINDA!" and rushed forward. I reached her in a second, Lucy at my side, falling to my knees in the blood-soaked sand. I cradled her head. My tears landed on her upturned face and my heart almost stopped to see her smile.

"Hey," she said, and that was enough for now.

Above us the World-Ender's spinning maw began to contract. I saw spidery legs sheared off and fall to the beach. I saw them crawl away towards the nearest darkness. The slithering sound of their passage would haunt my nightmares forever.

Johnny came to stand over me, his hand fell on my shoulder, and we launched another devastating power wave. Lucy sent forth a tornado of primal force.

Gorgoth screeched in pure animal rage, a kid thwarted and venting his fury, and then his core disintegrated like a collapsed black hole. The edges of his cloud snapped together with a crack that shook the earth. The sky healed itself in that moment.

We were left stunned by the immediate silence, our ears ringing, unable to believe that we had survived.

I clung to Belinda. Beside me Marian Cleaver fell to his knees and cradled Devon's body. I wept for the girl from Maui. In the end Loki *had* gotten his kill.

The hateful Destroyer's body lay prone before us. I watched Lucy crawl through the wet sand to Devon's body and lean over to kiss the healer's forehead. Ken collapsed near her and doubled over, his body wracked with sobs. When I glanced around, still numb, still choked, I saw Tanya scratching her head and staring in surprise at a distant running figure.

"Emily Crowe," Tanya replied to my unasked question.

"This is unreal. Cheyne said she had a connection to the Hierarchy demons, and when Gorgoth fell she just took off."

Weird. I cast around again as Belinda struggled to sit up. Behind us the exhausted Trevochet's, along with Lysette and Giles, were in earnest conversation with Cheyne and Ceriden. Near me, a shattered and battle-worn Jade sat with glazed eyes. Even in her agony Jade wept aloud for her fallen King. Eldritch lay dead in the sand. His Queen had died days before. The Elven race was shattered. They had done everything possible to help us and now...what would they do? Were there any more elves left in the world?

Felicia stood near Ken, her head down. I watched as Felicia's shoulders shook.

My God. Think of all we have lost. Of the *people* who gave their lives.

Then I heard Ken cry out. My heart performed somersaults. I followed the direction of his disbelieving gaze.

To see Dementia, the crazy bitch-demon, sitting nonchalantly on a fallen, still-smoking palm tree to the left of the wide-open, still-pulsing, Gates of Hell. Nothing came out of there now, but Dementia twirled a dirty lock of hair around one finger and observed us with a mocking intensity.

"I killed you!" Ken shouted. "For Ryan and Myleene! I killed you, you fucking bitch!"

My eyes blurred with tears. How many good people had we lost today? How many more?

"*Ken Hamiltonnnn,*" Dementia hissed as glee twisted her face. "*I challenge youuuuu. If you dare come and get meeeeeeee-*"

And with that the insane demon leapt into the Gates of Hell.

Ken screamed and made to follow, but Tanya blocked his way. "NO!" she shouted along with almost everyone else on the beach. Our chorus stopped him.

"Not into Hell."

The crazy demon was gone. Back to whatever vileness she called home.

Vampires and Lycans were walking past us now, trudging wearily up the beach, nursing their battle wounds. Marines and cops in their hundreds were mixed in among them, comrades joined through battle.

Then someone cried: *"Eliza!"* I saw a huge bear of a man stand up, the chef from Ceriden's house named Milo, with Eliza's body cradled gently in his massive arms.

Milo, this enormous man, weeped uncontrollably.

Eliza's body was limp but moving. I saw her feet kick, and the weak raising of her hand.

"Oh, Eliza!" Ceriden cried out in hope and flew past me as if the pit-born hounds of hell were at his heels. "Devon must have saved her," he shouted to anyone who would listen. "Devon protected her."

Tears welled in my eyes. It seemed Eliza was another of Loki's victims that he'd overlooked in his arrogance. Thank God. No. . . thank poor Devon.

I started as Lucy slipped her small hand into my own. I smiled into her tear-streaked face and hugged Belinda to me. We'd won. So why did our victory feel so empty?

Lysette suddenly screamed, her voice a knife in the dark. Everyone on the beach turned to her.

"Seven demons," she said, leaning her weight on Giles. "I...I read Crowe as she ran away. God, for my future sanity, I wish I hadn't," she groaned into Giles' arm. "I know everything. It all comes down to the text Crowe stole from the Louvre. The Text of Seven. Including Dementia, there are seven major demons. And seven Hells." She paused, shaking her head in confusion. "The Hierarchy and Black Chapter manipulated everything. There are seven places on Earth where seven ancient artefacts are hidden. I gleaned that. . ."

"We should have known," Ceriden sounded as crushed as if Cameron had just called to cancel a dinner date.

"Known what?" Belinda asked weakly. Felicia and Ken turned towards us.

"It was their plan all along," Cheyne cleared her throat. "As we kept saying, no demon, and especially the Hierarchy demons, would destroy this world. Because it is also *their* world."

"So the mall *was* a distraction," Lysette said. "Or rather – a simple distraction in *Gorgoth's plan* and in the minds of his Destroyers, but Crowe was a *double agent*. For her the distraction was everything, allowing her to engineer the Hierarchy's summoning at the mall."

Marian Cleaver nodded. "Whilst we were busy with Gaines?"

"Yes," Cheyne said. "In a normal world the witches council would have stopped any Hierarchy summoning. That is our job, to monitor magical activity. But with the finding of the Text of Arcadia and its message – that Gorgoth was coming – it grabbed every ounce of our attention. I believe now that the Hierarchy themselves, or Emily Crowe, arranged that we find the Text of Arcadia to keep us focused on Gorgoth."

It made sense. "But why?" I asked. "What does the Hierarchy want?"

"They are already seeking these seven artefacts,"

Lysette said slowly, speaking from memory. "Two of these artefacts are in Hell. The other five are scattered across the far reaches of our world-" as Lysette paused to think a profound silence settled. "We must get to those artefacts before the demons do."

My initial thought was: *a race.*

"But why?" it was Ken's tortured whisper.

"Their plan all along," Cheyne told us. "was to be summoned whilst this whole Gorgoth thing distracted us. To disguise their ultimate agenda."

Ken prompted, "Which is?"

Cheyne paused. "To bring Satan Himself, in all his hellish glory, back into our world."

I felt my jaw drop. "They're trying to raise the Devil?"

"They *will* raise the Devil," Lysette said. "If they manage to collect all the artefacts."

"And the Devil is worse than Gorgoth because-" I had to ask.

"Imagine Hell on Earth," Ceriden said tonelessly. "With all of us alive. Forever. I mean, Gorgoth was just going to destroy it."

And now memories of my visions rose like black thunderbolts. I had seen Belinda captured by a demon, among corpses piled high. They hadn't been visions of the coming of Gorgoth. They had been *premonitions* as I had feared, precursors to the coming of Satan. The Devil.

The very embodiment of mankind's deepest fears. And he would bring Hell to Earth.

Ken turned once again towards the Gates of hell, hefting his sword. "It comes down to Dementia and me." he started forward, and my heart went out to him. "I will go into Hell and find the two artefacts. Someone *has* to."

"No," I heard the Jade, the elf, say. "Not without me."

Then Felicia looked straight at me and flicked a glance off Belinda to Ken. "And not without me, too."

I felt my heart break as our fellowship broke apart. I remembered Felicia sat at the kitchen table, sipping coffee, playfully mocking Belinda and explaining to me the ways of her kind. She loved life; she loved the freedom of the run. And she had just volunteered to walk the dread paths of Hell.

Together they stood, these new companions, brushed themselves off, and walked towards the Gates of Hell, kicking sand as they went. Moonlight and starshine glittered from their eyes and in shimmering shards from their readied weapons.

Humility brought tears to my eyes. One swift glance at Belinda and I knew that if she had been able, she would have accompanied them.

But still there was more. I saw Eliza wriggle out of Milo's grasp and land on steady feet, breathing harshly, but determined. "I will help you, Ken." Eliza spoke up, and Milo also grunted in agreement.

And finally Mai walked up to the little group. "And I," she said with venom. "I also owe Dementia a painful death."

"There are still five artefacts to race for on earth," I said, mainly for Belinda's benefit.

Marian Cleaver added. "The Hierarchy has a head start on us."

Cheyne nodded. "And we will need everyone's help. There is a copy of the Text of Seven at the library. I'm sure there are riddles to solve, codes to crack. The search must start now. Without delay. We must determine the location of the five artefacts on Earth before the Hierarchy finds them," she glanced behind her. "Come Brethren, timing is everything now. We must begin."

Behind Cheyne, the coven gathered. As a group they passed beyond the exhausted Johnny Trevochet and his wife, Natalie, who clung to one another, just happy to be alive. I studied the approaching coven. All twelve witches wore dark cloaks that covered their bodies and deep cowls that concealed their faces. Almost as one they reached around their necks for their platinum talismans, the source of their powers, as I had seen Cheyne do a dozen times already.

They were ready to cast their spell. Where would they send us?

I held tightly to Belinda and promised myself we wouldn't be separated anytime soon.

Some promise.

THE END

Authors Note

Chosen, is the first part of a trilogy. Part 2 – GUARDIANS – is now available for the Amazon Kindle with part 3 due for release in 2019. All helpful, genuine comments and advice are welcome. I would love to hear from you.

davidleadbeater2011@hotmail.co.uk

Visit my website for the latest information:
www.davidleadbeaternovels.co.uk
Facebook – davidleadbeaternovels

Other Books by David Leadbeater:

The Matt Drake Series
A constantly evolving, action-packed romp based in the escapist action-adventure genre:

The Bones of Odin (Matt Drake #1)
The Blood King Conspiracy (Matt Drake #2)
The Gates of hell (Matt Drake 3)
The Tomb of the Gods (Matt Drake #4)
Brothers in Arms (Matt Drake #5)
The Swords of Babylon (Matt Drake #6)
Blood Vengeance (Matt Drake #7)
Last Man Standing (Matt Drake #8)
The Plagues of Pandora (Matt Drake #9)
The Lost Kingdom (Matt Drake #10)
The Ghost Ships of Arizona (Matt Drake #11)
The Last Bazaar (Matt Drake #12)
The Edge of Armageddon (Matt Drake #13)
The Treasures of Saint Germain (Matt Drake #14)
Inca Kings (Matt Drake #15)
The Four Corners of the Earth (Matt Drake #16)
The Seven Seals of Egypt (Matt Drake #17)
Weapons of the Gods (Matt Drake #18)
The Blood King Legacy (Matt Drake #19)
Devil's Island (Matt Drake #20)
The Fabergé Heist (Matt Drake #21)

The Alicia Myles Series
Aztec Gold (Alicia Myles #1)
Crusader's Gold (Alicia Myles #2)
Caribbean Gold (Alicia Myles #3)
Chasing Gold (Alecia Myles #4)

The Torsten Dahl Thriller Series
Stand Your Ground (Dahl Thriller #1)

The Relic Hunters Series
The Relic Hunters (Relic Hunters #1)
The Atlantis Cipher (Relic Hunters #2)

The Rogue Series
Rogue (Book One)

The Disavowed Series:
The Razor's Edge (Disavowed #1)
In Harm's Way (Disavowed #2)
Threat Level: Red (Disavowed #3)

The Chosen Few Series
Chosen (The Chosen Trilogy #1)
Guardians (The Chosen Trilogy #2)
Heroes (The Chosen Trilogy #3)

Short Stories
Walking with Ghosts (A short story)
A Whispering of Ghosts (A short story)

All genuine comments are very welcome at:

davidleadbeater2011@hotmail.co.uk

Twitter: @dleadbeater2011

Visit David's website for the latest news and information:
davidleadbeater.com

Made in the USA
Middletown, DE
26 September 2022